FREEDOM'S RANGERS

Patrolling the past to protect the future

Hunter looked down the line of his men standing at the foot of the portal ramp. All were outfitted for a night commando raid. Jaeger carried his Walther Wa-2000 with night vision scope attached. Anderson shouldered an RPG rocket launcher. The others carried assault rifles.

"Full power! Portal open!"

Light engulfed them as they stepped back through ninety years and several thousand miles of space . . .

FREEDOM'S RANGERS

FREEDOM'S RANGERS

KEITH WILLIAM ANDREWS

BERKLEY BOOKS, NEW YORK

FREEDOM'S RANGERS

A Berkley Book/published by arrangement with
the author

PRINTING HISTORY
Berkley edition/July 1989

ISBN: 0-425-11643-3

A BERKLEY BOOK ® TM 757,375
Berkley Books are published by The Berkley Publishing Group
200 Madison Avenue, New York, N.Y. 10016.
The name "BERKLEY" and the "B" logo
are trademarks belonging to Berkley Publishing Corporation.

PRINTED IN THE UNITED STATES OF AMERICA.

10 9 8 7 6 5 4 3 2 1

FREEDOM'S
RANGERS

One

The sentry was bored. MIT's campus was silent; as silent as the inky expanse of the Charles River beyond the line of trees to his right. To the east, Boston's lightless skyline could barely be seen against an overcast sky. There was a chill breeze coming off the river, but the sentry scarcely noticed. Early March at home was much colder than this, and his jacket took the sting of the wind. He shifted the AKM slung from his shoulder to a more comfortable position, considered lighting a cigarette, then decided the risk of his sergeant finding him smoking on duty was not worth the warmth of the smoke.

Service with the U.N. Peacekeeping Forces stationed in the former United States had so far offered little of the action and excitement Vasili Nikolaevich had pictured when he'd first received his orders. Still, the duty had its compensations . . . plenty of available loot, and the girls were pretty, if not exactly willing. There were worse things in a soldier's life than boredom, and crawling around after guerrillas in the Ozarks or getting shot at by survivalists in Oregon was not his idea of excitement.

Vasili needn't have worried. He had only a few seconds left to live.

A shadow detached itself from deeper shadows at the sentry's back, one long arm coming up from behind, a hand clamping down across his mouth. The point of a combat knife descended, piercing with expert control through jugular and carotid and spine. The Russian's arms and legs jerked once, then fell limp.

Lieutenant Travis Hunter wiped the blade on the sentry's jacket, returned it to the reversed sheath on his black combat vest, then rose, checking left and right for other signs of movement. The parkland grounds around the university buildings remained silent. He peeled back the cover on his luminous watch and noted the time: 2241:12. Hunter signaled then, a sharp, quick motion of his hand to the darkness. Three men slipped from the shadows by the river. Like Hunter, they were shrouded in black, faces smeared with camo greasepaint, armed with automatic weapons. One of them dragged the Russian's body behind bushes next to the building he had been guarding. The numbers set into the wall overhead read "82." The buildings of MIT were notorious for their lack of logic or order, but according to their informant, this was the university's Computer Department Research Annex.

Silent hand signals gave orders. *You . . . to the left. Watch for sentries. You . . . take the door. . . .*

The door was a service entrance in the rear. Hunter took the right side of the door, sliding his silenced Uzi around to where he could hold it at the ready. Sergeant Roy Anderson took the other side, scanning the surrounding rooftops for signs of the enemy. Master Sergeant Greg King crouched over the lock, the meter in his hand, scanning down the doorjamb for hidden wires of alarms or traps, before he started in with the lockpicks. The door clicked open, and Anderson stepped through, probing ahead with the leveled snout of his H&K MP5SD3. The fourth member of the team scurried from cover, a heavy canvas bag thumping at his side.

Inside, light spilling past the corner of a bend in the hallway gave warning of possible habitation. Anderson dropped to his belly and inched forward, extending a dentist's mirror at floor level to cautiously peer around the corner. Above him, Hunter reslung his Uzi, quietly unholstered the silenced 9mm hush puppy automatic at his hip, and flicked off the safety. Anderson pulled back, twisted to look up at Hunter, and signed his report. *One sentry . . . fifteen feet . . . facing out . . .*

Lieutenant Hunter nodded and readied himself. With his back to the concrete-block wall, he took a deep breath, counted to three, then swung around into the lighted passageway, his heavy-barreled pistol dropping into line with the sentry in a double-handed grip. Two shots coughed with a harsh *phht-phht* before the surprised sentry could react, splattering blood from his head and throat. He twisted toward the commando, then sagged sideways against the door, slumping to a bloody, half-seated sprawl on the floor.

Behind the dead guard was the security door to the computer labs. The raiders ran gloved hands across smooth metal. There were no locks to pick here, and a quick check of the sentry's uniform pockets produced no magnetic cardkey to operate the door from the slot mounted on the wall nearby.

Hunter waved the fourth team member forward. Sergeant Eduardo Gomez hunkered down before the door, ignoring the sentry next to him as he rummaged in his pouch to produce a small ball of clay-like plastique. Swiftly he measured handsbreadths across the door, selected a spot, and began working the high explosive putty into a broad, flat ring around the locking mechanism.

Hunter checked his watch and grimaced at the 2243:30 displayed there. "Let's hustle, Eddie," he whispered, reholstering his pistol. "Time! Time!"

The team's demolition expert said nothing but continued working, embedding fuse and blasting cap into the putty and humming softly to himself under his breath.

Standing at the far side of the door, Master Sergeant King glanced at his watch. "He'd better be here, after all this!"

Hunter shrugged as he checked his H&K's safety. "They said he's in here working late every night, Greg. It's our best shot."

Gomez finished crimping the end of the fuse to the M-60 igniter and looked up at Hunter. "Ready."

"Right. Stand clear."

The strike team moved well back on either side of the steel door, as Gomez pulled the safety pin, then yanked a pull ring to ignite the fuse. The explosion was certain to alert every Russian in the building. They would have to move fast.

The blast rang off the concrete-block walls in noise and concussion, filling the passageway with smoke, and punching a neat hole through the door's lock mechanism. Standing side by side, King and Anderson exchanged glances and checked their MP5SD3s. Then the master sergeant pushed the door in with his foot.

Freed when the explosion severed its locking bars, the massive steel door swung inward on oiled hinges. The two raiders' submachine guns spat chuffing bursts of silenced fire. Two blast-dazed Russian sentries at the far end of the inner passageway toppled backward with flailing arms and a clatter of helmets and rifles on the bare tile floor.

In the inner sanctum now, the team made their way to a more ordinary door, one with "Computer Lab One" etched into the brass plate set into the wood. Gomez and Anderson took their places on either side, SMGs at the ready, while King tried the door. With a nod to Hunter, he paused, then threw his shoulder to the wood. The door smashed open, and Hunter and King burst into the room, weapons leveled.

King nearly collided with a technician in a shapeless white lab coat. Hunter swung to cover movement across the room, half masked by a desk and ranked computer terminals. King reached out with one hand to shove the technician to the floor. There was always the chance the KGB had placed security people inside the lab. . . .

The technician spun, hands flashing in a karate

strike at the sergeant's arm, and King jumped back with a bitten-off "Aw, shit!" Hunter dropped into a crouch, swinging his Uzi to cover King's attacker.

The lovely face, the dark and angry eyes, the cascade of raven hair reminded Hunter of no KGB agent he had ever known. Her lab coat might be shapeless, but there was nothing at all shapeless about what it contained. The girl stood facing them, breathing hard, her body fluid in a classic karate stance.

Further thoughts were interrupted by a shaken "Who *are* you people?" from a short, white-haired man rising from behind the computer terminals. He adjusted his wire-rimmed glasses and peered at the invaders uncertainly. Though his features appeared somewhat more gaunt now than they had in the three-year-old photographs Hunter had memorized, it was unquestionably David Stein.

"U.S. Army Rangers!" Hunter looked about the room. Stein and the dark-haired girl were the only people there. "Ditch that white coat, Doctor, and let's go. We're here to rescue you and we're double parked." He studied the girl, his Uzi still aimed at her as she relaxed from her martial arts pose. She looked uncertain. Was she KGB or simply a karate-trained lab assistant?

"Sorry to intrude, miss, but we're taking your boss with us."

"I am damn well not going anywhere without my daughter," Stein said.

"Your daughter?"

"Rachel Stein," the girl said, as Hunter redirected the muzzle of his submachine gun toward the ceiling. She regarded the black-garbed, camo paint-smeared commandos with distaste. "I didn't realize it was Halloween."

"Oh, bloody hell," King muttered, rubbing his bruised arm. He did not sound pleased. "The boss didn't say anything about *her*."

"So we're even," she said. "Nobody told us about *you*. Father, just what the hell is going on? These bozos are supposed to *rescue* us?"

Stein looked at Hunter, questioning. "I take it Brian got through?" he asked.

"If you mean your assistant, yes, sir. He made it to The Hole last month. Now, can we save the introductions for later? Your former employers are going to be all over this building any second now."

"My daughter is coming with me. She knows the transformation equations as well as I do."

"Right." Hunter was not about to argue the point. He could imagine what would happen to the girl if the Soviets found Stein missing, whether she knew anything or not. "But shuck that coat and those heels, lady. A white lab coat makes too good a target in the dark, and you won't be able to run in those shoes."

His words were underscored by the spat of automatic fire from the passageway. "Company's coming, Lt.!" Anderson said outside.

Stein turned to his daughter. "The files, Rachel. Dump the files."

"Doctor . . ."

"Patience, Lieutenant. My notes must not be left for the Soviets."

Hunter weighed the liabilities two rescued civilians presented his team as opposed to one. Dr. Stein wore a light gray suit which was nearly as visible in the dark as the lab coats had been. His daughter wore a white blouse; just as bad. And she would be limited in how far and how fast she could run in her stockinged feet.

Why hadn't they told them about the girl back at The Hole?

More gunfire sounded in the hall, the loud banging of AK fire overwhelming the softer hiss of short, silenced bursts. Stein's daughter tapped rapidly at a computer keyboard, watching the results scroll up the screen in front of her. "Done!" She said. "Dumped and forgotten."

"If you people don't mind," King snapped, gesturing toward the door.

Hunter smiled as she rummaged through a closet, producing a pair of dark raincoats. The coats, obviously the property of people larger than either of the Steins, would cover their light-colored clothes and give them a chance to blend into the dark. His assessment of the girl rose several notches. She was smart.

She caught him watching as she stepped out of her shoes and tucked them into a coat pocket. "I wasn't planning on playing commando tonight," she said.

"Gomez!" he called. "Anderson! Cover! We're coming out!"

"We're clear out here," Gomez yelled from outside. "Hurry it up, Chief!"

The smoke-filled hall was momentarily clear, though a sprawl of still shapes at the far end showed the results of the firefight a moment before. They could hear the shrilling of an alarm now, somewhere in the distance, and the muttering echo of large numbers of running, shouting men. They hurried back the way they'd come, Gomez and Anderson behind the group, their weapons ready, facing to the rear. Then they were through the outside door and into the dark chill of the evening. The MIT campus was coming alive around them with lights and noise as the alarm sounded.

A cluster of Russian soldiers appeared out of the night. *"Ahstahnahveet'yes!"* someone yelled. "Halt! Halt or we fire!"

King chopped into the group with rapid-fire bursts from his H&K. Someone screamed, and Russians crumpled onto the grass in twisted heaps.

A single shot barked somewhere in the darkness nearby, followed by the long, drawn-out rattle of AK fire. The fleeing party threw themselves to the grass, Anderson and King firing short, precise bursts at muzzle flashes and running shadows.

Hunter touched Gomez's arm. "Get our guests down to the river, Eddie. We'll be along in a moment."

"Right, Chief."

The firefight seemed to be spreading now to embrace much of the MIT campus. Hunter suspected that wandering bands of Russian soldiers had begun firing at one another in the confusion and dark. Hunter took careful aim at a pair of running figures backlit by the lights now coming on in a campus administration building and tapped the trigger of his Uzi once . . . twice. The pair dropped from view. Another long roll of automatic fire stabbed from the darkness off to their left, directed at a band of troops moving across the administration parking lot.

"They can kill each other," Hunter said to the other two. "They don't need us here. Fall back."

"Right, Lieutenant," King agreed.

The commandos stayed on their bellies as they backed away from the battle now being waged intermittently across the MIT campus. The U.N. Occupation Forces were jittery, firing at anything that moved or shot back. Hunter could hear shouted orders in Russian, however, and it wouldn't be long before the officers got their troops back under control.

Buildings and campus gave way to the narrow strip of parkland and the double concrete ribbon of Memorial Drive along the bank of the Charles.

Gomez and the rescued scientists had already reached the pair of whaleboats drawn up on the riverbank under a clump of trees. Those boats, low and broad, fiber glass painted black, had brought the team from their insertion point. One boat would get all of them back.

The team's demolitions man had already eased one of the boats into the water, hauled it around until it pointed upstream toward the black mass of Harvard Bridge, started its powerful electric outboard with the press of a button, then waded clear as it began moving against the sluggish current.

Hunter could see the boat's wake as it picked up speed. Empty, traveling slowly upriver, it might buy them time. "All aboard," he said, helping the elder Stein into the flat-bottomed craft. "It's not elegant, but it'll get us where we want to go."

"And where is that?" Rachel asked. Her eyes widened as Hunter jabbed his thumb over his shoulder, pointing downstream. "Are you sure you Neanderthals know what you're doing? That way is Boston . . . and the Charles River Dam!"

Anderson grinned in the darkness. "Well, ma'am," he said, in his best cowboy's drawl, "they won't be expecting us to go that way, will they?"

On the shore to their left a searchlight snapped on, its beam sweeping low across the water. "Everybody down!" Hunter said. With luck, the black whaleboat would pass unnoticed on black water.

They had luck, but the wrong kind. The beam came to rest with the whaleboat pinned in the center of its glare. There were shouts, and the sense of men running somewhere behind the dazzle of the light. *"Tahm! Vohzl'yeh ryehkah!"*

Gunfire stabbed from across Memorial Drive, and spurts of water geysered on each side of the boat. Anderson, standing knee-deep in the river alongside the boat, brought his silenced MP5 up to his face and opened fire, sending short, measured bursts across the water.

There was no effect. "Damned popgun," he muttered, as he pulled the sling off over his head. "Time for the heavy artillery, Lt.?"

"Let 'er rip," Hunter replied. Anderson was already reaching across the gunnel into the boat and peeling canvas off a metal shape in the bottom. A moment later, he hefted the massive bulk of an M-60 light machine gun out of its hiding place, slipped the sling over his shoulder, and checked the feed for the belt of ammo dangling from the weapon's left side. His first burst roared like thunder, and with an unheard scream Rachel covered her ears. Unlike the Uzi and the H&Ks, the M-60 was not silenced, and its slow, methodical hammer echoed from the buildings of MIT, its tongue of flame probing toward the searchlight.

The light flared briefly and died. Shouts and gun-fire turned to screams as Anderson swung the ma-chine gun to rake the darkness just below and on either side of where the light had been. By the time the last of the ammo belt had been chewed away, the enemy gunfire from the campus had ceased.

Gomez and King hauled the M-60 into the boat, then helped Anderson roll in, dripping. Hunter trig-gered the near-silent electric outboard and leaned back on the tiller, swinging the boat smoothly out into the center of the Charles.

For a blissful moment, the night was quiet. Then gunfire barked again on the shore, off among the MIT buildings. None of the fire seemed to be directed toward the river, at least for the moment.

"Okay, Gomez," Hunter said to the small man in the bow of the whaleboat. "Let's give them some-thing more to think about."

"Right you are, Chief." He chuckled once as he fished around in a tackle box, producing a small, flat battery casing set with buttons and a long antenna. He touched a button, and orange flame fireballed into the night against the Cambridge skyline. Another press of a button, and a second blast erupted from the direction of the Soviet motor pool behind the MIT administration building. Gunfire broke out afresh as Soviet occupation forces panicked and began gun-ning one another down in the flickering, orange light of burning vehicles.

"We left a few calling cards," Hunter explained for the benefit of the team's guests. He gestured over his shoulder, beyond the fires. "That ought to con-vince them we're heading off that way."

They were silent after that, the six of them huddled

over as though that act could somehow make the small, black boat completely invisible as it slipped through the night. Hunter peered into the darkness, intent on landmarks more sensed than seen. The city was so dark! With electricity strictly rationed and a curfew stringently enforced, any lights which showed from the city would be those of official vehicles or guard posts. So far, all activity seemed to be behind them, up the river.

The Storrow Lagoon and Boston were on the right, the darkened skyline of the city visible against the stars of a clearing sky. Hunter remembered attending Fourth of July festivities there as a child; the crowds and the music and the fireworks. It would be a long time before Independence Day would be celebrated along the Charles again, he thought. The knowledge brought pain, and a soft curse.

There was more gunfire in the distance as they slipped quietly under the Longfellow Bridge close by the Cambridge shore. The hollow ululation of a siren drifted after them, mingled with the raw, distant thutter of a helicopter following the river west. More gunfire sounded, and then the dull, flat boom of another explosion came to them across the water. Gomez snickered again.

"They found our diversion," King replied to the Steins' blank and questioning looks. "Clear up by Boston University Bridge, from the sound of it."

"Fifty pounds of C-4," Gomez added. "With a detonator set to go off when the boat is hit by gunfire or tampered with. It makes a very nice bang."

Ahead of them, the buildings of the old Boston Science Museum, flanked by the white dome of the Hayden Planetarium, stretched across the river at the spot where the Charles River Dam blocked the way. To their left, the shells of empty oil storage tanks and burned-out warehouses and industrial plants rose from the ruins of the Cambridge side of the river.

"How do you propose to keep following the river?" Stein asked.

"I don't," Hunter replied. Under the empty windows of the Science Museum, Hunter brought the tiller sharply over and guided the whaleboat up the Lechmere Canal. Once under the abutments of the Cambridge Parkway Bridge, vague shapes hemmed them in, a narrow canyon of concrete and rusted steel. The boat thumped up against a jittery wooden pier, and King and Anderson jumped out and flattened on their stomachs to haul the boat against the rickety structure as the rest of the party scrambled out. Anderson retrieved his M-60, then the small group moved off at a jog across concrete pavement and gravel, past the silent and empty ruin of an industrial park.

"Ouch!" Rachel said. She stopped, leaning against a sheet metal wall with one hand while she pulled her shoes on with the other. "Hold it a minute."

"Not much farther." Hunter came up beside her. He reached out to take her arm, to help steady her, but she jerked away with a violence which startled him.

"Don't *touch* me!" From the set of her jaw and the wild look in her eyes, he realized her reaction had surprised her as much as it had him. She turned away with a grumbled, "You soldiers should learn to keep your hands to yourselves!"

"Sorry." He dropped back, scanning the surrounding ruins for signs of Russian occupation. A moment later, they rounded a corner. Fifty yards ahead, King and Gomez were helping a third man pull yard upon yard of camouflage netting off a squat, giant insect of gray-green metal.

"A helicopter!" Her eyes widened as she made out the painted blue flag of the U.N. Occupation Forces. "A *Russian* helicopter!"

"Polish, actually," Hunter explained. "An Mi-2 utility chopper, forty years old at least. Best we could steal on short notice. It'll be crowded and she's not armed, but flying that thing is simpler than trying to explain what a U.S. chopper is doing over occupied territory."

The others were already on board as Hunter and Rachel reached the helicopter's door. The engine coughed and whined, and the main prop began keening into motion.

Anderson slammed the door shut, the pilot brought the engine up to speed, and the aged helicopter lifted from its hiding place in the ruined industrial park and chugged low across the railway yards and burned-out warehouses of Charlestown. The spire of the Bunker Hill monument was just visible against the waters of Boston's Inner Harbor. Beyond, Logan Airport was alive with lights and moving vehicles.

"Went okay?" the chopper's pilot yelled over the drumming din of the props.

"We're clear," Hunter yelled back. "But stay low and out of their radar, just in case."

"No sweat." The pilot hauled the stick over, then they dipped to the left, skimming rooftops as they circled well north of the city. Twenty minutes later, they were on the ground at Hanscomb Field, an old Air Force and Guard strip just west of Lexington, abandoned since the Collapse, but not yet occupied by foreign troops already stretched thin. There they abandoned the helicopter and hustled aboard the black, streamlined shape of a stealth transport.

Rachel Stein buckled herself into one of the transport's narrow, straight-backed passenger seats. "By the way . . . just where are you taking us?"

"West, miss," Hunter grinned. "Ever been to Wyoming?"

Two

It had been a resort area once, a national park just west of the Continental Divide, tucked in south of Yellowstone where the Snake River flowed through a fertile, flat-bottomed valley almost completely enclosed by mountains. A dam on the Snake had created Jackson Lake, and a handful of communities—Moose, Moran, and Coulter Bay were the largest—had flourished for years on income from summer campers and fishermen and winter skiers. The area was properly called Grand Teton National Park after the most prominent of the mountains to the west, but most people, tourists and natives alike, referred to the valley by the more descriptive name of Jackson Hole.

There had been scant recreational camping in the United States since the Collapse, though survivalist bands and resistance groups camped and trained in deadly earnest at a thousand hidden sites across the Rockies and anywhere else where terrain and isolation kept the Soviets at bay. Since the beginning of the occupation by U.N. Peacekeepers, Jackson Hole had been one of the principal cantonment areas for what was left of the U.S. Army. The 3rd Battalion, 75th U.S. Rangers, or what was left of them after the fighting outside of Omaha, had been headquartered at Moran. For troops exerting linguistic privilege claimed by soldiers throughout history, Jackson Hole had, inevitably, become The Hole.

Hunter stepped from the stealth transport onto the runway of the airport just south of the original park boundaries, drawing in a deep, sweet lungful of mountain air. Around him Air Force personnel were already rigging camouflage netting over the sleek, black aircraft, while others hitched a tractor to its nose wheel in preparation for towing it to the shelter of rock-hewn hangar areas off the runway. Its landing had been timed to avoid the observation of Russian reconnaissance satellites, but it would have to be hidden before the next one was due to pass over.

There was no sense in tempting a Russian air raid or *spetsnaz* strike.

Officially, there was still only one United States of America, and the country's armed forces still took their orders from President Ashley and the American Congress. In effect, there were two nations and two governments. So long as the Soviet, Cuban, and Warsaw Pact Peacekeepers occupying the cities were unwilling to advance into the hazardous lands west of the Missouri, the Rocky Mountains offered a haven to those members of the armed forces who had

refused to demobilize when Washington had surrendered to the final Soviet ultimatum.

Much of the Free American Army operated out of
The Hole.

"Damned air smells funny," King said at Hunter's side.

"It's called 'fresh air,' Master Sergeant," Hunter
said with mock severity. "It's good for you."

King sniffed suspiciously. "Nah. No meat on it.
Bet you feel right at home, though, Lieutenant." He
looked around at the surrounding mountains, their
flanks clear and ice-covered, sharp in the spring air.
"Trees, mountains, cliffs. Wouldn't be surprised if
there were grizzlies out there for you to wres-
tle. . . ."

"Lost without any shopping malls around, eh,
Greg?"

King wrinkled his nose in distaste. "This ain't no
place for a city boy, that's all."

Hunter smiled. The joke was an old one. Greg
King had grown up in the Bronx. To hear him talk,
his life before he joined the service had been a cross
between *West Side Story* and a Chicago mobster
movie. In King's book, trees were what toothpicks
were made from, and mountains were made to be
leveled by bulldozers to make space for new parking
lots. He was a strange contrast to Travis Hunter, who
had been raised in the Alaskan backwoods; but despite their vastly different backgrounds they had a
friendship that broke all barriers of rank and upbring-
ing. Now that America was on the edge of extinc-
tion, the only home either of them had left was the
Army. After the rest of their old Ranger platoon was
lost fighting Cuban "advisors" at Omaha, the two

had been assigned together to a smaller, elite SPOT with Anderson and Gomez. Along the way, Hunter had lost track of the number of times the four Special Operations Team members had saved one another's lives. King was a lot closer to him now than his own brother, killed by the Russians during the annexation of Alaska in 2005, had ever been.

"Hey, Chief?" Gomez came up to them, his kit bag slung over his shoulder. "We s'posed to hike back to Moran now, or are they gonna send us transport?"

"We're to deliver our . . . guests, first, Sergeant." He gestured back to where Dr. Stein and his daughter were stepping off the plane. They looked rather small and lost in the midst of so many hurrying airmen. "After that, we'll have to see what our orders say."

Leaving King and Gomez to supervise the unloading of their weapons and equipment from the raid, he walked over to where Roy Anderson was talking with the Steins. The former Texan rancher, like the rest of them, had shed his blacks for more comfortable camo fatigues and had put on the white cowboy hat he always wore whenever he could get away with it.

Anderson saluted with a touch to the brim of his hat and a drawled "Howdy, Lieutenant." The formalities of traditional military courtesy were not strictly observed by members of the tight-knit team.

Hunter nodded. "Sergeant. Everything secure?"

"It is not, Lieutenant," Dr. Stein said. The rescued scientist appeared flustered and indignant. "Where is our transportation?"

"Sorry, sir," Hunter replied. "That's not our job.

Someone from FREAMCENCOM is supposed to meet you here and take you . . . wherever it is you're supposed to go. If they're not here to meet you, it's probably just a short delay.''

"Short delay!" Stein removed his wire-rimmed glasses and smeared at them with a loose shirttail. "I don't have time for 'short delays'! Such inefficiency is inexcusable!"

Hunter bit off a sharp replay. Stein could have had no idea before the previous evening that Hunter and his team would break into their MIT lab that night, but now that he was here, and free, he acted as though it were their fault they were being kept waiting. Hunter glanced once at the girl. She was aloof and cool, still draped in the too-large raincoat she had taken from the MIT lab.

"Our work is extremely important, Lieutenant," she said. "We need to reach a General Thompson as quickly as possible."

His eyebrows crept up. Major General Thompson was the senior-ranking officer at The Hole, and, at the far, far end of the intervening layers of command, his own commanding officer.

He returned his gaze to the elder Stein. Hunter's orders and pre-mission briefings had been disturbingly vague about just what the Free American Central Command wanted with the peppery little scientist; had not even hinted at what kind of a scientist he might be. Unbidden comparisons to Einstein and Fermi came to mind, but Hunter dismissed them. What kind of latter-day Manhattan Project could possibly help America now?

A growl of vehicles interrupted his thoughts. "Comp'ny comin', sir," Anderson said.

A trio of battered Army HMMWV squad carriers approached across the runway. They had obviously seen years of hard service; most of them, Hunter decided, spent wallowing through rivers of liquid mud.

A man in sharply-creased camo fatigues and a precisely-angled black beret dismounted from the lead vehicle and approached. His black, red, and yellow shoulder patches indicated he was a survivor of the armed forces of what had been West Germany before it had vanished into the Communist maw which had consumed Europe.

Hunter studied the familiar face for a moment, then grinned in sudden recognition. "Karl! Karl Jaeger! What are you doing here?"

The two men shook hands. Three years before, Hunter and his Ranger SPOT had completed the last mission to be carried off by U.S. forces in a Europe overwhelmed by revolution and Soviet interventions. Karl Jaeger, once a professor of history at the University of Hamburg, had been the leader of an anti-Communist guerrilla unit rescued by Hunter moments before the KGB closed in on his band in Wilhelmshaven. At one point there had been a question over just who was rescuing whom. Jaeger's deadly accuracy with a sniper rifle had held the Russians off long enough for Gomez to blast open a lock on the Ems-Jade Kanal, creating a watery diversion which had given them their chance to reach their boat and the safety of a submarine off Helgoland.

That had been before the Treaty of Washington and the virtual shutdown of the U.S. Navy.

"At the moment I am here to escort you and your guests on an outing to the mountains," he said.

"Us?" His orders had directed him to turn Dr. Stein over to FREAMCENCOM officers at the Jackson Hole airport, then await further orders.

"If you wish to come. I was directed to tell you that you and your men are being asked to volunteer."

"Volunteer? For what?"

Jaeger's mouth pulled slightly in what might have been a smile. "Ah. That I am not at liberty to tell you. It is dangerous . . . and very, very important, but more than this, I cannot say."

"And we're being asked to volunteer for it . . . just like that?" He glanced at the Steins, who were standing close by. "Does this involve them, by chance?"

"As I say, I am not at liberty to speak more." Jaeger reached inside his fatigue blouse and pulled out a folded piece of paper. The Orders of the Day dated two months previously had been crossed out on one side—paper shortages had hit hard at the Army bureaucracy—but the orders typed out on the reverse side directed him and his men to report to COFREAMCENCOM—the Commanding Officer, Free American Central Command. The final paragraph indicated he could refuse the orders, at his own discretion, and report instead to Major Cromwell at Moran, but it was signed "A. Thompson, Maj. Gen.," and included a scrawled, hand-written note at the bottom: *We need you—Thompson.*

He looked up, meeting Jaeger's ice-pale eyes. "Why'd they send you to fetch us, Karl?"

The German's expression was unreadable. "I presume because you knew me. This . . . project they ask you to volunteer for, I have already volunteered.

Perhaps we will be working together, you and I, once again.''

"But you can't tell me what it's all about?''

"Believe me, my friend, I know very little more than you. What I do know . . . well . . . I doubt that you would believe me. You must see.''

He read the orders again and shook his head. They did not appear to be the sort of orders that could easily be refused. He turned and saw the three men of his team watching him expectantly from where their gear and weapons were piled up on the runway.

Alexander Thompson wanted them? For what?

It appeared there was only one way to find out.

The three Hum-Vees crept slowly along the steep, snow-banked mountain road that wound up the heights above the town of Moose. Behind them lay the spectacular panorama of Jackson Hole, the sunlight glinting off scattered glacial lakes and the meander of the Snake River far below. To their right was the near-vertical thrust of the triple peaks—the *Grand Tetons*—which gave the park its name. Why some early French explorer should name them "the Big Breasts'' was beyond him, though. They looked hard, razor-edged, and metallic in the midday sunshine.

Directly ahead was a less spectacular mountain, flanked by the wilderness sprawl of endless white-clad pine forests. Mt. Bannon lay on the very edge of what had been national park land and could still be reached only by tailbone-thumping travel up Jeep trails and clay roads which turned to quagmires after a rain. Even for the rugged Hum-Vees it was slow going in low gear.

Hunter rode in the middle vehicle with the Steins and an Army driver. Gomez and Anderson had gone with Jaeger in the lead, while a small security force brought up the rear. Master Sergeant King sat across from him, scanning the terrain outside relentlessly. So far, Soviet troops had come no closer to the Rockies than their token occupations of Denver and Cheyenne, but King had survived a good many years of war and anarchy by never letting down his guard, even in the heart of "secure" territory.

He shifted his gaze to the Steins, father and daughter. Their low-voiced conversation during the jouncing ride up the slopes of Mt. Bannon had steadfastly excluded the two soldiers. Hunter, who considered himself brighter than average, couldn't begin to follow the complex technical discussions the Steins had kept up almost constantly since their rescue.

During a lull in the barrage of equations, Hunter tried to enter the conversation himself. "Ah . . . are you a doctor too, miss?"

She regarded him without emotion. "The Soviets moved in a year before I completed my graduate work, Lieutenant," she replied after a moment. She turned back to her father and continued speaking a nearly foreign language. Hunter exchanged glances with King, who shrugged and grimaced.

Hunter grinned. The memory of the stocky, powerful King rubbing his sore arm was not something he planned to let the master sergeant forget any time soon. *Smart, fast, easy on the eyes, but not exactly the typical helpless female. . . . Pity she thinks Rangers are throwbacks to the missing link.*

The Hum-Vee gave a thump and a lurch, and King cursed. "It'd be nice if they filled us in once in a while," he grumbled. "Escorting scientists through the middle of nowhere ain't my idea of a mission."

"Not exactly the middle of nowhere, Sergeant," Stein said dryly. He sounded like a teacher correcting an erring student, an effect promptly ruined with a soft chuckle. His ill temper seemed to have evaporated completely now that he and his daughter were finally on their way to their destination, and he seemed relaxed and quite at ease. "I believe you'll soon change your mind about this particular mission, too."

Hunter was surprised. "You know where we're going, sir?"

"I have no idea of how fully your superiors have briefed you or your men, Lieutenant. I trust you'll not take offense if we change the subject. I have never been fond of military secrecy, but it is not my place to discuss such matters unless I am given specific permission to do so."

"Of course, Dr. Stein," Hunter said politely. Inside, he was more anxious than ever to know the scientist's secret. For the past two years most of his missions had been based around the Jackson Hole area. In all that time he'd never heard of anything going on in the area that might involve a man like Stein.

He returned his attention to the spectacular mountain scenery passing outside the window. They had climbed a long, long way up the face of Mt. Bannon.

The Hum-Vee veered to the side of the road and lurched to a stop. "What's the problem, driver?" He could see that the other two Hummers in the little convoy had stopped as well, engines idling.

The corporal in the front seat turned and pointed

at his watch. "Timing, sir. According to the schedule, Cosmos-3427's due overhead in a few minutes now."

Hunter was puzzled. "So? They'll see us sitting here on a mountain road."

The driver merely said, "Yes, sir," and returned his attention to the road ahead.

Hunter frowned. "I don't think I'll ever get used to all this spy stuff," he told King.

After a moment, the lead vehicle pulled out ahead of them once more. Their driver put the Hum-Vee in gear and gunned the engine, following. They were entering a stretch where pine trees overshadowed the road. Sunlight flashed through from patches of blue sky only intermittently.

Hunter leaned forward in his seat. Ahead of the lead vehicle, the road widened well back under the trees, and another trio of Hum-Vees was turning into line ahead of them. For a moment, he wondered if this might be some sort of diversion or ruse, prelude to an ambush . . . until he realized that their own vehicles were swinging off to the right, leaving the newcomers to vanish down the main road in dust and shadows.

They faced a sheer rock wall; a dead end.

"What's with those other Hum-Vees?" Hunter asked.

"Security, sir," the driver replied.

Hunter nodded. The Soviets had maintained an absolute mastery of space since the mid-'90s, and there were few things happening in the unoccupied regions of which they were not almost immediately aware through their surveillance satellites. For a convoy of squad carriers to vanish on a particular stretch of mountain road might attract unwanted attention here. Someone, Hunter decided, was going to a lot of trouble to misdirect the Soviets, timing the switch for a moment when known Soviet spysats were out of range, and making sure that three Hum-Vees were visible farther up the road when the next satellite came over.

A dull, throbbing sensation, like heavy machinery moving far underground, transmitted itself through the Hum-Vee's body.

"Bloody hell!" Master Sergeant King commented to no one in particular.

Ahead of them, the bare rock cliff was moving, splitting down the middle, and opening outward with a low, grinding rumble. Twin steel doors camouflaged outside to blend into the rest of the mountain swung open to reveal an opening five yards wide and almost twenty yards high. It gaped darkly like the mouth of Hell itself. Slowly, the squad carriers drove forward, stopping only when the darkness surrounded them and the towering doors were behind, closing ponderously. They came together with an echoing clang, leaving the car and its occupants in darkness.

An instant later light blazed from every direction as spotlights stabbed through the darkness. Hunter blinked, squinting, unable to pick out any details of the chamber.

A booming PA voice echoed around them. "All occupants will leave the vehicles immediately."

They climbed out. The cavern felt large, though they could see nothing against the lights. Gomez, Anderson, and Jaeger dismounted from the lead vehicle and joined them. Uniformed figures moved against the light, soldiers with weapons closing in on the party. One figure detached itself from the rest, striding toward Hunter, heels clicking on the concrete floor.

"Dr. Stein!" the figure said. "You don't know how good it is to see you."

In the midst of so much strangeness, the sight of General Thompson was reassuring, to say the least. The Rangers snapped to attention, rendering crisp salutes. Thompson stepped out of the dazzle of the floodlights, a spare, white-haired, impeccably uniformed man. He returned the salutes. "And Lieutenant Hunter. Good work. Very good work, all of you."

"Thank you, General."

"I'm glad you took us up on our invitation. We'd like you to be a part of all this." Thompson turned to Rachel, smiling. "We were relieved to find out that you were with your father, Miss Stein. Dr. Fitzpatrick wasn't very clear on where you were being kept, so we had to plan the extraction assuming we couldn't get to you."

Her father answered him. "They wouldn't let Rachel work with me until Brian got away. Then I needed someone who could understand the direction the work was taking. . . . I suppose they decided she was worth more to them as a scientist than as a hostage to my good behavior. It might have taken weeks more work to wrap things up if she hadn't been there."

"Then Dr. Fitzpatrick was right about the breakthrough?" Thompson asked.

Stein nodded. "Everything I hoped for. I think we

can guarantee better than ninety-nine percent accuracy now.''

''Excellent!'' Thompson turned piercing eyes on Hunter. ''I suppose you feel a bit in the dark, Lieutenant.'' It was a statement, not a question, but something in the twinkle in Thompson's eye made it clear he expected a reply.

Hunter blinked into the lights. ''Mine not to reason why, sir. You point 'em out, my boys'll knock 'em down.'' He didn't quite succeed at keeping the curiosity out of his voice.

Thompson's mouth twitched in a smile. ''Well, I think you'll be getting some answers to your questions soon. We've kept the Project isolated for security purposes, but now that Dr. Stein is with us again, it's time we brought some Special Ops people into the picture. Your team has the best record of all the SPOT units in this district. You'll do perfectly for what we have in mind.''

''Sir?''

Thompson ignored him. He turned and addressed the darkness beyond the spotlights. ''Jenkins! Take us through!''

''Sir!'' A voice replied from somewhere, rich with echoes. ''Security team, stand to! Lights!''

Spotlights died away as banks of ordinary lights came on overhead. For the first time Hunter and the others could see details; the huge, empty chamber with encircling catwalks thirty feet above the floor, and the dozens of men positioned to cover the new arrivals. They were dressed in Army uniforms; M.P. armbands and helmets prominent.

A staff sergeant with a badge proclaiming him

Chief of Security saluted the General. "We'll try to make it fast, sir."

"Don't cut corners, Jenkins," Thompson replied. "You know the drill."

Jenkins motioned the newcomers to follow him. Hunter glanced back at the car and wasn't surprised to see men checking it over thoroughly, obviously searching for intruders or surveillance devices.

Thompson saw his glance. "We take security seriously here, Lieutenant Hunter," he said quietly. "This installation's sealed up tighter than SAC or NORAD ever were."

"Didn't help them when push came to shove," King muttered sourly.

The General heard him. "True, Sergeant," he replied. "That's why we've never advertised ourselves the way they did."

They reached the end of the chamber, another high wall with large, heavy steel doors set in reinforced concrete. A smaller, man-sized door was near them, with a small console mounted in the wall adjacent. Thompson walked up to it and placed his hand on a glowing panel. "Thompson, Alexander," he recited. "U.S. Army, serial number 657-86-2119. Commanding Officer, Free American Central Command. Request admittance for myself, six visitors, one staff."

He withdrew his hand and looked at the others. "We'll process security clearances for the rest of you later. I'm afraid your records were pulled after the east coast went, Dr. Stein."

"Perfectly understandable, General. You couldn't know what they might be doing to me."

A green light flashed on the console, and a seductively female voice spoke from a grill overhead. "Identity confirmed. Authorization granted." The small door slid open. "Welcome to the Chronos Project Complex."

"Chronos Project?" Anderson wondered aloud as Thompson led the party through the door and into an elevator car.

"Yes, Sergeant Anderson," Jaeger said. He smiled faintly. "From the Greek word for time."

"I don't get it, sir," Gomez said, shrugging. "Just what is this place, anyway?"

"It could be America's last hope for freedom, Sergeant Gomez," Thompson said seriously. "Our chance not just to survive this war, but to erase everything it has done to our country. Literally." He pressed a button and the elevator started a fast descent deeper into the heart of the mountain. "Inside this complex, gentlemen, we've spent damn near thirty years putting Chronos together, thanks largely to Dr. Stein. Now we're getting ready to go on-line."

No one responded. The elevator continued to slide smoothly downward. Finally, Thompson continued. "Gentlemen, you are about to see the world's first operational time machine."

Three

"Officially this is the Main Control Room," Thompson explained as they stepped through the door. This, it seemed, was the final stop on the long tour through the Chronos Complex. The General, Jaeger, and the Steins preceded the team into a broad, brightly lighted chamber. "Officially, I say, because most of our people call it Time Square."

The room was square and cavernous, with a ceiling lost far above in a blue haze of neon lights. The layout reminded Hunter of pictures of Houston's Mission Control back when there had been a NASA, with bank upon bank of instrument panels, computer displays, and communications consoles. They walked into the room along the central aisle. Groups of white-coated technicians clustered at various consoles on either side, where wiring spilled from open panels in spaghetti tangles across the linoleum floor. Something like the press booth at a sports stadium, a glassed-in balcony overlooking the stage, jutted above the entryway from the concrete-block wall behind them. Railed catwalks ringed the room at the level of the balcony. A security camera rotated to follow their progress.

The stage, as Hunter thought of the low platform at the far end of the room, was dominated by a flattened, egg-shaped structure of ceramic and dull metal, encased in layer upon coiled layer of power cables and cooling fluid conduits. One end of the egg was open, the entrance sheathed in heavily-insulated busbars and power leads. The interior was dark, but Hunter sensed that there was power there. Something about the egg, a haze or a shimmer across the entrance, suggested vast power held tightly reined, like the ozone-sharp expectancy in the air just before a summer's thunderstorm.

"A time machine," King said. "You have got to be putting us on." He paused, realized who he was speaking to, and added a belated "sir."

"Not at all," the general replied. "We've been after this for a long time, now. Remember all the Star Wars funding, before Congress shut it off? Part of that money came here, though the appropriations reports mentioned things like underground cyclotrons for particle beam research."

"And all this is your work, Dr. Stein?" Hunter looked around the room, impressed.

"Hardly, Lieutenant," Stein said. "Dr. Emil Lorenz started the original work back in the '60s. Of course, there was no way to apply his equations to the real universe until the breakthroughs with high temperature superconductors, twenty years later. It was a great pity he didn't live to see what we've built here.''

''Dr. Stein was Lorenz's protégé,'' Thompson added. ''He's been refining Lorenz's original time travel equations for years, now.''

''Is that what you were doing in Boston, Doctor?'' Hunter asked.

''More or less. Rachel and I were caught there when the Collapse came. I continued to work at MIT on their academic staff, and I used the Crays in their computer labs at night for my own work.''

''But it was close,'' Thompson added. ''The Soviets had already shipped a number of the doctor's colleagues off to Russia to work on their projects, and others were shot or imprisoned. For a while there, we were afraid we were going to have to send you in to yank him from a prison camp, Lieutenant.''

''Worse than that,'' Stein said. ''As I worked with the MIT computers, accessing files, performing data searches, and such, I had the definite impression our Soviet friends were aware of what I was doing; perhaps even trying to follow my work by eavesdropping through the system. I know someone was trying to read my files. They kept tripping safeguards we wrote into the access programs.''

Thompson stopped in mid-stride and turned to face Stein. ''Who?''

Stein shrugged. ''I have no idea. Possibly the Boston office of the KGB. They questioned me about my work on several occasions.''

''You think they may be working on the same lines of research?''

Again a shrug. ''Hard to tell, General. But it's

possible. To tell you the truth, I don't know why else they would have allowed me to remain at MIT so long, with access to MIT's files, unless they had . . . um . . . other motives.''

''Hmph. We'll have to check into that. The thought that the Soviets could be developing a time machine, too . . . that's scary.''

''It is not to be contemplated, General.''

Hunter shook his head. ''Sorry, General, but all this talk about time machines is beyond me. What's it all for?'' He gestured toward the massive egg in its nest of wiring and cables. ''Does that thing let you look back into the past somehow?''

Thompson started to reply, but Rachel answered first. ''Much more than that, Lieutenant. That *thing*, as you call it, is a portal . . . a door. Though it, we'll be able to enter the past . . . and change history.''

Hunter swallowed, but the sudden lump forming in his throat would not go away. History had long been a hobby of his. As a boy his childhood heroes had been men of the past: Davy Crockett and Daniel Boone, Robert E. Lee and Douglas MacArthur. Much of his dedication to the Rangers and what was left of the United States was dictated by his vision of what America and her people had been: at Bunker Hill, Gettysburg, and Leyte Gulf.

Change history? Actually go back and rewrite the history books? How could such a thing be possible?

Disbelief mingled with an uncomfortable chill spreading up his back. If it was possible, what might be done with it?

''You look like you don't believe it, Lieutenant,'' Thompson said. He smiled. ''Can't say I blame you.

It's hard for me to believe, and I've been running this nuthouse for eight years now.''

"Dr. Stein!"

They turned at the exclamation and looked up. A short man in a rumpled lab coat was waving a clipboard at them from the catwalk next to the booth above and behind them.

"Victor!" Stein replied. "Hello!"

"I'll be right down!"

The man swung onto one of the spindly ladders connecting the booth and catwalks with the main floor and made his way down, hand over hand. "That's Dr. Phillips," Thompson explained as they waited. "He's been running the scientific end of things here in Stein's absence."

Phillips hurried across to Stein, extended his arm, and pumped the scientist's hand vigorously. "It's good to have you back!" he said, beaming. "We had no idea you were coming until this morning! Damned military never tells us anything!" He paused, caught his breath, and took in the entire room with a wave of his clipboard. "Well? Well? What do you think?"

Stein nodded, looking around. "Impressive. You've made good progress."

"Now that you're here we can *really* move! It works! Splendidly! If your equations are as good as Fitzpatrick says they are, we should be able to establish accuracy to within an hour or two!"

Thompson turned to the others and explained. "Our single largest problem has been in the accuracy of our transmissions across time."

"Precisely!" Phillips said. "Up to now, we could

generally hit to within a couple, three years and within a few tens of miles of the target.''

"I suppose that could be embarrassing,'' Hunter said, "if you were looking for a particular date. Set out to visit the Boston Tea Party and arrive a year late."

"Or worse, you materialize in the middle of Boston Harbor," Phillips added. "Stein's transformation equations should give us marvelously precise control. Ah!" He seemed to see Rachel for the first time. "You must be Miss Stein."

"It's nice to meet you, Doctor," she said. "Father's told me a lot about you."

Phillips peered at Stein over his glasses, then looked back at Rachel. "Nothing good, I hope? Ha! I understand you've been helping my learned colleague here with his sums."

Rachel grimaced. "Something like that."

Stein chuckled. "More than that, Victor. I never got to see much of Rachel back when we were setting up the Project; she was still doing her graduate work at MIT when I went to get set up with the Institute's computer department. But she has an intuitive ability with temporal calculus which is positively astounding . . .''

"Oh, Father . . .''

"Let me show you the new matrices!" Phillips said, waving the clipboard again. "How long do you think it will take to incorporate those equations?"

"It should not take more than a few days," Stein replied. "Now, with the basic Lorenz Transformations, the third integral . . .''

Rachel, Stein, and Phillips began wandering toward the stage, already immersed in technicalities.

Hunter turned to face Thompson, then hesitated.
How does a lieutenant tell a general that he's crazy?

"Question, Lieutenant?"

"Uh . . . well, sir . . ."

"You may speak freely. This must all sound a bit
crazy to you, eh?"

"Frankly . . . yes, sir. Are you serious? You're
going to change history?"

"Dead serious, Lieutenant. But we just provide
the means. You, Lieutenant, you and your people,
are the ones who are going to do the changing."

Hunter looked at him blankly. "Sir?"

"You men know the situation as well as I do. It's
not good. America is on the ropes, and we don't
have much time left."

Hunter nodded slowly. The past five years had
been a long series of holding actions against a Communist world grown overwhelmingly powerful. Free
America consisted now of the Rocky Mountain states
and a scattering of hold-out enclaves in places where
rough terrain and a determined resistance made Soviet forays unhealthy.

The Collapse had occurred with frightening speed.
Once Mexico had gone Communist, the north-bound
stream of illegal immigrants was transformed into a
flood, an unstoppable horde riddled with Communist
agents, terrorists, and provocateurs bent on destabi-
lizing a United States already reeling from reverses
elsewhere around the world.

The nation's military response to this unofficial invasion had resulted in the U.N. branding the United
States as an outlaw nation. Riots inspired by both
left and right had destabilized the country as the government declared martial law and a dozen political

fringe groups proclaimed revolution. The occupation began shortly thereafter, when a handful of leftists in Congress seized power long enough to formally invite a U.N. Peacekeeper force. Soviet propaganda about irrational American military leaders with their fingers on the nuclear triggers had long since set the stage for the intervention. In fact, Soviet orbital laser stations rendered America's nuclear arsenal largely obsolete, but by this time the world believed—or pretended to believe—that it was American nuclear warheads alone which threatened world peace.

So far, the Soviet-controlled peacekeeping forces were restricting themselves to America's major cities. Russian advisors in Washington controlled the government through their puppets in the newly formed All-American Party. America's rural and small-town populations were too scattered, too numerous, and too hostile to what they perceived as a betrayal by the politicians for the Soviets to bother with as yet.

The operative word in that statement was "yet."

"Our best estimates suggest that the Soviets will begin tightening the screws within the next three to five years," Thompson continued. "With no industry, with damn little agriculture left, it's just a matter of time."

Hunter gave a wry smile. " 'A matter of time.' And that's where all this comes in, I suppose?"

"Precisely." Thompson nodded. Suddenly, he was all business. "This will be a volunteer assignment, of course. We are forming a small strike team, an Intervention Force, which we can project back through time to certain crucial points—crucial turning points of history—where a small change could make a big, big difference for us here, today."

Hunter nodded slowly. Basic doctrine for Ranger SPOTs held that a small, elite, well-trained body of men could exert force far out of proportion to their numbers. A handful of specialists could change the course of a battle . . . or bring down a government.

But through *time?*

"And you want us to be that Intervention Force," Hunter said.

"After hearing what we have in mind, you may still refuse the mission. However, we will have to assign you to our staff here at the Chronos Project, at least until we do form the team and it completes its mission."

Hunter nodded. "Okay, General. I can see the need for that. Just what is the mission, anyway?"

"We've worked out a series of missions, actually," Thompson said. "Phase I is the most important, the key to the whole project. Later phases will be designed to fine tune things, to make sure the new history falls into the proper shape."

"And what is Phase I? We go back and stop World War III?"

Thompson shook his head. "That's something I can't tell you . . . not until you've given me your final answer about whether or not you want to be a part of all this."

"That's kind of hard, not knowing what you want of us, General."

"Agreed. But it's big . . . and it's important. The Chronos Project is going to give America a second chance."

• • •

Jaeger led them to the mess hall, then showed them to their quarters four levels above Time Square after dinner. The Chronos Project facility was far larger than any of them had first suspected. Over a thousand men and women were quartered beneath the flanks of Mt. Bannon, and the various levels spreading out from the central elevator shafts resembled a small, subterranean city.

Their quarters were a suite of rooms opening into a common area. The five of them gathered there late in the base's artificial evening and talked. The topic of conversation was, quite naturally, centered on their part in what Thompson had called Operation Second Chance.

"Can't be done," King said with a confidence the others found unnerving. "Can't be! If we went back and changed history somehow, it would've already been done, right?"

"Aw, heck, Master Sergeant," Anderson said. "Trouble is, you don't read enough science fiction. We go back to—oh, I don't know—say fifteen years back. We pop into the Oval Office, say 'Hi there, Mr. President! We're from the future!' Then we tell him to stand up to the Russkis. No big deal."

Jaeger nodded. "And all of history changes from that point on. World War III never happens."

"It would help if we knew exactly what it was we were supposed to do in the past," Hunter said. "Karl . . . haven't they told you anything?"

"No more than you, my friend. They only brought me in last week."

King shook his head. "I just don't buy it. You can't fool around with history that way."

"How about you, Eddie?" Hunter asked. "What do you think?"

"Me?" Gomez's dark eyes met Hunter's. "It makes me wonder if the brass really knows what they're getting into."

"What do you mean?"

Gomez shrugged. "I don't know the first thing about history, Lieutenant. I don't really care about it, one way or the other. What I do know is demolitions. I know the formulas for working out exactly how much TNT you need to make a hole in . . . oh, say in a concrete wall two feet thick."

"Yes? So?"

Gomez spread his hands. "Seems to me history is a hell of a lot more complicated than blowing holes in walls. Do they really think we could change things . . . and be sure the change would be better than we have it now?"

Anderson chuckled, stretching himself out in his chair to his full six feet three inches. "How in the hell could things be any worse, Eddie? Russkis occupyin' our cities? Dictatin' to Congress? Our whole army turned, demobbed, or hiding out in the mountains? Seems to me, it might be worth the chance."

"Greg?"

"I just don't know, Lieutenant." King shook his head. "Damn, it's tempting. If it works, it'd be worth . . . anything. Anything at all. But I don't see how it'd work. How it *could* work."

"Karl?"

"I have already made my decision, Lieutenant. I will go back with your team, or another." He shook his head. "If there is any chance to change things from what they are . . . any chance at all . . ."

"What do you think, Lieutenant?" Gomez asked.

Hunter thought about the question carefully. Going back in time . . . rewriting history . . . The whole idea sounded crazy.

But if Thompson and his people were right . . .

His Rangers training had prepared him for an idea he would otherwise have immediately dismissed as pure science fiction. A handful of trained men, in the right place, at the right time . . . they could change history, literally!

"I think," Hunter said after a long, thoughtful pause, "that we're being offered a chance to restore America to what she was before the Collapse. That sounds to me like something that's worth fighting for . . . no matter what the price. Maybe it'll work, maybe not. But we *have* to find out!"

There was a murmured chorus of assent from the others.

No military force can ever operate as a democracy, but the four Rangers were close, brothers bound together by blood and trust and the fire of more battles than any of them could remember. Hunter asked for a show of hands. The decision was unanimous.

Hunter reached for the phone and punched in a set of numbers. Thompson had given him the code to open a secure line to his quarters, with instructions to call at any time once the team made its decision. The others sat quietly, listening to Hunter's end of the conversation. "General? It's Hunter. We've decided. We want in."

The silence in the room grew as Hunter listened to the reply.

"Yes, sir," Hunter said after a moment. "May I ask, sir . . . just what *is* our mission?"

As he listened to the response, Hunter's eyes widened slightly. His knuckles whitened as they gripped the phone. "Yes, General. I understand." He struggled to keep his voice level. "I'll tell them."

Very, very slowly, Hunter set the phone back, then turned to look at the others.

"Well?" King asked. "What's the op?"

"I'm not sure I believe this," Hunter said. "Our orders are to go back to Germany, in the year 1917. We're to kill Vladimir Ilych Lenin."

Four

The idea was admirably direct and simple. Lenin's death in 1917, before he could organize a Communist government in Russia, would be more than just a victory in the long war. It would, in fact, transform the world.

The heavyset man sitting across the table from them leaned back in his chair, rubbing his chin with one finger. "It all hinges on the Russian Revolution," he said. His name was Leonard Todd, and he was giving them their first introduction to the time the Intervention Force was to visit.

By April of 1917, the first Russian Revolution had already more or less succeeded. Russia was in chaos, and the Czar in abdication. The Provisional Government was already beginning to pull things together, however, despite the wrangling between dozens of factions struggling with and against one another for control of the fallen empire. By summer, the young and dynamic Aleksandr Kerensky would emerge as the leader of a coalition government, bearing the promise of a western-style democracy in Russia.

Early in April a German government anxious to see Russia knocked out of the war gave free passage to a Marxist revolutionary exile named Vladimir Ilych Lenin. Put aboard a so-called "sealed train," he and his party were smuggled across Germany from Switzerland to the Baltic port of Sassnitz. From there, his party took a ferry to Trelleborg, then made its way through Sweden and Finland to the Russian city which one day would bear his name.

Over the course of the next few months Lenin brought new life and organization to the most radical of the feuding revolutionary parties—the Bolsheviks. By October Lenin had managed to win unprecedented support within the Russian military. That month would see the *second* Russian Revolution . . . the fall of Kerensky and the triumph of the Bolsheviks.

"Lenin was the key," Todd continued. "On April seventh he left Zurich, changed trains at the border, and set off across Germany. We have a precise timetable for the Lenin party . . . to Frankfurt, Berlin, and Sassnitz. On the tenth, at six in the evening, he arrived in Sweden. On April sixteenth, his train pulled into Petrograd—uh, that's Leningrad today— where he was welcomed by the Bolsheviks." He looked up from his notes. "These dates are according to the modern Gregorian calendar, of course. At the time, the Russians were still using the old Julian calendar, so they remember Lenin arriving in Petrograd on April third.''

"Whatever the date," General Thompson said, "our history people say Lenin's train trip is the best time to hit him."

Todd frowned. "I still think you should reconsider, General. Surely the military option should be delayed until we have a better idea of just what it is we're dealing with."

Thompson shook his head. "Reservations noted, Leonard. But right now, the military option is the only gambit we have left."

Hunter looked from one to the other. *So, even all the Chronos Project people don't agree yet. Interesting.*

Thompson had introduced Todd as Phillips's chief administrative assistant. According to Dr. Phillips, the man had become absolutely indispensable as the Project's chief research historian. On several occasions, Todd had adopted the persona of a writer for the newspaper *American Truth* and, with FREAM-CENCOM-forged credentials, slipped into occupied Washington solely to gain access to historical records in the Library of Congress.

"Just what other options are there, General?" Hunter asked.

"Only one, really," Thompson said. "We know Lenin's address in Zurich before he returned to Petrograd. He shared a room with one of his supporters . . . right across the hall from his mistress. We have discussed the possibility of sending a couple of men back to, say, February of 1917 and hanging around Zurich until they find a time to catch Lenin alone."

King chuckled. "Get him in a dark alley, eh?"

Thompson nodded. "Pretty much."

"Seems a slicker way to go than blowing up a whole train," Hunter said. If there was one particular nagging problem for him with the concept of time travel, it was the knowledge that the Intervention Force's actions in the past were going to have one hell of an impact on countless lives. How much of that impact could be foreseen? The fewer chances they took with the past, the better, so far as he was concerned.

"My point, precisely," Todd said.

"Normally, I'd agree." The General looked at his hands, folded on the table before him. "But history gets fuzzy sometimes. There are so many unknowns. The train gives us an exact time and place to hit it. If we send you to Zurich, you might have to wait around for weeks before you got a shot at Lenin."

"Isn't that a bit drastic, General?" Todd asked. "Blowing up a train with hundreds of passengers aboard . . . passengers who would survive that trip if we don't interfere?"

General Thompson smiled. "You haven't been in on the final stages of our planning, Leonard. We have that covered."

Todd grunted and looked unconvinced. Hunter thought that the researcher's point was valid, though. *There must be other people on that train besides Lenin. How are we supposed to get him . . . and no one else? I hope these people know what they're doing.*

Thompson watched Todd for a moment more, as though expecting further discussion. When the researcher remained silent, he unclasped his hands, placed them squarely on the table, and cleared his throat. "Very well. Let's get to specifics. . . ."

The mess hall for the Chronos Complex was located one level up from where Hunter and his men had spent the entire morning and part of the afternoon being briefed on their mission. Much of their time had been spent learning the history and politics of the early twentieth century. Their last session had been spent poring over photographs, portraits of the thirty Bolsheviks who, with Lenin, would be aboard the special train which was their target. Lenin was the one they were after, of course, but Thompson's Operations Staff had felt that identifying even one of the other people on the train would be a final proof that they'd accomplished their mission.

One face haunted him; that of a pretty, blond woman. Inessa Armand had been one of Lenin's converts in Paris and by 1917 was one of his most dedicated disciples . . . as well as his mistress. Devoted Bolshevik or not, it seemed a shame that she must die with Vladimir Lenin. Hunter had no idea what had happened to the woman in history as he knew it.

The bizarre nature of this new type of war nagged at Hunter. A person who would live in one universe would die in another . . . and that second universe would be of Hunter's making. He was not comfortable with the thought.

By the time he'd reached the cafeteria, the place was almost empty. His team had already eaten hours earlier and was now down in the Complex armory going over the weapons which were to be available to them on the mission; but Hunter had been delayed discussing the mission with Thompson, Todd, and Phillips, and so had missed lunch.

He didn't mind eating alone. It gave him time to think.

The moral issues of time travel were bad enough. Even worse was the basic complexity of history. Travis Hunter did not consider himself to be a historian, but he knew enough to have a profound respect for its intricacies. History was *not* an unending list of dates and kings and events. Each was a part of a whole. Change one event, and there was no telling what effect that change might have on the entire structure.

Wiping out communism, for example. Hunter had asked Thompson early that morning whether consideration had been given to the rise of Nazi Germany in the 1930s. As terrible a threat as communism was to the free world, there was no denying that the Soviet Union had helped destroy the Nazi menace in World War II. If Hitler's legions had not bled themselves white on the eastern front, what might have happened to the rest of the world? Surely, a world dominated by a fascist state and the Gestapo was as much to be dreaded as a world Communist state and the KGB? The politics might be different in theory . . . but the methods and the results of the two extremes were chillingly similar.

Thompson had merely smiled and replied with a phrase Hunter was coming to dislike. ''We've got it covered.''

On the other hand, had Lenin been all that important? Certainly, history remembered him as the one indispensable shaper of Russian communism in its infancy, but he had not acted alone. Trotsky and Stalin were two names he remembered—what of them? Perhaps the vacuum left by Lenin's death would have been filled by some other demagogue or political theorist. Perhaps nothing would change at all. . . .

"Mind if I join you?"

Hunter looked up, startled. Rachel stood beside the table, holding a tray. He stood, gesturing to a chair. "Of course not."

She sat but did not immediately pick up the sandwich on her plate. Hunter had the impression that wheels were turning behind that pretty face, but he felt at a loss in knowing how to start the conversation. "Uh . . . haven't seen much of you since we got here," he said at last.

She smiled, and the effect was dazzling. "I haven't seen much of myself," she said. "I've been working with Father, writing new software for the Chronos computers."

"His equations?"

Rachel nodded. "They incorporate a much better understanding of how time works mathematically."

"Time and math? So far as I know, two days plus two days equals four days."

She laughed. "Maybe in third grade. Not in the *real* world!" She sobered as she stirred sugar into her coffee. "Actually, I wanted to talk to you. I never had a proper chance to . . . thank you."

"Eh? For what?"

"For rescuing us, of course."

"Oh, that." So much had happened in the past two days Hunter had managed to put the events of the MIT raid completely out of his mind. He fought the urge to say something predictable about duty or just doing his job. He grinned. "Not bad for a bunch of Neanderthal bozos, hey?"

She looked up sharply, then shook her head. "I guess I was pretty awful, wasn't I?"

"Not at all. Oh, maybe you didn't seem all that eager to be rescued at the time." He chuckled. "Greg King's arm still hurts."

There was an intensity in her dark eyes that was almost frightening. "Oh God." She passed one slim hand across her mouth. "That night in the lab . . . For one moment there, I thought you people really were going to take Father and leave me behind."

Hunter was surprised to see she was trembling. "It was pretty bad in Boston, huh?"

She nodded. "You can't know, if you haven't been back there these last couple of years."

Rachel seemed alone and vulnerable. Hunter reached out to take her hand.

She jerked away. "Don't . . . !"

"I'm sorry . . ." Hunter felt an uncomfortable sense of trespass, as though he were intruding on some deep and savage grief. He pushed back from the table. "Maybe I should leave."

"No, please!" There were tears in her eyes. "Don't go, Travis. I'm . . . sorry. . . ."

"Would you like to tell me about it?"

She shook her hand. "No, not really." She used her napkin to wipe her face. She took a deep breath, obviously struggling for control. "It's not your fault," she said. "For a while, the Russians were holding me hostage, to make sure Father didn't run away. They . . . they were letting him keep on working at MIT. I'm not sure why. But they were afraid he would slip away, especially after Brian made his escape, and I was their guarantee that he wouldn't.''

Hunter nodded. He thought he knew what was coming.

"They had me in an apartment near the campus, with guards outside. Anyway, one night four of them got drunk. They broke into my room. They . . . they . . .''

He closed his eyes. "I know.''

After a moment, she was able to go on. "When Father found out, he was so furious . . . He insisted I be allowed to stay with him after that. The KGB major in charge of our security wasn't really a bad sort. Or maybe he just went along to keep Father working. We stayed together at the lab, after that. That's why you found us both there that night, instead of just him.''

"I'm glad we did.'' He decided to try to change the subject. "What did they know of your father's work, Rachel? They didn't know he was working on time travel stuff, did they?''

"They knew he'd been working on temporal theory. I think they may have been trying to look over our shoulders electronically. Father thinks so, anyway. Officially, Father was just on the MIT payroll as a physics professor. With no classes to teach, he could putter with the computers to his heart's content.'' She shrugged, then took a sip of coffee. "They must have known.''

That was disquieting. Hunter remembered Thompson's concern about a Russian time machine. He was only now beginning to realize the power time travelers might wield. Given the opportunity, what would modern Communists do to change history in their favor?

Rachel set the coffee cup down, then stared at her uneaten sandwich a moment. Finally, she looked up, her eyes meeting Hunter's. "Anyway, Travis, I am grateful. I wanted to tell you." She glanced at her watch. "I've got to go."

Hunter stood up. "Can't you stay?"

"I've got to get back to programming. As it is, it'll be another two or three days before we have the changes installed and the projector on-line. I'll see you tomorrow, though."

"Oh?" Hunter was beginning to hope he could see more of this fascinating woman.

"They have me scheduled to go over temporal theory with you tomorrow afternoon. See you then."

She carried her tray away, leaving Hunter to return to his half-eaten meal. Somehow, a briefing on temporal mechanics had not been quite what he had in mind.

Rachel seemed colder the next afternoon, wearing a strictly-business professionalism as though she wanted to keep them all at a distance. "The rate of change is implicit in the Lorenz-Stein equations," she said, pacing at the front of the room. "When you change history at a particular point, the effect we call the Transformation Wave sweeps forward at a rate which varies according to the Lorenz Uncertainty Factor. Eventually, on the order of several days later, the change will reach us here in 2007."

"By whose watch?" Anderson was leaning far back in his chair, his boots propped one atop the other on the conference table.

"I beg your pardon?"

"What watch are we usin', Miss Stein? I mean, if it takes several days for the change to reach you folks here, is that by your clocks here, or by ours, back in 1917?"

"Both, actually. If we project you back in time at, say, 9:00 A.M. our time . . . if you spend three hours in the past, you'll return to the complex at noon."

"Then, if we return to the present soon enough," Jaeger said slowly, "we will return before the change takes effect."

"That's what the numbers seem to be telling us," she replied. "By our calculations, your . . . interference in April of 1917 will take six days to reach us here in 2007."

"Ninety years in six days?" King said. "Not bad."

"Actually, the change moves slowly at first. It'll take three days to move the first fifteen years . . . and three more days to come the rest of the way. A logarithmic function is involved." She made a face. "It's easier to explain using a couple of blackboards covered by equations. But you people won't need to learn the math to understand it. Just take our word for it. It'll work."

"If we're going to be allowed to run around loose in 1917," Hunter said, "maybe we should understand what we're doing."

She shrugged. "I don't understand the aerodynamics behind that helicopter that took us out of Boston. This is the same thing."

"Not quite. If we have a limited amount of time in the past before some change we introduce takes effect, I'd like to know about it." Hunter spread his hands. "Suppose we succeed? I mean, we kill Lenin and wipe out communism before it gets started. Would there still be a Chronos Project? It was built to fight the Communists, after all. Without them, maybe none of this would have been built in the first place!"

"And you want to know if you'll be stranded in the past? No way to return?"

"Something like that."

"Good question." She paused. "I'll be honest with you. There's no way to predict the final structure of the new present . . . not with absolute precision. That's why we've structured these missions to be quick. We'll put you in, let you make the change, and pull you back before the transformation effect reaches us."

"And what then?" Gomez asked. "Do we all vanish? Just like that?"

She managed a thin smile. "Not quite. As I said, we can't predict exactly what will happen. Probably, all of us will still be here . . . but since we haven't spent the last twenty years or so fighting the Russians, we'll be living different lives, doing different things." She gestured, the motion taking in all of them and the subterranean workings around them. "That's what all of this is about, after all. Each of us will have different memories . . . since everything that's happened because of the Communists will never actually have happened."

King shook his head as though trying to clear it. "Whoa, there. And if none of this happened, who is it who turned off the Reds in the first place? No time machine to send us back, to stop the Commies, who made us build the machine, to send us back . . ."

"Sure!" Anderson said. "Go back and kill your grandfather . . . and then who is it that killed your grandfather?"

She held up her hand. "Right. The basic Temporal Paradox. But the physics don't work that way. There is one universe: ours. It contains certain . . . events, which we know as history. Go back and change things, and the events will be different. In the new universe, we don't need to build a time machine to go back and change things, because the change is now one of our remembered events . . . our new history." She looked back at King. "Does that answer your question?"

King growled something unintelligible. Jaeger leaned back in his chair, pressing his hands over his eyes. "I have this picture," he said quietly, "of one stray bullet taking out a German soldier on that train while we're after Lenin. I had a great-grandfather in World War I."

"Zap," Anderson agreed. "Hey, Karl. Don't you go leavin' us in the middle of a firefight, hear?"

There was laughter around the table. Rachel smiled. "Your actions will not cause huge chunks of the population to disappear, no," she said. "Presumably, your great-grandmother would have married someone else in the new universe you're creating. Oh, there will be changes, certainly; but small ones. You might wind up with brown eyes, instead of blue. You might remember your great-grandfather's name was Heinrich instead of Wilhelm."

"Lutz," Jaeger said softly.

"Whatever. The point is, you needn't worry about depopulating modern Germany. The genetic pool will remain the same, whatever happens to a few individuals.''

"I wonder," Hunter said.

"Pardon, Lieutenant?"

"However you look at it, we're taking one hell of a lot on ourselves . . . rewriting history. People who die in one history live, people who would have lived die. . . ." He looked up at Rachel, trying to interpret what he saw in her eyes. "I wonder if we have the right."

"Take a look at the world, Lieutenant." Her eyes closed. "The portal is an absolutely fantastic weapon, a weapon of unbelievable potential. With things as bad as they are, do we have the right *not* to use it?"

But Hunter was not entirely convinced.

"Now," Rachel said, picking up a briefcase and opening it on the table. The case was lined with foam padding and contained a book-sized box. "Let's talk about how we're going to get you back after the mission. This is a recall beacon. . . ."

Five

"You have the recall device?" Thompson looked worried, the strain showing in his eyes and in the quick, nervous motions of his hands. Above them, at the top of the ramp, the portal shimmered behind its curtain of shifting blue light.

Hunter patted the canvas pouch slung from his combat vest and hanging at his hip. "Right here, General." The small control unit, sealed in its shockproof case, would be their only link with their own time once they arrived in 1917. Their briefings of the past week had included numerous sessions with the device.

The science of the thing was beyond him. All Hunter knew was that unlocking the device and pressing a button would transmit a pulse of energy, somehow, forward through time. Stein and the others

at Chronos Complex would be able to reestablish the
link, allowing the team to return to their present. It
would take some time, they'd explained, to build up
power sufficient to open the portal. Hunter just hoped
that when it came time for them to leave 1917 Germany, they weren't in a terrible hurry. He could picture facing an attacking platoon of German soldiers
and saying, "Please wait, *bitte*. Our time machine
isn't quite up to full power yet."

Hunter looked down the line of his men standing
at the foot of the portal ramp. All were outfitted for
a night commando raid; black clothing and tactical
vests, watchcaps, and faces. Jaeger carried his bullpup Walther Wa-2000 which looked even more like
something out of a science fiction movie than usual
with its night vision scope attached. Anderson shouldered the 15-pound bulk of an RPG rocket launcher,
plus a pair of rocket grenades. An H&K SMG was
strapped across his chest as his backup weapon. The
others, less heavily burdened, carried assault rifles,
Hunter and Gomez H&K 33A2s, King an FN-FAL.
On this mission, any firefight the team ran into would
be in the open and at fairly long range, where submachine guns would lose their effectiveness. All of
them wore backpacks laden with the other gear they
would need for the mission.

Thompson clasped his hands behind his back,
looking at each of them in turn. "I won't make a
long speech, gentlemen. I don't need to remind you
how vital this mission is to . . . to all of us. To
America. If you succeed, you five men will have the
singular distinction of having created a new world
. . . a world free from the horrors of communism.
We can't say yet with any certainty what that new

world will be like, but we know it will be a better
world, one that has not been drained by the terrible
cost of preserving our dwindling freedoms against
the Soviet empire.''

Hunter kept his face expressionless. There were
still unanswered questions about that new universe,
and he was still worried about them. At the moment,
all he could do was assume that Thompson's assur-
ances that they ''had it covered'' would indeed deal
with any problems the absence of a Soviet Russia
might cause during the course of a rewritten twentieth century.

''If all goes as planned,'' Thompson continued,
''you will find yourselves near the Werra River in
central Germany. The date will be April 8, 1917; the
time somewhere close to midnight. You should be
able to complete your mission and return within three
hours.'' He glanced momentarily up to the control
booth, where Stein and Phillips were at the main
controls. ''We have absolute confidence in the math-
ematics of this process, of course. We know we can
place you quite close to the place and time we select.''

Stein's equations had been absolutely vital for that
aspect of the Chronos Project, Hunter knew. Indi-
vidual men sent into the past before Stein's rescue
had reported missing their target by years, in some
cases. During one of his briefing sessions, Hunter
had seen a collection of newspapers acquired by the
Project's volunteer scouts. One man sent to 1910 had
emerged in 1864 and returned with a newspaper telling of the upcoming presidential race between Lincoln and McClellan. The historian in Hunter had
been fascinated, but he had wondered what that scout

had thought, finding himself off target by over fifty years. Hunter had not been able to ask the man about it, since he'd been sent out on another test run and never come back, one of the twenty or so casualties the Chronos Project had suffered while trying to calibrate the time portal's control settings.

At least, the IF team were not the first to travel in time. It gave them fewer things to worry about.

"It will be up to you to get in, hit your target, and get out," Thompson continued. "We expect to have you back in this chamber three hours from now, your mission accomplished . . . and with a new and golden age about to dawn, thanks to your efforts." He hesitated, as though trying to think of something more to say. "Good luck, men. Our prayers go with you."

He paused a moment more, then turned abruptly and strode toward the back of the room.

"Not bad as send-off speeches go," King muttered at Hunter's side. "Sounds like *he* believes all this, at any rate."

Hunter grinned. "Let's hope he's right." *God, I hope he is!*

Thompson paused at one of the main floor computer consoles to speak with Leonard Todd and one of the Project technicians. *Todd seems to have made peace with the idea of sending troops into the past at least,* Hunter thought. *We'd never have been able to pull this thing together without his maps and research. Good Lord . . . finding one train on one bridge in the whole of Germany ninety years ago . . .*

There was a touch at his elbow. He turned and

found himself looking into large, dark eyes framed by a cascade of black hair. "Hello, Miss Stein."

"Travis, I . . ." She stopped and looked away. "Oh, damn. A moment ago I knew just what I was going to say." The cold and distant professional manner of the briefing sessions was gone, and she seemed embarrassed.

"How about 'have a nice trip'?"

She tried to smile but did not entirely succeed. "I just wanted to say . . . be careful. Take care of yourselves."

"We sort of had that in mind."

"Sure, we're always careful," Gomez said from the end of the line a few feet away. He tugged at the strap securing his demolition gear to his back. "It's in the bag!"

"Ahh . . . right," she said with an ironic tone and a sidelong glance at Gomez. She hesitated, then reached out her hand, awkwardly, and Hunter took it. Her fingers were cold. "Hurry back, Lieutenant."

She turned and was gone. Hunter looked after her, wondering about the change in her manner.

A blast of sound from the PA speakers interrupted his thoughts. After a squeal of feedback, Phillips's voice echoed through the chamber. "Full power in thirty seconds."

Hunter looked up at the booth, where Stein gave him a thumbs-up sign. Hunter waved, then turned to his men. "Stand ready, people."

The team took their positions on the ramp. There was room for two to pass through the portal at a time, and their marching order had been worked out during the previous week. First through would be Hunter and King, their assault rifles at the ready just in case they were met by any unforeseen reception committee. Gomez would be next, his demo equipment and skill essential to the plan. Jaeger and Anderson would bring up the rear. A throbbing hum which seemed to rise from the floor beneath their feet filled the room, and the auroral displays playing about the portal's mouth grew in intensity. As Hunter stared into the opening, he became aware of a growing swirl of light within light, a whirlpool of cold blue fire obscuring the portal mechanism at the top of the ramp.

Hunter had never seen the device running at full power. *They want us to walk into that?*

"Ten seconds," Phillips announced over the PA. "Good luck!"

The hum grew, a palpable droning in the air. Hunter shifted the H&K assault rifle to the ready position. He wished he could wipe the sweat from his face, but there was no time.

"Full power! Portal open!"

Hunter strode forward up the ramp. Light engulfed him, cold fire clinging to him and gathering in pulsing nodes along the barrel of his rifle. He was aware of no particular sensation as he stepped back through ninety years and several thousand miles of space . . .

It was night on the far side of the portal, star-studded and clear, with a chill breeze bearing the scent of mountain pines and fresh water nearby. Hunter turned to watch his team file through the faintly luminous, swirling pool of blue light. A moment later, the whirlpool seemed to wind itself up into a glowing blob of luminescence which faded away, leaving no trace at all that anything unusual had been there. Beyond where the portal had existed was a boulder-studded bluff almost invisible in the dark. Frogs creaked and croaked in the distance. Otherwise, it was completely silent.

Could this be Germany, ninety years in the past? Hunter shook his head, still wondering if it could be true. Somehow, even right at the end, he had doubted. He reached down and touched damp moss, then glanced up as a bat darted and swooped overhead. It was peaceful here, rugged and tree-covered. But if they were where and *when* they were supposed to be, the thunder and trench-mired hell of the western front lay less than three hundred kilometers to the west.

And a train was approaching through the valley below them bearing the man who held in his mind the destiny of Russia . . . and of the twentieth century.

Jaeger pointed to a cluster of lights partly obscured by trees and rolling hills off to the southeast. "That should be Eisenach."

Anderson gestured in the opposite direction. "That would put the Werra down there."

"The terrain fits what Todd told us," Hunter said. "Looks like they got the location right, anyway." It was an odd feeling. They were standing on a hillside which, in thirty more years, would lie just to the east of the barriers between East and West Germany. And in his own time . . .

He looked up at the sky. There was no way to be absolutely certain that they had arrived at the right date, or even the right year, but his Ranger training had taught him to estimate time from the stars. The constellations were right for early April. With Leo almost straight overhead and Orion setting in the west, it was probably about midnight—right on target. Lacking any other precise time, he set his watch to 2400.

King studied the sky beside him. "Could be they hit it right." Then he grinned in the darkness. "Okay, Lieutenant. Now look at the stars and tell us what *year* it is."

"That, Master Sergeant, we're going to have to find out for ourselves," Hunter replied. "First we find the railroad bridge. If that special train comes through at 0300, if the serial numbers match what Todd told us, I think we can assume this is 1917."

"And pray to God those scientists know what they're doing."

Hunter thought about the twenty men who had died getting the data necessary for calibrating the portal's accuracy. "We have to assume they do," he said. "Let's move out, gentlemen. We have a train to catch."

Six

Hunter lay on his belly on a partly wooded ridge-top east of the Werra, studying the view through starlight binoculars. Below him, railroad tracks crossed the river on a bridge of iron girders set on concrete pylons. The ravine was an inky slash through the valley, fifty yards wide.

"Any sentries?" King whispered.

"Not a one," Hunter replied. "Looks clear."

"Wasn't likely there would be," King replied. "Not unless they put sentries on every damned bridge in Germany."

Hunter lowered the binoculars. "You sound worried, Greg."

"Ah . . . I dunno, Lieutenant. I just don't like the whole bloody idea. The past is the past . . . and I don't see how we're gonna change it."

That still? "Orders is orders, Master Sergeant. Let's get on with it."

Following the plan worked out in step-by-step detail during the previous week—and *that* was a linguistic tangle Hunter did not care to examine closely—Hunter and King began unpacking explosives from the packs they wore, helping Gomez unwrap and place them, kneading each lump of plastique into key spots under the railbed along the bracing on the east bank. Anderson and Jaeger slipped across the bridge to the west side to search for a good observation site. From there, they would be able to warn the others by the small headset radios they wore if the train was seen approaching. Telling time by the stars was accurate only to within an hour or two . . . and it was always possible that the train would be early.

They worked quickly but with exaggerated care. The rocks they clung to were damp; the soil of the embankment muddy clay which could be treacherous under a misplaced boot. The only light came from a moonless sky and the small, red-lensed flashlights they clipped to their shoulder straps. The Werra at this point was normally only a couple of feet deep, but the spring melt and heavy rains had swollen the creek to a sizeable and swift-flowing stream. The waters of the ravine were impenetrably black and invisible even when their lights were directed into the gulf, but Hunter could hear the constant roar and hiss of the flood below him. The bridge spanned the ravine perhaps fifteen feet above the water's surface. By the time he was done, his clothing was damp from the fine mist sprayed up from the river's coursing against concrete supports and water-smoothed boulders.

Finally Gomez placed the last of the small, radio-activated blasting caps he carried and gave a thumb's up of satisfaction. They scrambled up the bank and made their way along the wooden plank deck of the bridge between the double set of rails.

Jaeger had found a lookout point on the spur of a ridge south of the tracks, rising from the west bank of the Werra. Though heavily wooded, the north slope was clear and afforded an excellent view across the low-lying land to the west. In the east, a third-quarter moon was rising clear of the hills above Eisenach, spilling light into the valley. With their eyes already dark-adapted, they could make out endless details of forest and rocky slope, the unnatural angles of an isolated farmhouse miles away, the spidery tangle of girders supporting the railway bridge. Hunter found a convenient boulder which he designated as their primary rendezvous and hid the recall beacon there, still wrapped in its canvas satchel. If he should be killed in the coming action, the others would still be able to recover it and make their escape. Gomez found a sheltered spot among the rocks just above the Werra, where his radio detonator would have a clear line of sight to the explosives on the far side of the ravine. Anderson joined him, his RPG unslung, loaded, and ready. The others lay spread out and silent on the crest of the ridge, watching for the train.

By Hunter's arbitrarily-set watch it was 0240 when they saw the lone, baleful eye of light far off to the southwest. They watched it through their binoculars long enough to verify that it was a train locomotive, traveling toward them along the rails which curved around the northern flank of their ridge.

"Stand by, Eddie," he said into the slender mike extending from his headset. By this time, the distant rumble of the train could be heard against the night noises and the far-off brawl of the Werra.

Time seemed to crawl for them. The locomotive, a massive 4-6-2 engine, appeared to move faster as it grew closer, an inverted pyramid of smoke boiling above its stack and iluminated by light reflected from its headlight. The rumble of wheels was augmented now by the chuff and bellow of steam belching from the driver pistons on either side of the engine.

Hunter studied the chugging beast through binoculars. "I have the number," he said. "Twelve-oh-four. It checks." He swung his binoculars to the last car in the line. It was dark, the shades of every window drawn. He could make out a number on the side, under the line of blank windows. "Car number eight-one-one-five-zero-four. Check again."

"Verified, Lieutenant," King's voice was an awed whisper at his side. The master sergeant dropped the binoculars from his eyes, then raised them again as if expecting an illusion to vanish.

It did not.

The engine thundered around the curve north of the ridge. Behind it were the tender and four cars, as expected.

"We have our target, Eddie," he said into the microphone. "Last car in line is verified."

"We're ready here, Chief," Gomez replied in his ear. *"Charge armed."*

"Right. At your discretion, Eddie. The target is

yours.'' He touched King and Jaeger. ''Let's move, people.''

A hundred yards below them, the train rounded the slope and entered the straightaway leading to the bridge. The blast of the locomotive's steam whistle, piercing and lost-soul mournful, shrilled above the chuff-hiss-chuff of the engine's drivers. Jaeger, King, and Hunter hurried across to the opposite side of the ridge and began sliding down the steep embankment toward where Gomez and Anderson were waiting. They emerged from the trees as the locomotive thundered across the bridge, steam billowing through the iron girders and out across the black chasm beneath. The whistle wailed again, dopplered down a note as the train moved away from them. The tender was clear of the bridge now . . . and the first car . . . and the second . . . Gomez gripped the firing lever, safety off, waiting as he counted the railroad cars off the east end of the bridge.

What if Greg's right and we can't change history? The thought was a small, nagging agony in these last seconds. *If history can't be changed, then something's going to go wrong. The detonator won't work, or the charges won't fire. . . .*

Gomez's arm moved convulsively. Orange flame erupted from the top of the far abutment, as thunder echoed down the ravine and off the east slope of the ridge. The flare blossomed, fireballing up into the night as the bridge gave a sickening, slow-motion shudder and jerked back from the far embankment. Bits of wood planking and chunks of iron and concrete spun out through fire-edged darkness. The last car of the train broke free from the next car ahead, rearing back on its rear wheels like a living thing burned by the flame. Momentum kept it moving forward. The railcar crumpled into the shattered abutment as its trailing end followed the twisting bridge debris into the gulf, smashing against the rocks at the bottom and raising a vast spray of water and shattered wreckage. Part of the bridge structure burned, illuminating the ravine. The car lay twisted and torn, on its side and half submerged in the foaming water. Most of its windows were shattered and, faintly now, the screams of people trapped inside could be heard above the waters roar and the clattering racket from the far bank.

In the far darkness, the locomotive was braking to a halt, the surviving cars derailed and striking sparks as they ground along rails and ties and rocks. It would be long seconds before so many tons of metal came to a stop. The third car broke free of its coupling and landed on its side, sliding a dozen yards with a shriek of steel on steel. Already, it was evident that the blast had been perfectly timed, that Gomez had calculated those charges with precision. There might be injuries among the passengers of the rest of the train, but no fatalities.

But the Bolshevik car must be a charnel house by now.

Roy Anderson sighted along the heavy tube balanced on his right shoulder and squeezed the trigger. The RPG flashed at both ends, and the five-pound missile kicked forward, falling free until its fins snapped open and its rocket motor fired. The projectile was visible by the burning point of light at its tail as it swooped down into the ravine and impacted squarely on the wrecked railway car, just above the water. The explosion nearly tore it in half, and the wreckage slipped further down the embankment, wreathed in smoke and boiling water. Anderson began loading his second missile.

Hunter brought his binoculars up. The car, what was left of it above the water, was burning now, and the river around the wreckage was well lighted. Movement caught his eye . . . a head! Someone was swimming . . . or rather, someone was struggling against the foaming current, trying to reach shore.

The crack of raw sound close to Hunter's ear startled him. Karl Jaeger was standing a few feet away, the boxy Wa-2000 raised to his shoulder, the rubber eyepiece of its telescopic nightsight pressed against his eye. The head disappeared.

"Did you get a positive ID?" Hunter asked.

For answer, Jaeger tracked his rifle a little to the left. Hunter brought the binoculars back to his face and saw the target, the head of another swimmer. This one was a woman, her long, blond hair a tangled mask across her face as she clambered from the water. Briefly, he wondered if that might be Lenin's French mistress, Inessa Armand . . .

The crack sounded again, and the figure lurched, toppling back into the water. Hunter spun on Jaeger. "What in hell are you doing, Karl?"

Illuminated by the distant flame, Jaeger's face was a sallow mask, without emotion. Hunter reached out and pushed the sniper rifle's muzzle up until it pointed at the sky. "Karl! What are you doing?"

"I . . ." The man's pale eyes focused uncertainly on Hunter. "Killing."

"I can see that, dammit. But you're looking for Lenin, got it? He's the one we want! The others don't matter!"

Jaeger looked at him, blank incomprehension in dead eyes. Hunter turned away, shuddering. Jaeger had acquired a reputation for icy deadliness in the years he had fought with the Free German underground, a ruthlessness Hunter had seen before in Wilhelmshaven. But this was worse . . . far worse.

The only targets Hunter had seen the West German take down before had been Soviet troops and an arrogant KGB major. This slaughter of helpless survivors from the wreck they'd engineered, Bolsheviks or not, was something entirely different.

Disturbed, Hunter left Jaeger and made his way farther down the embankment. The slope grew steeper and more crumbly as he neared the water. He reached a point where he was balanced on a boulder extending out into the water. He pulled his H&K assault rifle around to the ready position and searched the far side of the ravine.

Another figure limped from the wreckage, silhouetted by flame. Anderson's second rocket hissed down from the slope above and slammed into the wreck, smashing the charred target into splintered, burning fragments. For a moment, Hunter thought the survivor had been swept away by the blast. Then he saw the figure again, closer now among the rocks on the opposite bank, a man's figure waving a heavy revolver and shouting across the water. He strained to catch the man's words above the roar of the flames and the water. *"Dah z'drahfst'vooyet Bolshevyestskey reval'yutseyah!"*

Russian! If further confirmation that they had the right train car was needed, this was it. Gunshots banged across the water. A bullet snapped somewhere above Hunter's head. The man's aim was wild; he might not even be able to see Hunter at all, but the IF team commander decided to move back onto the slope and out of the light of the burning wreck. Another sharp crack came from above. The silhouetted figure spun wildly, the revolver spinning out and into the water. The crack sounded once again, and the man pitched forward into the water and vanished.

The last of the wreckage was sinking into the river, extinguishing the fire from the RPG rounds. Hunter was aware of a new sound now, the crackle and snap of small arms fire.

"Things are getting hot, Lieutenant." King's voice over the radio headset sounded worried. *"We're taking fire."*

"Pull back across the ridge," he replied. "We're done here."

From the bottom of the embankment, he had not been able to see the rest of the train, but as he climbed the slope, he could turn and look back to where the derailed train lay on the far side, still belching steam and smoke as half-glimpsed figures jumped from the cars. Intermittent flashes of light marked where troops were firing at the west side of the ravine, evidently convinced that the attack on the train had come from there. Voices called to one another in German, giving orders to spread out, to advance on the river, to fire. A spark of light flared into the sky, then exploded in flickering, day-bright radiance. The Rangers froze in place as the flare hung from its parachute far overhead, bathing the ridge in actinic light. So long as they didn't move, the Germans across the river would not be able to see them.

Probably.

After a long minute, the flare burned out and
Hunter began racing up the slope, grabbing at tree
roots and bushes to help him up the hillside. Then
he was at the crest and dodging into the shelter of
the woods as small arms fire continued to probe and
bang from the far side of the Werra.

He joined the others at the rendezvous site, where
King had already recovered the recall beacon. Hunter
activated the device, unlocked the switch cover to
expose a single large, red button, and pressed it with
his thumb. Now they needed only to wait for Stein
and the others at the Chronos facility to pick up the
message, build up the portal's power, and open the
way for their return to their own time.

Eighteen minutes later, blue fluorescence sparkled
into being above the beacon, thickened, and began
revolving, a familiar and welcome whirlpool of light.
One by one, the commandos stepped through.

Strange. As he stepped into the harsh light of Time
Square, it felt as though he'd been gone for years,
instead of barely three hours.

Seven

Hunter found himself looking around the cavern-ous expanse of Time Square, as though he expected to see some physical evidence that they had indeed transformed history. The change was not due to hit the present for another six days, but the *reality* of what they'd done—utterly destroying the railway car carrying Lenin to 1917 Russia—needed some tangible proof to be believed at all.

But the final proof had not yet arrived.

"Mission accomplished," he said as Thompson walked across the gleaming floor.

"Excellent! Excellent! Did you manage to make a positive ID?"

Hunter shrugged. He was terribly tired, now that the strain of the mission was past. "There was a woman . . ." He paused. It had been dark, and she had been more than fifty yards away. "No, Sir. Not on any of the people. The numbers on the engine and on the passenger car matched with what we'd been told."

Thompson nodded. "That's all we could really hope for. It would have been nice if you could have *seen* Lenin's body . . . but then, we'll see the proof of it in a few days, eh?"

Anderson came up next to them "Can't be too much doubt about it, General!" He was excited, almost jubilant. The end of a mission always affected him differently than Hunter. Where Hunter felt only a profound and crushing exhaustion as the adrenaline charge left him, Anderson became positively buoyant. "Man, you should've seen the way we lit into 'em!"

"It made a nice bang," Gomez agreed.

Hunter looked across to where King stood with Jaeger. The Master Sergeant caught his eye, grinned, and gave an exaggerated shrug. Perhaps Greg King was finally coming to grips with the notion that it *was* possible to change time.

Jaeger did not seem so pleased. The grim coldness of the ridgetop in Germany was still there. *I've got to talk to him about what happened,* Hunter thought. *But later . . . later. God I'm tired.*

"I'm glad you're back." He turned, and there was Rachel.

"Hello . . ." Further conversation became impossible, however, much as Hunter wanted to pursue it. Phillips and Stein stepped off the ladder to the control booth and approached, all smiles and congratulations.

"Well?" Phillips asked. "Well? How did it go? How was 1917?"

"Dark," Hunter said. "And unfriendly."

"But you found the train?" Todd was at his side. "Did you get a clear identification?"

Hunter merely nodded.

He glanced up at a clock on the wall beside the control booth. It was only late afternoon . . . after three hours of creeping through the German night. His body still hadn't caught on to whether it was actually day or night. He felt as though he could sleep for days.

"That's enough, people," Thompson said. "Let's let them get some rest. We're not done with this yet."

"Time for Phase 2?" Anderson asked. "What's next on the agenda?"

With an effort that was almost physical, Hunter made himself think about Phase 2. They'd been given no details as yet, beyond the fact that further missions into the past were necessary to fine tune the effects of their meddling in 1917. With Lenin dead, a few minor adjustments would be needed to ensure that the Communists would never be able to gain a firm foothold in Russia.

The team had still not been told who or what their next target would be, and Hunter had become irritated at Thompson's refusal to give them any specifics until after the Lenin mission was completed. Who would it be next? Trotsky? Stalin?

"We don't need to go into all that now," Thompson replied to Anderson's question. "We have to execute Phase 2 before the Lenin transformation hits us, but we've still got six days in which to act. The way we have it plotted out now, you'll spend to-morrow and the next day briefing for Phase 2 . . . and go out Thursday morning.''

Hunter pursed his lips. It was Monday afternoon now. It would take six days for the changes brought about by Lenin's death to reach the present, some-time Sunday afternoon. After that, there might not be a Chronos Complex to come back to; they could end up stranded in the past. If they went out Thurs-day, they would have three and a half days to carry out their mission . . . if they wanted to come back.

What did Thompson have in mind for them?

"Afraid we won't sleep nights, knowin' what's comin' up?'' Anderson said, grinning.

"Oh, not at all,'' Thompson said, an enigmatic smile spreading across his face. "I know you men can handle it.''

"So, what's the target, General?'' Hunter asked.

"Adolf Hitler.''

"What I want to know,'' King said, "is what the hell Hitler had to do with helping the Communists! I always thought the Reds and the Nazis hated each other.''

"Correct,'' Todd replied.

It was the day after their return from 1917, and the team was gathered once more in one of the Com-plex's briefing rooms, with Leonard Todd and Gen-eral Thompson filling them in on the next phase of the operation.

"In fact,'' Todd continued, "Hitler built the Na-tional Socialist Party on anti-communism as much as he did on anti-Semitism. The Communists were an extremely serious threat to Germany in the years immediately after World War I.''

''They were a fairly serious threat to Germany other times, too,'' Jaeger said *sotto voce*. The former German guerrilla still seemed moody, and Hunter made another mental note to talk with him before Phase 2 began. The mission plan so far called for Karl Jaeger to take out Hitler with his telescopic sniper's rifle, and Hunter wanted to be certain that the West German could be depended on. Something was bothering the man, but Hunter couldn't tell what.

Todd ignored Jaeger's comment and continued with the briefing. ''As you know, we expect Lenin's death to eliminate any real danger to Russia from communism in 1917. Without Lenin to unite the Bolsheviks, Aleksandr Kerensky will pull together a coalition government during the summer, and by winter, it is likely that a reasonably stable democracy will emerge.'' He looked up from his notes. ''Kerensky's government was socialist, of course, even by our standards today, but the groundwork had been laid for a multi-party government built along a western-style parliamentarian system. So long as the Reds weren't organized and trying to pull it down, they should have been fairly secure.''

Thompson cleared his throat. ''What we have asked ourselves here is, was there a threat to Russia, some power or agency which might have forced the new Russian government to give up its democratic reforms?''

''Hitler,'' Anderson said, a faraway look in his eyes.

''Hitler,'' Todd agreed. ''Our projections suggest that a democratic Russia would be seriously threatened by the rise of Nazism in Germany in the '20s and '30s. We can't predict exactly what would happen, but one good possibility is a Russian Communist coup in the early '30s as a reaction to Hitler's suppression of the German Communists. Another is that Hitler would start nibbling at a Russian federation which wasn't all that strong . . . interfering in the politics of the Ukraine and Byelorussia, for example. A German-oriented Ukraine in 1930 might raise enough of a scare to bring the Communists into power.''

''So where and when are we supposed to take Hitler out?'' Hunter asked.

''At the first point where we have a clear shot at him,'' Todd replied. He exchanged an unreadable glance with Thompson. ''I still don't entirely agree with this, General . . .''

''It's our best opportunity, Leonard.''

''Yes, sir.'' He looked back at the commandos. ''There are several possible times and places available to us, since his life is well documented, but the general has insisted on one in particular. You men are going to Munich, late in the year 1923. You will be taking part in the amusing little charade known to history as the Beer Hall Putsch.''

The story of the Nazis' rise to power was as bizarre and as twisted as that of the Communists. Again, one man held the key to that power, the slight, stoop-shouldered artist-*cum*-politician from Austria, Adolf Hitler.

He had entered politics in 1920, when he took over the leadership of the tiny German Workers' Party and transformed it into the *Nationalsozialistiche*

Deutsche Arbeiter Partei—almost immediately abbreviated as "Nazi." The term *"der Führer"*—the Leader—was applied to him almost from the start. Under Hitler's leadership, the Nazis had become the most powerful of the numerous right-wing groups seeking the overthrow of the tottering Weimar Republic, the end of war reparations to the Allies, and the destruction of the Communist party.

In 1923, the situation in Germany was critical. The First World War and the Treaty of Versailles had left Germany torn and bloodied, hopelessly in debt to France and England, swamped with unemployed former soldiers, ravaged by an inflation gone totally out of control, and battered by continuous risings by both left and right.

A state of emergency in Bavaria had led to a massive crackdown by the military on various political groups, and with it, the threat of civil war and Bavarian secession from Germany. A meeting called by Bavaria's political leaders in a Munich beer hall provided Hitler with the chance to grab power for himself and the Nazis. Hurriedly gathering his forces, he took over the beer hall during the meeting, on the evening of November eighth. Bullying a handful of politicians at the point of a gun, he forced them to go along with his plans for a revolution. Once Munich was secured, Hitler would march on Berlin . . .

"The attempt failed," Todd said. "The next morning, he led his troops from the beer hall into the center of Munich. The march ended at a plaza called the Odeonsplatz, when police opened fire and the Nazis, Hitler among them, ran for their lives. The Beer Hall Putsch, as it came to be called, totally discredited the Nazi movement. Everyone was certain the Nazis would never again be a force to be taken seriously.''

"Famous last words," Gomez said.

"Indeed. Hitler was sentenced to five years in prison, but he served only eight months. The speeches he delivered at his trial made him famous throughout Germany and won the sympathy of many who had mistrusted the Nazis before. And while he was in prison, he wrote a book . . .''

"*Mein Kampf,*" Hunter said.

"Yes. *My Struggle.* It became the cornerstone of the new Nazi Party, which Hitler began building on the foundations of the old as soon as he got out of prison. Those men killed on the Odeonsplatz became the first martyrs of the new order.''

"So we're supposed to shoot Hitler during the Putsch?" Jaeger asked.

Todd nodded. "We know where he was on the evening of November eighth . . . and on the morning of November ninth. He was surrounded by thousands of people in both cases, but there should be opportunities for your team to take him out with sniper fire from a comfortable distance.''

"We will insert you near Munich on the afternoon of November 7, 1923," General Thompson said. "That will give you a day to orient yourselves, find the . . . uh . . . what was the name of the beer hall, Leonard?''

"*Der Burgerbraukeller.*''

"Right. You should be able to locate a convenient sniper position, spot Hitler as he either enters or leaves the place, and kill him there." He looked at each of the commandos in turn. "We're allowing some extra time on this one, though, since you'll have to be moving among the locals instead of in a German forest. You'll have clothing that will let you fit in. We've even printed up inflated Reichsmarks for you. If you miss your chance at Hitler on the eighth, you'll have another chance the next day during the march. He was prominent, out in the lead, and should make an excellent target."

"Let me get this straight, General," Anderson said. "You want us to kill Hitler before the Nazis amount to anything . . . just so he doesn't push Russia into the Communists' hands later on?"

"That's about the size of it, Sergeant."

"Well good Lord . . ." He shook his head.

"What's the matter, Sergeant?"

"Not a thing, General. Not a single damned thing. Looks to me like you folks are setting up a regular utopia here. I mean, two quick trips, and we're wiping out the two nastiest dictatorships of the twentieth century!" He leaned back in his chair and laughed. "We're making the whole damned world over new!"

"I'd like to talk with you, Karl." It was Wednesday evening, and they'd spent two solid days preparing for the Hitler mission. Both men were exhausted from long hours of planning, studying maps of pre-World War II Munich, and memorizing photographs of a whole array of politicians and other players in the events of 1923. This was the first opportunity Hunter had found to sit down with the German expatriate since their return from the Lenin mission.

"Yes?"

"I want to talk to you about what happened at the

bridge, when you were killing those people in the water.''

Jaeger's eyes were expressionless blue ice.

"Don't look at me that way. I want to know what was going on in your head." *I have to know I can trust you!*

"Orders . . ."

"Bull. Our orders were to kill Lenin. Your orders were to scope any survivors and shoot Lenin if you saw him. You were shooting everything moving."

"This was bad? They were Communists . . . Bolsheviks."

"Maybe." Hunter struggled with an inner turmoil. "But my understanding of this time travel stuff is that we're to interfere with the past as little as possible. If we're told to kill Lenin, we kill him . . . and try not to gun down a hundred others just for fun! Why do you think we worked it out with Gomez to destroy only Lenin's special railcar? I didn't want to wipe out everyone on the train, because they might have a place in this new future we're building, too."

Jaeger didn't answer.

"Well? Nothing to say?"

"I . . . I apologize, Lieutenant. It won't happen again."

"Dammit, man, that's not good enough!" He remembered the blond woman. Inessa Armand, perhaps? Dedicated revolutionary or not, what harm would she have been capable of in this brave new world without dictators? Certainly, she could not have taken Lenin's place. There had been only *one* Lenin. "What the hell were you thinking of, shooting that woman?"

Jaeger hesitated a long time before answering.

Hunter thought he might not reply at all. "It was part of my count, Lieutenant," he said at last.

"Your count? What count?"

Jaeger sighed. "You would think it . . . uncivilized."

Hunter shook his head. "I doubt it."

"You do not know, perhaps, that I was a university professor at Hamburg, before the War."

"I knew, yes."

"Then perhaps you know I had a family in Hamburg."

"No."

"Ah. I did. Marlene, my wife. My sons, Kurt and Lutz. My daughter Frieda."

Hunter closed his eyes. He had heard this story before. His own brother, in Alaska . . . "Dead?"

"There was a major of the KGB. Andrei Viktorovich Druzhinin, his name was."

"That major you shot in Wilhelmshaven?"

"No. Unfortunately. I thought it was him at the time, which is why I risked our position to take him out. You see . . . I *had* to kill this man."

"Your family?"

Jaeger nodded. "Druzhinin had a considerable . . . reputation. He was the district KGB commander, in charge of rounding up subversives and counterrevolutionaries. They . . . we called him the Butcher of Hamburg. Two years before you brought me out, he rounded up hostages throughout the city in order to control the . . . I believe the phrase was counterrevolutionary hooliganism. I was arrested as a suspect in the disturbances. My family was picked up because . . . they were my family."

"And he killed them."

"Kurt and Lutz were shot in front of us. At least, their deaths were clean. Marlene . . . she took a long time to die in their interrogation cell, and I was forced to watch . . . everything. Frieda . . . they told me they gave her to the regiment's officers. I never saw her again."

"God . . ."

"While I was being transported to a new prison, I broke a guard's neck and escaped. My glorious career as a guerrilla began from that point."

"I . . . see . . ."

"Do you, my friend? I swore twenty of the bastards for each of my children, and forty for my Marlene. When you rescued me, the count stood at forty-eight. In America, I killed thirty-one more. At the bridge at Eisenach, I got three, for a total of eighty-two." His mouth worked in a caricature of a smile. "You see, I only count those I can see when they die . . ."

"Those three in the river, they had nothing to do with . . ."

"They were *Communists*, Lieutenant. Bloody, red-handed Communist bastards!" The hatred in Jaeger's pale eyes was a living thing. Hunter wondered how the man would be able to stop killing, once he raised his tally to one hundred.

He took a deep breath. "I can understand your feelings, Karl . . ."

"Indeed, Lieutenant?" The voice was harsh and urgent. "I doubt that very much!"

"Okay, so I don't feel what you feel! Maybe nobody can! But I'm telling you this, mister. If you're going to be in on this party tomorrow, you damn well are going to do what I say!"

"There was never any question of that . . ."

"No? That means I will designate your target, Karl, and I will tell you when to fire. You shoot *what* I tell you, *when* I tell you, and nothing more! This thing is too big, too important to have you running off after your own personal vendettas! Am I clear?"

"Clear; yes, sir."

"Remember it, then. I . . ." He broke off as the whoop of a siren sounded in the passageway outside the quarters area. "What in the hell is that?"

"An alarm," Jaeger replied. His eyes widened. "It is a full base alert."

Eight

"*Intruder Alert! Intruder in Main Control! Intruder Alert!*"

The voice coming over the PA speakers strung along the passageway sounded shaken. Security personnel in brassards and helmets were boiling into the corridors like maddened hornets as Hunter and Jaeger made their way to the elevator.

"Main Control?" Jaeger asked. "Level Nine?"

That would bring them out on the main floor of Time Square. "Make it Eight," Hunter replied as Jaeger pressed the button. He wanted to come out at the control booth overlooking Main Control. If there were intruders in Time Square, they could come in on them from above.

Leonard Todd had gotten there first.

"What the hell's going on?" Hunter asked.

"I don't know," Todd said, gesturing toward the huge, glass windows of the booth. "I just got here myself. I was up in Archives when the alarm sounded."

Hunter leaned across the booth console and looked down onto Time Square. Sergeant Jenkins and ten armed security men were already there, together with General Thompson, Dr. Stein, and Rachel. Other people continued to arrive, many of them showing signs of having dressed in haste when the base alert woke them up.

If there had been an intruder, he was long gone.

"Let's get down there." Todd, Jaeger, and Hunter stepped through the booth's side door and made their way along the catwalk to the nearest ladder leading to the main floor. The aisle leading from the main level door to the time portal was crowded with other people arriving to find out what was happening.

"Good God, General," Hunter said as he reached Thompson's side. "What's the ruckus?"

"Someone's been tampering with the computer," Thompson replied. The general eyed the growing crowd with distaste. "Jenkins! Post guards. Let's clear some of these people out of here. Don't let anyone else come in here until we know the score."

"Sir!"

"You want us to leave, General?"

"No, Lieutenant. This involves you and your people, I'm afraid. You should be in on this."

Tampering with the computer? Hunter looked across the aisle. Rachel was seated at one of the computer consoles, her father looking over her shoulder. Hunter did not understand exactly what those banks of computer consoles on Time Square's main floor had to do with the portal, but he knew that Rachel and her father had been working hard to rewrite some of the programming which controlled its operation. Did the tampering have something to do with the equations which had brought the Steins to the Chronos Complex? He moved closer to the Steins and stole a glance at the display monitor they were studying. Rank upon rank of computer code was scrolling up the screen, all meaningless to Hunter.

"There!" Rachel said, suddenly excited and angry at the same time. She pointed to a block of programming code on the screen. "That's different!"

Hunter squinted at the gibberish of letters and numbers on the screen. "How can you tell?"

Dr. Stein glanced at him. "Rachel has been writing the code which incorporates my equations into the portal's operational parameters," he explained. "How computer code is written is as personal as . . . as a person's handwriting."

"This whole block," Rachel said. "I wouldn't have set it up this way. Someone else must have accessed the program and made this insertion."

"If you say so." It looked more like magic than technology to Hunter, but then so did travelling ninety years into the past.

"What does the addition do to the program?" Thompson asked.

"We're working on that, General," Stein said. "Give us a moment. . . ."

Sergeant Jenkins approached with a young corporal in tow. "This is Roberts, sir," he said. "He had the duty up in the security room."

"Did you get the intruder on tape, Roberts?"

"Uh . . . no, sir. The Time Square camera is out, sir."

"Out? What do you mean 'out'?"

"There was a memo from Maintenance on my console when I took over, General. Said they'd pulled it for servicing yesterday."

Hunter glanced toward the back of the room. The camera mount high in the corner of the room was empty. "That seems rather convenient," he said.

"It certainly does," Thompson agreed. He walked to a console and tapped out a series of commands on the keyboard.

"What are you doing, General?" Todd asked.

"Calling up maintenance records for the last week. I don't remember hearing about any problems with the security system here. . . ." He studied the display screen. "Jenkins?"

"Sir!"

"There's a work order here, dated yesterday. It has your initials."

"Uh . . . sir?" The security chief craned his neck to see what was written on the computer. "I never wrote that order!"

"You didn't?"

"The security cameras were working fine yesterday morning, General! I checked them myself!"

"Hmm. Could've been anyone, I suppose. Accessed the system, wrote the order, and entered your initials. Damn!"

"Someone knows a very great deal about our

computer system, General,'' Stein said. ''This new code was slipped in as a trap.''

''Trap? What kind of trap?''

Rachel looked up from the screen, her face taut. ''This part of the program is what directs portal operation, General. It takes the procedure step by step . . . a chain of commands which controls the machinery. First power up . . . then set coordinates . . .''

''Yes, yes, I know how the damned thing works!''

''Yes, sir. What this code does is set up an extra step. It resets the coordinates to a new location, initiates the transfer, then resets the coordinates back to what they were in the first place.''

Hunter felt a growing chill. ''What new location? What do you mean?''

Rachel pointed at the indecipherable blocks of print on her screen. ''I'm not sure. Looks to me like it's north. Way north. The time is still set for the afternoon of November 7, 1923.''

Dr. Stein looked up from the console next to Rachel's. ''I've got it. It works out to latitude sixty degrees north . . . longitude one hundred eighty degrees west.''

Thompson closed his eyes. ''Oh, God . . .''

Hunter was worried now. ''Sir?''

''Someone just tried to murder you, Lieutenant. Those coordinates would have dropped the five of you . . . um . . . northern Pacific area. I'd have to check a map . . . but that's probably somewhere in the Bering Sea.''

Hunter tried to imagine dropping through the portal above the frigid, gray waters off the Alaskan coast in early November. He'd cruised the waters north of the Aleutians with his father and brother when he was a teenager, and he knew something of the conditions there. Cold and exposure would have killed them in minutes . . . assuming their heavy packs and weapons hadn't dragged them under immediately.

It would have been a cold and lonely death.

Rachel looked up at Hunter, her dark eyes showing fear. "Travis! Who would try to kill you?"

"Obviously, someone here doesn't want us going through that portal tomorrow."

Thompson nodded. "It certainly looks that way."

Jaeger stirred at Hunter's side. "That means then . . . a traitor is loose in the Complex?"

"Someone set it up to take out the security camera here, walked in, brought up the portal controller program, and started entering new code. It would have dropped our IF team into the ocean instead of sending them to Munich, then reset itself." Thompson paused, considering the problem. "We wouldn't have known anything was wrong. We'd just have been sitting here waiting for a recall signal that would have never come. Interesting that someone is trying to stop us from killing Hitler in 1923, but not Lenin."

"That is interesting," Stein said. "Tonight would have been his last chance to tamper before the Munich mission . . . and his best chance as well. The way this tampering was set up, we would not have discovered it before we projected the team into the past. I wonder . . . Do we have a closet neo-Nazi running loose down here?"

"That doesn't make much sense," Hunter said.

"Let's stick to what we know. How was the alarm set off?"

"That was my doing," Rachel said. "Back at MIT, we got pretty paranoid about the KGB snooping on our work. I got so I'd always set up a hidden security cut-out on the programs I was working on. It's called a tripwire. I guess using them is second nature for me now. Access to the Controller Program requires a code word. If anyone used the wrong word, or no code at all, it would trigger another program to alert the base security office."

Hunter felt a new surge of respect for the slim, black-haired girl. Her paranoia had just saved him, his team, and his mission.

"Doctor? How long to fix the thing?" Thompson asked.

"Perhaps no time at all. You made backups, did you not, Rachel?"

"Of course." The answer was sharp and impatient. "What I want to know is . . . can we trust *them*?"

It took all of them a moment to digest that. The traitor could be anyone in the Complex with a knowledge of computers. He probably knew that Rachel regularly made copies of everything she did to the Controller Program for storage in the fireproof vaults on Level Six. It was possible that whoever had made the changes to the program had hoped that the tampering would go unnoticed until after the IF unit had been sent out. It was just as possible that the intruder had already planted similar changes in the program backups. That way, if the portal technicians did discover the tampering, they might substitute a backup, not realizing that there was some deadly trap in the copy as well.

"This is getting pretty deep," Todd said. "Didn't you have your tripwire on the backups?"

"No. That's set up in the operating system, not in the file itself. The tripwire is just supposed to cover work in progress."

"Good God. If you can't even trust the back-ups . . ."

Rachel closed her eyes, then sighed. "I'll have to check the whole file, pretty much line by line. I can start by pulling a backup and comparing it with the working program. Then we can begin running test routines . . ."

"How long, Doctor?" Thompson asked.

Stein shrugged. "I'm afraid I will be of little help. I make the theories . . . but this is Rachel's program. I would just be in the way."

"Um. Miss Stein?"

She glanced at Hunter, then looked back at the General. "I don't know, General. I can delete the additions here in five seconds, but . . ."

"How long?"

Rachel shook her head. "Forty-eight hours?"

"Dammit, no! That takes us up to Saturday! We don't have that."

"If I work straight through . . . maybe thirty-six. General, there are at least ten thousand lines of code here!"

"That's probably the only change our intruder had time to make," Thompson mused. "We could probably risk it . . ."

"No!" Rachel's voice was sharp. She pointed to the display. "We don't know that that's the only change they made! It was easy enough to spot this change . . . but maybe it's a red herring . . . something to keep us from noticing some other change that's been slipped in. No, General! We can't let Travis and his men go through without checking it completely!''

''Hmm. Lieutenant?''

''General, if there's even a chance that that gizmo is going to send us somewhere we don't want to be . . .''

''I suppose you're right.'' Thompson looked thoughtful. ''But the time is awfully tight.''

''We still have our extra day, General,'' Hunter pointed out. ''We go out Friday instead of Thursday. We still have until Sunday afternoon.''

All of them were keenly aware that the changes brought on by Lenin's death could eliminate the Chronos Complex. Hitler's assassination, if it was to take place at all, had to be completed before Sunday.

''That's cutting things damned tight,'' Thompson said. ''But I don't see any options.''

''It took three hours to knock out Lenin's railcar. How much worse can this be?'' He thought for a moment. ''Look . . . as it's planned now, we'll have all day November eighth to set ourselves up in Munich, with a good shot at Hitler that evening. If we miss him there, we'll still have until mid-afternoon on the ninth, when we can catch him during his march through the city. Lots of opportunity . . . and lots of time.''

Thompson nodded. ''And if something goes wrong, the Lenin Change hits us Sunday afternoon and you don't have a Chronos Project to come back to.'' He sighed. ''Very well. Miss Stein, it looks like it's up to you. Let me know what you'll need. Every hour counts. If you can make it twenty-four, do it!''

Rachel was already tapping away at her keyboard. ''No promises, General. I'll do what I can, but miracles aren't part of my job description.''

Thompson grunted, then turned to his security chief. ''Jenkins, I want your people in this room around the clock. And I want to see you in my office in thirty minutes.''

Jenkins licked his lips and swallowed. ''Yes, sir.''

''I want a complete review of security procedures. And we're going to start pulling dossiers on everyone in the Complex with computer clearance.''

''Sounds like you have your work cut out for you, General,'' Hunter said.

''One of my people is a traitor,'' Thompson replied. His voice was cold steel. ''I want that bastard.''

''Yes, sir,'' Hunter agreed. He looked across the room at the time portal and suppressed a shudder. A short step through that blue shimmer, and a short plunge into icy water miles from shore. If it hadn't been for Rachel . . . ''Before he can take another crack at us.''

''This is getting to be a habit.''

Hunter set his tray down across from Rachel. The cafeteria was nearly empty. It was afternoon of the next day, but this far underground there was no way to distinguish day from night. It felt like the middle of the night.

She smiled at him, but her eyes were very, very tired. "What's the old line?" she asked. "We've got to stop meeting like this."

"Oh, I don't know. I rather like it." He took a bite from his sandwich and swallowed without tasting it. "You look beat."

"Unh."

"Any more surprises from our . . . mysterious friend?"

She shook her head. "I'm beginning to think that one change was the only one. But I've got to be certain."

"I appreciate that."

"You look like I feel," she observed. "What's been keeping you up all night?"

He shrugged. "We've been using the delay to go over pictures and histories again. Learning who's who and what's what in old-time Munich: Ludendorff, von Kahr, von Seisser. I'm beginning to feel like I know every thug, VIP, and politician in the city of Munich personally."

"And Hitler."

"Oh . . . of course. There'll be no missing *him*."

"Not unless he shaves off his mustache."

Her evident exhaustion worried him. "You'd better get some sleep, Rachel. I don't care what deadline Thompson wants . . ."

"Oh, I got a couple hours early this morning. I'm okay."

"You don't look it." He wondered how well she

could review the Controller Program when she was
half dead on her feet.

"You really know how to make a girl feel
good."

He paused, considering. He had never questioned
Rachel's devotion to the Chronos Project before.
After all, ever since the death of Dr. Lorenz, her
father had been the driving force behind the government's time travel program. But the way she had
been pushing herself since her arrival here under
Mt. Bannon made him wonder if there wasn't more
to it than that.

"You're driving yourself awfully hard, Rachel."

"I suppose we all are."

"Yeah . . . but why? It's not just because of your
father, is it?"

She glanced up sharply at him, an unexpected fire
in her eyes, and Hunter instantly regretted his
words. "Oh . . . right," he continued lamely.
"Sorry. I guess if we can wipe out the Communists,
what happened to you in Boston would never . . ."

She shook her head. "No, that's not it." She
stared at her partly-eaten meal for a moment, then
looked back up at Hunter. "I mean, I'd rather it'd
never happened, of course."

"I guess once the Lenin change reaches us here
in the present, it'll work out that we never rescued
you from Boston. Never had to rescue you, I
mean . . ."

"It *is* confusing, isn't it?" She said with a sad
smile. She raised her hands to her throat and un-
buttoned the top two buttons of her blouse. She was
wearing a small, golden pendant on a chain around
her neck. Rachel leaned across the table so she could

show it to Hunter without taking it off. As he bent forward to see, he became acutely aware of the perfume of her hair, of the swell of her breasts against the thin, polyester fabric of her blouse. *She is beautiful . . .*

"This is my mother," she said. It was an old-fashioned locket, the kind with a miniature catch which opened it to reveal a tiny photograph. The woman looked much like Rachel, with her black hair and large eyes. "She died nine years ago."

"The war?"

"No. Not exactly. She died in an auto accident not far from here."

Hunter raised his eyebrows but said nothing. After a moment, she continued. "I guess you didn't know. Emil Lorenz was my grandfather. My mother's father. We were living down in Jackson Hole . . . oh, ever since I was a kid. Father met her while he was working with Granddad. We lived on a government reservation in The Hole while the Complex was being built up here. Anyway, Granddad often went for drives with her up into the mountains. One day, they never came back. They found the car and the . . . bodies later, at the foot of a cliff." She snapped the locket shut and slipped it back out of sight. "I detested the Chronos Project for a long time after that. If Granddad and Father hadn't been working up here . . ."

"Dr. Lorenz and your mother wouldn't have had their accident," he finished for her. "But Rachel, how do you know they wouldn't have died anyway, someplace else? Doing something else?"

"Fair question. One of the theories we've tossed around while figuring out how time travel works is the notion that things are pretty much fated to happen, one way or another. You go back and stop John Wilkes Booth from killing Lincoln . . . but some other Southern sympathizer kills Lincoln later on.'' She spread her hands. ''Of course, that would invalidate everything we're doing here. It *must* be possible to change time. You guys have already done it, killing Lenin.''

''I guess so.''

''If we're successful here, there will be no Communist take-over, no Collapse, no World War III.''

''Yes . . .''

''There will also be no Chronos Complex. We will never need to have built it in the first place. If our ideas about technological developments in the last few years are correct, we won't even have been able to build it. I don't know what I will be doing in that . . . that other world, or where I'll be. But it won't be here.''

''And your mother will still be alive.''

''I hope so.'' Her voice was little more than a whisper. ''Oh, God . . . I hope so.''

Hunter reached out and took Rachel's hand. She did not draw away. Somehow, her revelation had drawn him much closer to her. He and his men had volunteered for this project in order to reverse the disasters which had overtaken America in the past few years. Rachel's war was a much more private one, a war to restore one person to life.

He hoped she would be successful.

There was only one problem that Hunter could see with her reasoning. If the Russians never turned Communist, if the time portal was never invented, then he would never have the opportunity to meet this fascinating and intelligent young woman.

And that, Hunter decided, was something he didn't even want to think about. He was beginning to suspect that he was falling in love.

Nine

Rachel leaned back from the computer console and stretched, trying to work the knots from the muscles in her shoulders and back. A time readout on her display read 0828 . . . almost eight-thirty in the morning. She had finished going through the Portal Controller Program two hours earlier, but as tired as she was, there had been no thought of sleep. The thin fabric of her white blouse clung to her body with an unpleasant clamminess. A shower would have been nice, at least, but since her arrival at the Complex, she'd been so busy programming that she'd never had the chance to pick up new clothes at the base exchange. With only the clothes she'd been wearing during her rescue from MIT, Rachel had been reduced to rinsing her blouse, slacks, and underwear in the sink in her quarters and letting them dry hanging up in her shower overnight. To take a shower that morning would have meant putting the clothes she'd been wearing continually for thirty hours back on afterward, a thought too horrible to contemplate.

"Hi there. How's it going?"

She looked up as Leonard Todd leaned his massive frame forward to look over her shoulder. "Oh, hello. It's fine. Debugged and ready to go."

"Did you find anything else? Any more traps?"

She shook her head. "No. I guess the . . . I guess whoever it was didn't have time before the alarm sounded. And the backup copies are clean after all."

He grunted, then took a seat next to her as he turned on his own computer display. She scooted her chair a bit farther from his. Todd was nice enough, if a bit rigid at times, but at the moment she couldn't stand the thought of anyone getting too close to her.

"Did you guys track the intruder down yet?" she asked.

"No," Todd said. "The General's had Jenkins and me going over personnel records pretty much nonstop. No clues yet." He leaned back and rubbed his eyes. "God, I'm tired."

"You too, eh?" Hunter's voice sounded behind them. "Doesn't anyone sleep around this place?"

Rachel swung her chair around and managed a smile. "Why, Travis! How distinguished you look!"

He grinned in response, tipping his gray felt fedora. "You like it? The latest style, they tell me . . . at least in 1923!"

She looked past him to where the other four commandos were gathering in the aisle. All of them wore similar clothing, short-tailed suit coats and vests, with hats which had not been in fashion for decades, overcoats draped over their arms, and heavy-looking travellers' satchels by their feet. Unlike their approach to the Lenin mission, they were going to have to move through one of Germany's biggest cities without attracting any more attention to themselves than they could help. The Chronos facility employed a small army of tailors who had spent months researching clothing styles of the early 1920s.

"You look like a bunch of gangsters on your way to Al Capone's Chicago," Rachel said. "What do you have in those satchels . . . machine guns?"

"Yes, actually . . . now that you mention it." He laughed. "And Eddie's carrying a couple of pounds of plastique in his money belt. We'll be the best-armed gangsters in Munich!"

"Well, maybe," Todd said. "Unless you want to count the S.A.!"

"There is that." Todd's briefings had covered the various army and paramilitary organizations they might encounter in Munich. The *Sturm Abteilung*, or Storm Troopers, were perhaps the strongest group outside of the army itself. "We won't be looking for trouble, but we're going to have to wander around Munich for a while to get set up." He brushed at the lapel of his jacket. "Camouflage."

General Thompson approached them. "Well, Lieutenant. Is your team ready?"

"Just about, General." He drew open his suit jacket, revealing a small box clipped to his belt. He closed a switch. "Yankee Leader to all Yankees," he said, speaking softly. "Radio check."

Rachel saw the others murmuring replies one at a

time. The Rangers were carrying some sophisticated technology into the past, three-piece personal transceivers which should pass unnoticed in the streets of Munich. The microphones were tiny devices pinned behind their lapels, the receivers worn almost invisibly in their ears. Power and control were handled through the belt units, without the need for wires.

Hunter listened intently for a moment. "Right," he said at last. "All set, General."

"You still need your operating capital," Thompson said. He gestured to a private carrying an armful of currency. "Hot off the presses."

Each of the commandos accepted stacks of money, which vanished into various pockets of their jackets. Rachel suppressed a startled exclamation when she saw the denomination on one of the bills as Hunter rifled through a sheaf of currency . . . a bundle of one hundred million mark notes.

Hunter caught her expression and grinned. "This is the small change," he explained cheerfully. "They're having a bit of trouble with inflation where we're going."

"Well, it ought to keep you going for the day or two you have to be there," Thompson said. "Remember, though . . . don't have any more contact with the natives than you can help."

"No problem, General. If we stick to our plan, we'll be fine." Hunter glanced at the clock next to the control booth. Phillips and Stein were there, making adjustments to the controls. "Are we about ready to go out?"

"I suppose," Thompson said. "Damn . . . I wish

we'd been able to spot our traitor. I don't like sending out an op with him still loose.''

Hunter nodded toward the sentries spaced every few feet along the catwalk and at strategic points around Time Square. ''Just keep this place guarded, General. As long as this room is secure . . .''

''And a few others, like the reactor room.'' Thompson nodded. ''We're covered as well as we can be. All the same . . .''

''Attention!'' Stein's voice blared from the booth PA speaker. ''Full power in one minute. Stand by!''

''Time to go, General. Don't worry. We'll pot Hitler . . . and then we can all relax in that utopia Roy was talking about.''

Thompson extended his hand. ''No speeches this time,'' he said. ''Just . . . good luck.''

Hunter shook hands, then shrugged into his trenchcoat. Rachel stood up and walked next to him.

''Please be careful, Travis.''

Hunter looked down at her. Rachel knew her eyes were red and glassy from thirty hours with little sleep, knew her hair was limp and tangled, but she didn't care.

It looked like he'd been up most of the night as well.

''This mission is a lot more dangerous than the last one,'' she said. She kept her voice low, so no one else would hear.

''Not really,'' he said. ''We'll have to deal with the local people this time . . . but we all know the language and the city. We have cover stories.'' He looked down and tugged at his jacket lapel. ''We'll make out okay.''

''You'll come back?'' She was still puzzled and a

little surprised at her growing feelings for this man. She wanted to let him know how she felt but was afraid to say too much, and even more afraid of her own feelings. *I need time to get this straightened out,* she thought. *Time . . . but there's never enough of it . . .*

"We'll be back."

The thirty-second warning sounded, and Hunter took his place with his men. Each drew a handgun from a shoulder holster concealed under his jacket and checked it. This time, they would pass through the portal with handguns at the ready and heavier weapons stowed in the hand luggage. The target was a wooded area two miles northwest of Munich, at three in the afternoon, November seventh. That far from town, there should be no one around to see them emerge from the portal.

"Full power!" Phillips's voice said from the PA speaker. Blue fire throbbed across the portal entrance.

Rachel sat back down in her chair, watching as Anderson and Hunter stepped forward into the portal. Jaeger and Gomez were right behind them, and King followed an instant later. The blue light shimmered, coalesced, and danced . . . but the men were gone.

Gone.

Weariness swept over her. She wanted a shower and about two days' uninterrupted sleep . . . but how was she supposed to sleep until she knew that Travis and the others were all right? She was certain that the program had been cleared of traps, but so much could still happen to them, eighty-four years in the past.

It was going to be a long day or two before they returned.

And when they did, the Lenin change would arrive, and she would become . . . who? Somebody else entirely. A Rachel Stein who had never met Travis Hunter.

But Mother will be back . . . and if it never happened, I'll never know what . . . what might have happened . . .

She stood and looked about the room. The technicians at their consoles were relaxing now, their part in the operation complete until the recall signal was received from 1923. In the back of the room, Dr. Phillips stepped off the ladder and started forward. Her father was overhead, still in the control booth.

A huge hand damp with sweat swooped over her shoulder and across her throat. "All right!" Leonard Todd's voice bellowed close by her ear. "Nobody move!"

Todd!

There was an agonizing delay of seconds before others in the control room realized that something was hideously wrong. Todd gripped her from behind. She felt cold metal brush against her neck. A spreading ripple of shocked murmurs spread across Time Square. Technicians turned toward her, their eyes widening at the sight of Todd holding a gun to her head.

"Todd!" Thompson's face was a mask of fury. "What the hell do you think you're doing?"

"Don't move, General! None of you move! I mean it!"

Rachel brought her right foot up sharply, ready to strike back at her captor's kneecap.

"Don't even think about it, bitch!" The man's voice was harsh, with a distinct tremor. She felt him move his body a step back to avoid her kick. His hand tightened against her neck and jaw. "You try anything like a karate move and you'll wish to God you hadn't!"

She gasped for air, pulling at his arm with both hands, unable to dislodge his grip. "That's . . . carrying the . . . melodrama a bit . . . a bit far, isn't it?" she managed at last. "You don't want . . . want to kill me. . . ."

"Who said anything about killing you?" She could hear the grim smile in his voice. "I'll shoot you in the kneecap and drag you out. You!" She felt him gesture with his pistol toward Phillips. "You! Stay away from that panel! The next son of a bitch to move without my say-so dies!"

"Leonard . . ." Phillips's voice was low, his words slow and precise. "Leonard, we have to power down. There might be damage if the portal . . ."

"No! Leave the power settings where they are!"

Rachel tried to concentrate on slowing her breathing, slowing the pounding of her heart. That Todd was the traitor was obvious. What he wanted now was not, but she could sense his desperation, and his fear.

"Everyone!" he yelled. "Drop your guns. Now!"

"Do as he says," Thompson ordered, and a metallic clatter echoed from around the room as guards set their weapons on the floor. "What do you want, Todd?" The general spread his hands slowly. "Let's talk about . . ."

"No talk!" He raised his voice. "Stein! You hear me, Stein?"

"I hear you," the doctor's voice replied through the PA speaker.

"Come down!"

"I . . ."

"You want your girl to keep breathing, you come down here!" His voice was shrill, his hand slippery with sweat under Rachel's chin. Todd was much larger than she was, and he was pulling up and back so hard that she could barely keep her toes on the floor. Her father descended the ladder in the back of the room. Absolute silence lay across Time Square. She wondered if Todd's hands were slippery enough that she might wrench free and scramble to safety.

Too late. Todd took several steps back, dragging her along as he moved up the ramp in front of the portal. He shifted his grip, squeezing his arm across her chest.

At least she could breathe now.

Stein approached, his hands held carefully out in full view. "Right!" Todd snapped. "There are co-ordinates written on my computer screen, Stein. You copy them down, number for number, then enter them into the Portal Control up in the booth."

Stein shook his head very slowly from side to side. "It won't work, Todd . . ."

"Don't you tell me what won't work! You enter those coordinates, and you'd better be damned sure you don't make any mistakes! You try to dump me in the ocean, and Rachel here'll be right there with me! You understand?"

Stein nodded, torture showing in his face.

"You be real careful about what numbers you enter! If we step through and find ourselves in the wrong place, I'll take your little girl apart piece by pretty little piece! Hear me? No tricks!''

"No tricks," Stein agreed, his voice dead. He leaned over Todd's console and copied figures into a pocket notebook. Then, with one lingering look at Rachel, he walked back up the aisle and climbed the ladder to the control booth.

Phillips stepped closer. "Listen, Leonard. Don't you think . . .''

The pistol came up sharply a few inches in front of Rachel's eyes. She could not keep her eyes off the weapon, a sleek 9mm Beretta from the base armory. The fluorescent lights gleamed off its black satin finish. "One step further and you're dead, Phillips."

"Please . . . don't!" Rachel twisted under Todd's arm. "Don't hurt anyone . . .''

"Shut up and quit squirming! Stein! You have those coordinates entered?''

"Yes," came the voice on the PA. "But I don't understand . . .''

"You don't have to understand anything. Don't try! Now get ready to send us out!''

The general looked up at the portal with growing horror. "Todd! No!''

"Shut up! Now . . . all of you! Listen to me, and listen sharp! I'm not repeating myself! The girl and I are going through the portal. When we're gone, shut down everything, *everything*, and wait. If I get even a hint that you people are trying to follow us . . . or trying to interfere with us in any way, the girl dies! You hear me, Stein?''

"I hear you."

"Follow us, and I'll do my best to see that she takes a long time to die! You see to it these soldier types don't try anything, if you want to save your girl a lot of pain! Understand?''

"Yes.''

"Todd,'' Phillips said carefully. "You don't have a beacon. How do you plan to get back?''

"You leave that to me. Rachel and I'll do just fine. Right, Babe?''

She felt his breath hot against her neck and tried to pull away. His grip tightened as he took another step back. She could feel an eerie prickle across her skin as the powerful magnetic fields at the portal entrance shifted and intensified. The tang of ozone was sharp in her nostrils, and she could hear the low-throated hum of current flowing into the portal apparatus.

Desperately, she thought of possible karate moves. She was too short to snap her head back into Todd's face, and the way he was holding her she couldn't strike with arms or elbows. She might be able to break his knee cap, but she could not be sure of crippling him. Fear sapped her will, leaving her trembling and exhausted.

"The . . . the portal is set to your coordinates.'' The amplified voice broke. "Todd . . . please let my daughter go! We won't follow . . .''

"Nothing doing! You people are screwing around with things a lot bigger than you'll ever be able to imagine!'' He pressed the barrel of his gun against Rachel's cheek so hard she gave a little gasp. "This is my guarantee that you won't meddle! Now . . . open the portal!''

"Todd!'' Thompson said. "We can work out something else . . .''

"Open the portal, dammit!''

"Portal . . . open . . ." Stein rasped.

"Don't, please . . ." She wrenched herself to one side. Almost, she broke free.

Phillips lunged.

The gunshot was a cannon's blast inches from Rachel's ear, impossibly, painfully loud. She screamed. Phillips stumbled against a computer console, his throat torn and bloody. Rachel screamed again as Todd squeezed the Beretta's trigger once more. A security guard diving for a submachine gun lying on the floor was punched back against a wall, blood splattering from his side. The yells and shouts and confusion seemed very far away through the ringing in Rachel's ears. The pungent smell of gunsmoke tickled her nose.

Through tears and terror, she saw her father leaning forward in the control booth, hands spread against the glass. Phillips slumped across a console. Blood bubbling from his neck and mouth, splashing across the linoleum floor. Over a burst of gunfire the general's voice shouted, "Don't shoot! Don't shoot!"

Blue fire engulfed her as something cold and hard smashed against the side of her head.

Ten

Travis Hunter did not believe in omens, bad or otherwise, but the road sign they encountered as they descended from a wooded hill toward the German country road was unsettling. One arm of the sign pointed southeast, with the words *München 10 km* . . . an easy walk of about six miles. The other arm pointed north to Dachau.

"The death camp at Dachau won't be opened for another ten years," Jaeger pointed out. "Dachau's just a village now. An artists' community."

"Maybe," Hunter said. "But it will be the first one. And ten years isn't a very long time."

"Yeah. If we miss pick-up, we may just have to live through all that," Anderson said, nodding. He patted at the sheaves of banknotes under his trenchcoat. "How much does a ticket from Germany to the States cost these days, anyway?"

"I'm more worried about the people who would let something like that happen," Hunter replied. "Or who would make it happen. They're the ones we'll be dealing with today."

The weather was well matched to Hunter's gray thoughts. November 7, 1923, was a grim, wet, and blustery day in southern Germany, and all five of them were glad they were wearing overcoats instead of their more usual combat gear. Working swiftly, they buried their recall beacon beside some prominent rocks within sight of the ominous road sign, then set out for Munich through an intermittent drizzle under a leaden sky. It was impossible to judge the local time from the sun, but the gloomy quality of the light filtering through the clouds suggested it was well past noon.

They approached Munich along the Dachauerstrasse through rolling, lightly-wooded hills. Above the trees to the south, they could just make out the red peak of the Nymphenburg Schloss, a seventeenth-century summer palace for Bavaria's rulers.

By the time they entered Munich proper two hours after their arrival, they had encountered a number of the local people. Beyond the few curious stares which might be expected from townspeople confronted by the sight of five well-dressed men walking in a group and carrying their luggage at the edge of town, their arrival seemed to have attracted little notice.

"It's awfully quiet," Gomez remarked at last. They had turned off the Dachauerstrasse just north of the ugly sprawl of Munich's train station. The chuffing wheeze of steam engines pulling into the

Hauptbahnhof reminded Hunter of the passenger train they'd attacked a few days . . . or years? ago. Hunter knew Gomez's comment did not refer to the hiss and screech of the trains or to the clatter of rattletrap trucks and cars and trollies on the city's brick streets. There was a heaviness to the late afternoon air above Munich, an oppressiveness, as of waiting tainted by fear.

"The people are nervous," Anderson observed.

"And desperate," King added.

Evidence of that desperation was everywhere. As they neared the center of the city they encountered more and more of Munich's inhabitants. Brawny-armed women argued with customers at street stalls displaying produce or secondhand clothing, but they glanced at the commandos with suspicious eyes as they passed. Men in grimy work clothes and short-brimmed caps slouched at street corners, talking or watching the traffic listlessly. More than one seemed warily intrigued by five well-to-do businessmen carrying their luggage along the street.

Beggars, many missing legs or arms, many wearing German army uniforms with iron crosses and other military decorations, occupied porch steps or pieces of sidewalk pavement, asking passersby for a few billion marks for a decent meal. Some people carried baskets, even pushed wheelbarrows filled with money. Hunter remembered that the current exchange rate in Germany was something like four billion marks to the dollar. It made the sheaves of bank notes in his own pockets feel heavier.

Blue-uniformed municipal police paced the narrow streets in twos or clattered along the street on horseback, always watching the people around them. Nu-

merous green-uniformed Bavarian state police were
in evidence too. There were other armed men as well,
members of the various *bunds* and paramilitary
groups which considered themselves to be police
auxiliaries. For the most part, according to their briefings, the police welcomed their help in a city grown
desperate.

The S.A. were the most visible of these groups;
tough-looking men in brown uniforms and short-
brimmed caps or steel German helmets. They appeared to be patrolling the streets no less vigilantly
than the police.

It was their armbands; red, with the black twist of
the swastika set in a white circle and worn above the
left elbow of the *Sturm Abteilungers* that jolted
Hunter the most. Nothing he'd encountered yet, not
the sudden transition from Time Square to the woods,
not the sign on the road to Dachau, not the clothing
worn by himself or the people on the streets had
driven home the realization of just where and *when*
he was as did the sight of those swastika armbands.

"Let's drop the tourist bit," King said nodding
toward a pair of S.A. troopers ambling down the
sidewalk. "We don't want to attract attention from
that lot."

"Agreed," Hunter said. According to their briefings, the S.A. was a fifteen thousand-man unit disguised as a youth sports group to sidestep the limits
imposed by the Treaty of Versailles on the regular
German armed forces. By 1923, the S.A. was completely under the control of the Nazis, who used it
as muscle to support their political ambitions. Most
of the Munich putsch marchers would be S.A., under
the command of a war hero named Hermann Göring.

"It feels like the city's ready to explode," King observed. "Like a pressure cooker. Like the Bronx just before the Riots of '98."

"I feel this, too," Jaeger said. A policeman nearby frowned at the five of them. "We should, perhaps, speak German," he continued in his native language, his voice scarcely above a whisper, "and be careful of what we say."

"*Ja, mein Kamerad,*" Hunter replied. "We want no trouble now."

The Königshof had begun its career as a baronial mansion in 1862. Jaeger told them that the old hotel had still been in business, after numerous facelifts and renovations, during his last visit to the Bavarian capital in 1997. It was ideally situated for their purposes, overlooking the plaza known as the Stachus less than two miles from the Burgerbraukeller. The dome and twin spires of the Theatinerkirche rose from the Odeonsplatz a half mile to the northeast, where Hitler's putsch was fated to end in two more days.

Unless they managed to kill him at the beer cellar first.

They paid for the night in advance—common practice in a city where inflation could double the price of a newspaper between the morning and evening editions—and, after insisting that they would carry their own luggage, followed the *Hotelpage* to their rooms.

"Beautiful downtown Munich," King muttered, looking out the window. It was growing dark already, and the lights of the city were coming on. The fountain in the plaza across the street below their window played under the glow of streetlights, as the steeples of the Theatinerkirche took on a faint luminosity from the lights spread out below them.

"Hey, we made it this far," Gomez said.

"Sure!" Anderson agreed. "Set yourself down and rest a spell, Master Sergeant. We got until tomorrow before we get our chance at Adolf."

But Hunter sensed King's foreboding. It matched what he himself was feeling. "No rest," he said curtly. "Not yet, anyway."

"We need intel," King said. "I don't like the . . . the *feeling* of the city."

"The political situation at this time is strained," Jaeger said. "There is the threat of Bavarian independence . . . of civil war against the Berlin government. That, after all, is what the meeting at the Burgerbraukeller tomorrow night is all about."

"Um." Hunter thought about the situation. "I agree with Greg. I don't like walking into this thing blind."

"No sweat, Lieutenant," Anderson said. "We're already set to check out that Burgerbraukeller place tomorrow during the day."

Hunter nodded. According to their plan, they were to spend November eighth finding a spot for Jaeger and his rifle. "You know," he said slowly, "it would be nice if we could see what the place looks like at night."

"Like now?" King asked.

"We're not going to get a better chance."

"We didn't have a chance to scope things out at that bridge," Gomez said.

"No, but the situation was different. Operating in the middle of a city always throws a few million new

variables into things. Where are the street lights? Are
they working? Are the entrances to the place well lit,
or should we use starlight scopes?'' He nodded toward the window. ''I think I'd like to take a little
evening stroll. Care to come with me, Karl?''

''*Ja wohl, mein Leutnant*. The lighting is important for this mission . . . much more so than at Eisenach. I, too, would like to see the place at night.''

''I don't like deviating from the plan, Lieutenant.'' King frowned. ''Too damned many things can
go wrong.''

Hunter stood, retrieving his trenchcoat and hat
from the rack beside the door. ''We'll be back in
three or four hours. You're in charge, Master Sergeant. Check the weapons.''

''You're not going armed?''

Hunter patted the .45 Colt Commander he had
drawn for the mission, tucked under his left arm in
shoulder leather. ''We'll have these . . .''

''You'd better not go looking for trouble,'' King
said. ''Sir.''

''Yes, Mother. Coming, Karl?''

''On my way.''

Rachel's first sensations of returning consciousness were only vague feelings of discomfort. Her
head hurt . . . but the pain was far away and fuzzy,
almost as though it belonged to someone else.

Then she was wide awake and the pain was very
real, a throbbing in her head, where Todd had struck
her with his gun, which pulsed in time with her
heartbeat. Slowly, she opened her eyes, wincing at
the fresh pain the light brought to her head. She was
lying in the corner of a large, empty room, on a

mattress which had been spread out on the bare concrete floor. There were men nearby, three of them, bending over what looked like maps on a folding table.

One of the men was Leonard Todd.

She remembered Todd grabbing her in Time Square, remembered him pulling her backward toward the portal. She had confused memories after that, of coming half awake in the back of what must have been a truck before losing consciousness once again. So, the coordinates Todd had given her father had opened the portal to somewhere, and somewhen . . . but where?

Rachel knew the mechanics of the portal well enough to know that once the lock on a particular time was lost, it took time—as much as several hours—to build up the power to establish a new one. Todd had ordered the spatial coordinates reset, but they had passed through the portal almost immediately. That meant that the *when* of her captivity was fairly obvious . . . the target date for the Intervention Force—November 7, 1923.

And the where . . . Munich? She didn't have as much to go on for that part of the puzzle. The coordinates had been different than those used to send Travis and his men out, but the change in target could have landed her across town or across an ocean.

But she was willing to bet that she was still in Germany, at least.

A fourth man entered the room, removing his overcoat. By the light of the single, naked bulb dangling from the high ceiling, Rachel could make out his brown uniform, and the glaring obscenity of his swastika armband. He flung the coat across others atop a crate by the door, then peeled the Nazi arm-band off with a sour expression.

"Otvratyeetel'niyee veshch!" the man exclaimed with feeling as he flung the cloth down.

"Sprich Deutsch, Narr!" The speaker was a tall, lean, hawk-faced man in civilian clothes.

So, this *was* Germany, and the S.A. brownshirt uniform was a confirmation of the date. Rachel was certain now that she had been brought to very nearly the same time-space coordinates as Travis and the IF team. She strained to listen. Her grandfather had taught her German when she was a child, and she had had three years of the language in high school. She was rusty, but she could understand enough to follow the conversation. She did not speak Russian, but she had heard enough of it in Boston to know it when she heard it. The storm trooper had said something in Russian. The hawk-faced man had called him a fool and ordered him to speak German.

Just what was going on here?

"Well?" the man snapped.

"There is no sign that they were followed, *Loew Herr*."

"I told you, *Kamerad Oberst*," Todd said. "They wouldn't dare come through. Not when we have *her* as hostage."

Rachel struggled with the title. *Oberst* sounded like a German military rank. What would it be . . . colonel? She thought so. But "Comrade Colonel" sounded more Russian than German.

"Perhaps." Loew gave Todd a long, hard look. "You were a fool to come here, Kulagin. You were a fool to bring *her* here. You have risked everything."

Kulagin? Rachel blinked. Leonard Todd was . . . Kulagin? Whatever his name, he sounded terrified. The hawk-faced man, Loew, was the leader of the group. The way the others deferred to him, there was no doubt about that at all.

"Sir, it seemed best at the time. She has valuable technical information we can use!"

"Then you should have left her at the *schloss*! We don't have the personnel here to guard prisoners!"

The other man standing between Todd and the leader placed his hands inside his vest pockets and rocked back on his heels. He was a small, neat-looking man, wearing the vest and jacket and somewhat fussy expression of a schoolteacher. His hair was thin, and he wore thick, rimless glasses and a trim mustache. "Kulagin could be right, Comrade Colonel."

"Oh?" the leader asked. "And what would you suggest, Major?"

"Only that the girl could be useful once we've captured the Americans. They are notoriously . . . squeamish about such things."

"She was responsible for programming the Americans' time machine, Comrade Colonel," Todd said. "She knows the Stein equations. We need her to improve the accuracy of our own device!"

"All the more reason she should not have been brought here." The colonel sighed. "Well, we shall have to act on Kulagin's information, in any case. We cannot afford to have American commandos loose in Munich, just when Rising Star is about to commence."

"Comrade Kulagin *has* done us a service," the

major pointed out. ''We know they are here and what their target is.''

''And if he had done his assigned task properly, the Americans would not be here at all!''

''That was not my fault, Comrade Colonel!''

''I disagree, Captain Kulagin. And you have compounded your sin by coming here, and *now* of all times!''

''Please . . . Comrade Colonel . . .'' Todd/Kulagin gulped for air. ''I felt it essential that I come here at once and warn you that the Americans had made it through after all! That they are here! I . . . I can be useful to you!''

''Hmm.'' The colonel appeared to be considering the point. ''Perhaps. We are short of manpower here.''

''I have a list of the Munich hotels where they might be staying,'' Todd/Kulagin added. He sounded eager to please. ''There was no way to guess which ones would be full, with all the political activity in town, so the actual decision was to be left to them. But . . .''

''We don't have the people to watch every hotel in Munich,'' the colonel said. ''But we know they plan to kill Hitler at the Burgerbrau. That would appear to be the place to pick them up.''

''Your orders then?'' the major asked.

''Place observers outside the Burgerbrau . . . immediately. I want to know at once if the Americans approach it.''

''Are they to be captured or killed, Comrade Colonel?''

''If we can get them all at once, eliminate them. If the chance to pick up one or two for questioning presents itself, however, do so.'' He turned his head toward Rachel's corner, and his cold eyes met hers. ''Ah! I see our guest is awake. Let us see what she knows about these Americans.''

The Burgerbraukeller sprawled across much of a city block in the Haidhausen District, just across the Isar River from central Munich. Several stories tall, its grounds included hedged-in *biergartens*, as though it were trying to introduce the feeling of space and country to an area of narrow brick streets and closely-crowded buildings.

''This isn't what we expected at all,'' Jaeger said. They were standing across the street from the beer cellar's entrance onto the Rosenheimerstrasse.

''The lighting seems okay,'' Hunter replied. The street was only dimly and intermittently lighted by streetlamps, but each of the Burgerbrau's entrances had its own light. ''But offhand, I'd say somebody goofed.''

None of their briefings had included detailed plans of the beer hall where Hitler's putsch was to take place. Leonard Todd had explained that the building, heavily damaged during World War II, had been razed afterward by a population eager to prove that it was not interested in preserving Nazi shrines.

And, according to Todd, no plans or diagrams of the original beer hall had survived.

''I had no idea the place was so large,'' Jaeger said. ''I see many places where I could set up the sniper's nest . . . but no place where I could cover every entrance, every door.''

''Agreed. We'll have to have a pretty good idea

. . . especially since the streets are going to be filled by Storm Troopers and police tomorrow night.''

''Which door will Hitler use?''

''Probably this one, on the Rosenheimerstrasse . . . but how can we be sure?''

They continued their stroll, two well-dressed German businessmen taking the evening air. One of Munich's blue-and-white trolleys clattered up the hill from the direction of the Isar and the Ludwigsbrucke. Music spilled from the lighted windows of the beer hall, the sounds of crowds and laughter, the clink of glasses.

''They're having a good time, it seems,'' Jaeger said as the trolley rattled past. ''Shall we join them?''

Hunter was tempted. Perhaps if they knew what the layout was like inside . . . On the other hand, the chances of discovery became higher if they directly mingled with the population.

''No,'' he said at last. ''No, I don't think so. Let's get back to the hotel.''

They turned around and started back down the hill toward the river. The Ludwigsbrucke crossed the Isar at a point where a long, broad island divided the river in two. On the bridge, a pair of Munich policemen in blue jackets and tall, flat-topped caps clopped past on horseback, eyeing them incuriously.

''You know, Karl, we need to have a man inside.''

''Inside the beer hall?''

''Right. He could give a yell on the radio and let you know when Hitler was coming out. And where.''

''True. Perhaps I could cover the Rosenheimer entrances with the sniper rifle, while the others guarded the other streets with submachine guns. One way or another, we would get him. But we cannot depend on seeing where he is arriving in time . . . and we would need warning of where and when he was leaving.''

''It's the only way we'll have a chance of pulling this thing off. Otherwise, we punch the recall button now and scrub the mission. And I'm going to want to have words with Leonard Todd when we get back. He should have told us more about what we were getting into here!''

They stepped off the bridge and onto the broad Zweibrückenstrasse leading into the heart of town.

A hundred yards behind them, shadows detached themselves from the deeper shadows of the bridge, and followed.

Eleven

"We're being followed, Lieutenant."

"I know. Not very subtle about it, are they?" Hunter said, glancing back.

This early in the evening, the streets of central Munich were thronged by large crowds going in and out of the endless lines of theaters and beer halls, of restaurants and cabarets. Their progress had become slower as the crowds grew thicker. There was a curious blend, Hunter noticed, of rich and poor here. Men in tails and top hats escorted women in low-cut evening gowns and expensive furs past crippled beggars and apathetic-looking men in workers' clothes. Garishly-painted prostitutes, many of them teenagers and many of them male, vied with one another for the street trade. Across the street, a well-dressed man on an empty crate bellowed at the passersby about

135

the evils of *der ewig Jude* and had already attracted a sizeable crowd.

"I make it four of them, fifty yards back," Hunter continued. "Holstered pistols, no long arms."

"There were only two a moment ago. Are they all S.A. ?"

"Yep. Armbands and all."

"Why are Storm Troopers interested in us? We've done nothing to attract their attention."

"Maybe we look like Communists," Hunter suggested.

Jaeger gave Hunter a sour look. "Uh. Or rich capitalists."

"Or Jews. Uh, oh. I think they're closing in." Their pursuers were moving forward rapidly now, shouldering their way through the crowd.

"Do we fight?"

"I'd rather not. We'd better try to shake them."

"Yes, but how?"

Hunter pointed to an entrance across the street. "There. Come on."

Das Kätzchen Kabarett was one of the hundreds of cabarets which had appeared in Germany in the years after World War I, a nightclub catering to the trendy rich. Such places were popular despite the nation's problems. With Germany's inflation rate, any businessman with access to foreign capital could become outrageously wealthy, and a night on the town was a way to ostentatiously display that wealth. Countless others, convinced that money was becoming worthless, chose to blow a life's savings on a single evening's entertainment. Too, Germany in 1923 was undergoing a sexual revolution the likes of which would not occur again until the '60s. The nightclubs of the major cities were, in the slang of a later day, where it was happening.

Hunter and Jaeger were less interested in Germany's morals or financial problems than in a place to quietly escape their pursuers. The Kitten Cabaret seemed to offer them their best chance.

They descended red-carpeted steps into the dimness of the main floor. The level of noise suggested a crowd, even though it was so dark they could make out few details. The decor was glitzy, hung with black and red curtains under a mirrored ceiling.

They gave their hats and coats to a cloakroom girl wearing sequins and little else and slipped a few hundred billion marks to the headwaiter for a quiet table at the edge of the crowd. Except for candles at the round tables filling the hall, the only light in the room was on stage, where a man in a top hat and tuxedo was acting as master of ceremonies. A rather bad orchestra in a far corner delivered blatts of sound and the rattle of drums and cymbals at more or less appropriate places in his monologue, and over it all was the raucous babble of conversation and coarse laughter.

"I doubt that they'll follow us in here, Karl," Hunter said after they were seated. "If they're waiting for us, we can sit here long enough for them to get bored and go away."

The comedian's routine seemed to be poking fun at a man named von Kahr, a name Hunter knew well from his studies of Munich's politicians. Gustav von Kahr was State Commissioner, the putative government leader of Bavaria. In the confused tangle of German politics, he was one of three men given emergency dictatorial powers over the troubled state by Berlin.

The irony was that it was von Kahr who would call the meeting the following evening in hopes of organizing a putsch against Berlin.

"I would like to know what it was about us that attracted their attention," Jaeger said.

"Um. Most S.A. were thugs, plain and simple. They probably had us figured as a couple of rich, out-of-town businessmen they could roll in an alley."

An argument was underway at the table next to theirs. Hunter had been aware of it as they entered, but it was getting noisy enough now to drown out the comedian onstage, at least here in the far corner of the cabaret.

"Maybe," Jaeger said. "But I . . ."

"Shh!" Hunter raised a finger. The argument nearby seemed to have taken a political turn, and Hunter was interested. "Listen!"

"Das ist Geisteskrankheit!" a burly man in an Army uniform exploded, red-faced and more than a little drunk. "Sheer lunacy!"

"Nein, Herr Major!" His opponent was a neat man with a vast, handlebar mustache and expensive-looking evening dress. His arm was around one of the two ladies at the table; both lovely in bare shoulders and décolletage. "I tell you, *Herr* Hitler will be Germany's salvation against the Communists!"

"The Communists are finished . . . a spent bullet!" the Army officer said. "It is this . . . this *verdammt Österreicher* who will be the ruin of us all!"

"Oh, don't be so pompous, Hermann," one of the ladies said. "We're not here to listen to you two argue politics!"

"Then tell this fool to keep his idiotic political ideas to himself!" the officer bellowed. "I will not hear them!"

Fresh antics from the comic on stage brought a roar of laughter from the crowd. The man was parodying another of Munich's notables, General Erich von Ludendorff, puffing his stomach out and mimicking a proud, Army strut to the oompah-pah of a tuba.

"I tell you, Hans," the Army officer said, his voice rising above the background noise once more. "If those damned Oberland Bund people of yours approach the Engineer Barracks tomorrow, there will be trouble! *Hauptmann* Cantzler will throw you out!"

"What do you mean, Major? The Bund must have its regular drill. . . ."

"Not if they're using the opportunity to steal ammunition!" The major stabbed his finger at the civilian. "Your people have gone too far this time, *Herr* Oemler. Stealing ammunition, smuggling weapons . . . It looks as if the Nazis are planning a putsch!"

"And perhaps a putsch is just what is needed, *Herr Major*!"

"Bah! A putsch now would be insanity!"

"Nonsense! How long do you think the people can allow those idiots in Berlin to govern us? Do you deny that it is the Army's patriotic duty to support the German people in this?" The civilian gestured toward the cabaret stage with contempt. "Look at that pig, insulting a great hero like Ludendorff. He is with us! And not one soldier, not one policeman in this entire city would stand against him. He is a war hero! They revere him!"

"Do either of you boys have a light?"

Hunter and Jaeger turned, startled by the low and seductive voice behind them. The girl could not have been more than twenty, but her low-cut gown, bleached hair, and heavy makeup were obvious attempts to make her look mature and sophisticated. She leaned toward Hunter as she extended her cigarette in its stylish holder, exposing her bosom in deliberate provocation.

"I'm sorry, miss," Hunter said. "Neither of us smokes."

"Oh, that's all right," she said, producing matches from her purse and seating herself next to him at the table. "I've got it here. Buy me a drink?"

"Uh, actually, we were just leaving . . ."

Jaeger interrupted Hunter with a warning hand on his arm and a nod toward the door. Two Storm Troopers stood there in their brown shirts and Nazi armbands. Hunter thought one looked like one of the soldiers he had seen following them in the crowd outside. The other was an S.A. captain.

Hunter forced himself to hold very still. The two men were standing in the entrance, hands on hips as they peered into the semidarkness. The girl burbled on. "Oh, you can't go yet! The show here is simply wonderful! So very—you know—*sophisticated*! So *modern*!"

A waiter appeared at their side, asking for their drink orders. The S.A. were still there, and Hunter wondered if it would be possible to slip quietly under the table. It felt as though they were the center of entirely too much attention.

"Oh, I'll take champagne, of *course*," the girl said. "Bring us a bottle of your very *best*!"

Considering Germany's inflation rate, the cost of

that champagne might well require a wheelbarrow to cart in the money. The situation would have been funny had it not been for the Storm Troopers.

The cabaret's headwaiter approached the two S.A. men. They discussed something, and the headwaiter gestured in their direction.

"Trouble," Jaeger said in a voice only just loud enough for Hunter to catch it. The girl continued to babble about how she loved champagne and seemed not to notice.

"Steady," Hunter replied. "They're looking for two men alone. And they haven't seen us without our coats."

The S.A. men approached, glancing at each table and its occupants as they passed. Hunter leaned back as they approached and let go with a hearty laugh.

"Well! I don't see anything funny about *that*!" the girl said, mildly offended. Hunter could not imagine what it was she had been talking about. The captain passed their table slowly, and Hunter laughed again. Jaeger joined in this time, and the girl looked indignant.

"Just what do you two think is so damned funny?" the girl demanded.

The Storm Troopers had passed them by and were working their way around the edge of the room, circling toward the stage. Apparently, their directions from the headwaiter had not been very explicit.

"I'm sorry, miss," he said. Her speech and behavior were bizarre, but Hunter couldn't tell what the problem was. "Something the comedian said struck me funny."

But the MC was no longer telling jokes. He was introducing the cabaret's kittens, a line of pretty girls wearing cat's ears and whiskers, black fur G-strings supporting long, erect, furry tails, and nothing else.

The girl lowered her eyelids in what must have been intended to be a seductive manner. "Well! I can show you guys something as good as any of that! I just *love* threesomes!"

"Uh . . . maybe some other time." Hunter could not tell whether the girl was a prostitute looking for business, or some wealthy industrialist's daughter out looking for kicks. The quality of her gown and the glitter of her jewelry suggested the latter. Whoever she was, she would never know the service she had performed by approaching their table. The *Abteilungen* were talking to two men seated by themselves closer to the stage.

The MC had begun singing, though it was hard to hear over the noise from the audience and the uncertain melody from the orchestra. Hunter was able to make out something in the words about "sleeping with the whole damned crew" while the bare-breasted girls clustered about him in an adoring tableau.

"Oh, you two are no fun at all!" Their companion pouted, then brightened. "I know! Have some *koks!*"

She produced a small, square envelope of folded paper from her purse. "It makes you so *very* clever!" she said as she opened it.

Hunter exchanged an alarmed glance with Jaeger. At that moment, the girl leaned forward, shoving the envelope into his face. Caught off guard, Hunter lurched back, his arm snapping up in an instinctive block against the sudden motion. His hand connected with the packet, scattering fine white powder everywhere.

The girl's shriek cut above the music and the conversation around them. "What's wrong with you people?" she wailed. "Don't you do coke? Everybody does coke!"

"Company, Lieutenant," Jaeger said. The two S.A. had heard the commotion and were making their way back toward the table.

"Damn!" Hunter looked from the girl to the advancing Storm Troopers and back again. His reaction had been purely reflex, triggered by the girl's lunge toward his face. She stood before him now, her tears turning her mascara to mud. He revised his estimate of her age downwards. She couldn't be more than eighteen.

"I would go home if I were you, miss," he said. Now he knew what was wrong with her. She was strung out on cocaine.

"Ja, Fräulein," Jaeger agreed, watching the S.A.'s approach. "This is not a healthy place for you. Quickly, Lieutenant!"

They started to go, but their way was blocked by the engineering officer from the table next to theirs. *"Hör mal!"* He growled. "You don't treat a lady that way!" Momentarily, Hunter wondered if the man had simply not heard the entire conversation, or whether everyone in this country had the same, twisted moral values. Other people nearby turned in their seats to see what was happening.

"Pardon me, sir. I left my time machine running." The two commandos pushed past, leaving the officer in some confusion.

"Uh oh," Jaeger said. The front entrance was blocked by another S.A. man. It appeared that he must have arrived with the others but remained out of sight in the entrance hall.

Desperate now, Hunter looked about the room. A glowing sign reading *Ausgang* caught his attention on the far side of the room, close to the stage. "That way," he said. "An exit!"

They tried to remain inconspicuous, pressing past the tables and indignant patrons. The light was dim, but it felt as though every eye in the room must be following them.

They had nearly reached the exit when the door swung open. Two more S.A. troopers were there, the light from a brightly-lighted hallway beyond briefly spilling into the darkened cabaret. Hunter grabbed Jaeger's arm and steered him aside. There was a small alcove with a curtain to one side of the stage, between the room's far wall and the orchestra pit. Behind the curtain, steps led up to the backstage area.

The two S.A. reinforcements recognized them . . . or perhaps they were simply responding to the sight of two men in civilian clothes hurrying away from them. They followed.

Backstage was a tangle of props and scaffolding, of cheap cardboard scenery and stacks of packing crates. Several stagehands goggled at them, then began making urgent shushing noises and go-away motions with their hands. They ignored the stagehands and set out across the floor. A burst of audience laughter warbled through the curtains to their left, where the stage lights beyond revealed the shadows of the MC and the girls. Apparently, he was telling jokes again.

They were nearly all the way across when the captain and the trooper with him appeared only a few feet ahead. "You two!" the man shouted. "Stop!" Two more troopers came up the stairs across the stage and behind them, trapping them.

A harried-looking man in a vest came up behind the officer. "Please, *Herr Hauptmann*! I want no trouble with the S.A.! But there's a performance going on . . ."

But the captain was already cross-drawing his Luger from the holster on his left hip.

Hunter's foot lashed out, striking the man's hand against his belly before he could get the pistol clear. The pistol clattered on the floor as Hunter slammed his elbow into the captain's chin.

The trooper behind the captain was already well into his swing before Hunter saw it coming. The man's fist smashed into the side of his head, sending Hunter sprawling backward and into the curtains across the stage. *"Bitte!"* The man in the vest seemed beside himself. *"Bitte!* There's a show on!"

The two S.A. who had followed them grabbed Jaeger from behind. Hunter, lying flat on his back by the curtain, groped inside his jacket for his automatic. Before he could get the weapon free, the trooper who had hit him landed on his chest. They grappled, rolling, as Hunter tried to draw his Colt.

He failed. The S.A. trooper threw a punch at his head, forcing Hunter to block it. Hunter's open-handed riposte caught the thug behind the ear and sent him sprawling. Then Hunter was on his feet again, an instant before the captain locked his arms around him from behind. Hunter feinted to the left, then twisted right with a sharp kick to the man's knee. The captain stumbled and fell through the curtains. Feminine shrieks sounded from the far side.

Somebody landed full against Hunter's back, driving him forward and into the curtains. He dropped to the wooden stage and rolled, coming up in a glare of lights as he broke his attacker's hold, rolling the man across his shoulder.

Showgirls in whiskers and fur tails scattered, or stood transfixed, mouths open. Several, in a curious twist of illogic, tried to cover their breasts with their arms as they stood there screaming, despite the fact that only moments before they'd been quite nonchalant about their nakedness before a huge audience.

The soldier staggered to his feet, swinging a heavy fist. Hunter blocked it and countered with the heel of his hand. The man's head snapped to one side, spraying the curtain and the torso of a screaming girl with scarlet from his shattered nose.

Something soft and black came down across his face, closing on his throat. The captain had caught him from behind with the tail and G-string torn from a passing showgirl.

The audience was on its feet now, cheering and applauding wildly, apparently believing that the violence on stage was all part of the show. The fur tail was stiffened with wire and Hunter could feel his eyes bulging as his attacker pulled the noose tight.

Ignoring the garrote, he reached behind his head, grabbed the captain's hair, then lunged forward and down. The captain's hold broke as he sailed with flailing arms off the stage and into the orchestra pit. There were shouts and curses from the orchestra, and a new round of cheers and clapping from the audience. He yanked the tail off his throat, gulping air.

It was time for his exit. Hunter turned to dash from the stage, colliding with the tuxedoed MC. He—no, it was a she—was standing there screaming with the rest of them, her hat gone and her hair dishevelled. "Here." He handed her the tail and its shreds of fur G-string. "One of your girls dropped this."

Hunter pushed through the curtains, looking for Jaeger. Behind him rose thunderous applause and shouts of "More! More!"

He saw Jaeger, rising above a limp brown form on the floor, a Sykes-Fairbairn bloody in his hand. Beyond the commando, another S.A. leveled his revolver at Jaeger.

"Down, Karl!" He shouted as he drew his Colt Commander. Jaeger dove forward as the Storm Trooper's pistol barked, plucking a hole in the curtain several feet above Hunter's head. Hunter brought his .45 up and squeezed the trigger twice, double thunder smashing the *Abteilunger* up and back and into a stack of crates with a splintering crash. There were more screams from beyond the curtain, followed by another round of applause. The patrons of *Das Kätzchen* seemed to be getting their money's worth this evening.

Booted feet pounded on the stairs at either wing of the stage. "This way!" Jaeger said. A door in the back wall led to dirty, narrow hallways lined with doors and cluttered with trunks, props, and scenery. Beyond was an exit. Shouts and sounds of pursuit followed them as they plunged through the exit and into a narrow back alley.

It was several minutes more before they could be certain that they had escaped.

Twelve

"There." Anderson indicated the direction with a nod of his head. "By the river."

Hunter turned his head casually, looking past the trunk of the tree that was sheltering them. A lone man in the uniform of an S.A. major stood on the walk beside the riverbank, his back to them.

"There's our uniform, Roy," Hunter whispered.

Since their scouting run of the night before and their escape from the trap at the cabaret, they had further refined and developed their plan for the attack on Hitler. They had moved from the Königshof that morning and rented an unfurnished apartment in an ancient and filth-stained four-story brownstone across the Rosenheimerstrasse from the beer hall. The one small window in their new headquarters gave them a perfect view overlooking the Burgerbraukeller's main entrance. From there, Karl Jaeger had a clear shot at the door Hitler was most likely to use.

But they still needed a man inside. Although three of them could cover the building's other entrances, they could not count on spotting Hitler's arrival in time to get a shot at him. A man inside the beer hall could alert those outside when Hitler left, giving them time to get ready and get into position. Their historical briefings had revealed that there had been a large crowd at the Burgerbrau that evening, that there was room only for Munich's most influential political VIPs. An officer's uniform might be the ticket they needed to get one of them inside. They had spent most of the afternoon wandering the Haidhausen district, looking for a likely target.

They were in Maximilian Park, a few hundred yards north of the beer hall on the east bank of the Isar. There had been a rather boisterous Nazi rally a few hours before, with cheers and waving swastika flags and thunderous *Sieg Heils* in front of the impressive Maximilianeum, but the park was mostly deserted now.

Except for this lone *Sturm Abteilung* major.

"Cover me," Hunter said. He was shivering a little in the wet, raw bluster of the November afternoon, since he and Jaeger had been forced to abandon their coats at the cabaret, but at least an overcoat wouldn't slow him down now. He stepped out from cover and walked briskly toward the major. He was within three paces of his target when an S.A. enlisted man swung into view from behind a clump of nearby trees.

Perhaps there was something about Hunter's expression, or his look of concentration, which telegraphed his intent. *"Achtung, Herr Major!"* the soldier shouted as he began fumbling with the bolt-action rifle slung across his shoulder. The major turned suddenly, his eyes opening with surprise, but his hand already grasping the butt of the revolver in its holster on his belt.

Hunter ignored the soldier and lashed out with the heel of his hand, catching the major expertly under the angle of his jaw with a sharp, upward thrust which snapped the man's neck. As the major collapsed, Hunter heard the sharp *phut-phut* of Anderson's silenced 9mm pistol a few feet to his rear, and the soldier flailed his arms backward and collapsed in a heap.

They looked up and down the river and studied the surrounding trees. Their act appeared to have gone unnoticed. Working swiftly now, they dragged the bodies into the shrubbery which lined the park walk.

"This guy's about my size," Hunter remarked as they stripped the major's uniform off. "Looks like I finally got promoted."

"Would've been nice if we could have saved the other uniform, too," Anderson remarked.

Hunter glanced at the other body and grunted agreement. Anderson's two shots, aimed at the target's center of mass, had rendered both coat and brown shirt unusable for any attempt at impersonation. "No problem," he said. "We only need one."

A distant, subdued roar floated across the Isar, making the commandos glance up. Large numbers of people were milling along the streets on the river's far bank, and the sound of thunderous cheering was rising from the direction of the Marienplatz.

"Another rally," Hunter observed. "They're holding them all over town today."

"A lot of the city is pro-Nazi," Anderson agreed. "We'll have our hands full making our E and E tonight."

"It's not the getaway that's worrying me," Hunter said. "It's getting that bastard Hitler in the first place."

Another volley of cheering drifted across the Isar.

"Get away from the door."

Rachel stepped back as the door swung open. An older, sour-faced man in civilian clothes stepped through, holding a bowl of soup. Another guard was visible beyond, a rifle in his hands.

Damn. That's not going to work either.

She had been waiting for her opportunity, crouched behind the door in hopes that she would be able to push past the guard and run for freedom. Obviously, her captors were not going to give her that chance.

At a guess, it was sometime past noon of the day after her arrival in 1923. She had been treated well enough—fed, given a mattress and a chance to sleep, and otherwise left alone with her thoughts in her bare, locked room.

The guard set the soup and a tin cup of water on the cement floor in front of her, then left without another word. She heard the jingle of his keys as he locked the door behind him.

Rachel slumped on the mattress, drawing her knees up within the circle of her arms. The bits and pieces of information she had won since she'd regained consciousness the night before were falling together

. . . and she didn't like the picture they were revealing.

Item: this was Munich, in November 1923. No other possibility made sense. Item: Todd was the saboteur, and his real name was Kulagin. Item: other people than those at the Chronos Complex were interested in 1923 Munich, and they had their own time machine. Item: though her captors spoke to her in English and to one another in German, at least some of them spoke Russian. . .

The conclusion was inescapable. The Russians did indeed have a time portal and were busily at work implementing a plan here in 1923, something they called Rising Star. She had as yet no clue to the nature of Rising Star; but, whatever it was, it was not likely to be in the best interests of America or the fallen West.

Travis has got to know about this, she thought. *He doesn't know the Reds are here, doesn't know they're after him, tracking him down . . .*

The thought brought a fresh burst of fear. She had to warn Travis, but how? In the movies, the prisoner could always be counted on to escape by smashing down a door, picking the lock, knocking the guard unconscious, or other improbable acts which Rachel knew were utterly beyond her. She had nothing on her person except her mother's locket, her clothes, and some wadded up tissue in one pocket of her slacks . . . hardly material for constructing a lethal weapon.

But if she was to escape, she would have to manage it herself. Travis had no idea she was here. She couldn't count on his arrival in the traditional nick of time. Her karate, she knew, was unlikely to be of much use. A brown belt friend had taught her some self-defense moves during her first year at MIT, but she was not about to trust her skill against, say, several men . . . or an armed one.

She *had* to escape, and time was running out. Finding Travis would be a problem; the only thing she knew for sure was that he would be at the Burgerbraukeller that evening, in time to catch Hitler's arrival at a meeting which would begin at sometime after 8:00 P.M.

Well, first problems first . . . and the first problem was escaping the Russians. How?

Rachel had spent a great deal of time lying very, very still, using her senses. There was a sharp odor to the air . . . paint, she thought, or turpentine. The sounds of people talking and moving about were indistinct and far off, which suggested that she might be able to escape if she could just get out of the room. Three times she heard what sounded like the rumble of a garage door opening and closing—almost certainly a door to the outside. She placed the sound carefully in her mind. When the opportunity came, she would have to go *that* way.

Several times, Rachel heard the creak-slam of a door close by and the hollow, running water sounds of a toilet being flushed. She remembered a glimpse of a washroom the night before, as she was being brought to the room . . . and a window! She'd not paid much attention at the time, but she was certain now that she had seen a frosted glass window through the half-open door of a bathroom, and the fuzzy glow of a streetlight beyond.

The window in the washroom seemed her best bet. Her captors were feeding her; presumably they would recognize her need to take care of certain other biological necessities as well. She had heard the toilet being flushed from her cell. It was *noisy*. If she timed the breaking of the glass with the flushing of the toilet, she might be able to scramble through the window and onto the street before her guards knew she was gone.

Rachel went over each step of the growing plan. She could smash the window with her shoe, protecting her hands by wrapping them in her knee-high stockings. A shard of glass might serve as a weapon if someone came in after her.

Once on the street, she was certain she could find a policeman who could get her to the Burgerbraukeller. Her German was good enough that she could make up a story that did not involve kidnappers from the future . . . something about having to find her brother, say, at the meeting that evening. All of the Rangers knew her. If they saw her outside the beer cellar, they would find a way to reach her.

The sooner she got away, the better.

"Hey!" She yelled, then pounded on the door. "You there! I need to use the bathroom! Hey! Is anyone there?"

Her door was unlocked several minutes later, which suggested that there was no one else close by, at least in this part of the warehouse. Her escort was the same dark-haired civilian who had brought her lunch. "Quiet down," he said in heavily-accented English. "Out."

"I was beginning to think you people had forgotten about me. . . ."

"No fear of that, *devoshka*," he said. They

reached the washroom door and he pushed it open. "Let's go."

"Now wait a moment. You're not going in there *with* me!"

Her guard grew an unpleasant smile. "You think I give you chance at window?" The smile broadened. "Anyway, I think maybe you wanting help . . . *da*?"

He grabbed her wrist, pulling her toward the small room. Rachel clutched the doorknob with her free hand and slammed the door hard on the guard's arm. He yowled and released her. She turned and ran. The garage door sounds she had heard had come from *that* direction. She dodged right around a stack of wooden crates and caught the gleam of daylight through a window on the far wall. Behind her, the injured guard was screaming something in Russian.

There was the sound of booted feet on concrete to her left. She swerved right around another stack of crates . . .

And collided head-on with Loew.

She tried to strike him but his hands took her wrists with practiced ease, twisting her around and holding her tight. She tried to kick but received a stinging blow to the side of her face in return.

"I see we have been far too lenient with you, Miss Stein," Loew said. There was nothing in his voice Rachel could identify . . . no anger, no disapproval, no compassion. "We will have to do something about that."

Thirteen

It seemed as if all of Munich had gathered in the streets outside the Burgerbraukeller, and Hunter wondered if he was even going to make it inside. If all was going as the history books claimed it would, State Commissioner von Kahr had called the meeting the evening before in an effort to make sense of the political mayhem which had descended on Munich. Revolution was in the air. No one was sure whether the commissioner was setting up his own independent Bavarian government, calling for a march on Berlin, or simply trying to keep a lid on the explosive situation in the city. All that anyone knew for certain was that von Kahr wanted to keep Hitler and his Nazis from twisting the revolution to their own purposes.

The Rosenheimerstrasse was so jammed with peo-

ple that the arriving automobiles of Munich's politicians could barely make headway. Horns blared,
pedestrians shouted, and mounted troops of police
struggled to maintain order. Hunter managed to
squeeze past the line of civilians filing into the beer
hall's front door and slip inside. His borrowed S.A.
major's uniform served him well. No one questioned
his right to enter the building.

On the other streets surrounding the block-wide
sprawl of the beer hall, King, Anderson, and Gomez
had taken up positions with their H&K MP5s hidden
under their trench coats.

"Yankee Base," Hunter murmured into his lapel
mike. "This is Yankee Leader. Radio check."

"*Yankee Leader, Yankee Base,*" Jaeger's voice
sounded in his earpiece. The German would be on
station now, waiting at the third-floor window of their
apartment across the street. "*I hear you. Ready to
go.*"

If anything, it was more crowded inside the building than out. The Burgerbrau was the second largest
beer hall in Munich, with an auditorium which could
hold three thousand people. Looking around as he
pushed his way from the vestibule into the main hall,
Hunter could well believe it. Patrons were already
jammed up against the rails which lined the open
balconies above the smoke-filled room. Every table
was taken, and every wall was lined with talking,
cursing, milling people pressed so tightly together
that the handful of buxom waitresses carrying trays
laden with half-liter tankards of beer above their
heads were having trouble getting through.

Most of the people were civilians, though Hunter
saw a number of policemen and brown-shirted S.A.

scattered through the crowd. The city's more prominent politicians were easily identifiable by their expensive tuxedos and morning coats, their women by layers of sparkling jewelry and low-cut gowns. The noise of the crowd was a steady, droning roar.

They're looking for leadership, Hunter thought to himself. *Von Kahr called the meeting, and they're expecting him to pull order out of chaos and make things right.*

What he had learned about Gustav von Kahr suggested that the man was more insipid bureaucrat than dynamic leader.

Hunter elbowed up to a part of the wall near the serving window, a position which gave him a good view of the entire room where he was not in immediate danger of being trampled. There were enough S.A. uniforms in evidence that he did not feel out of place, but none so close that he felt he was going to need to explain himself.

"All Yankees," Jaeger said over the radio. *"Looks like more politicians arriving. Some cars are trying to get through the crowds out front."*

It did not seem possible that one more person could squeeze into the auditorium, but a few moments later, the double doors at the back of the room opened and three men came through, making their way through the crowd toward the speaker's platform at the other end of the hall, thirty yards away. Hunter recognized all three from his studies of photographs back at the Complex: General Otto von Lossow, commander in chief of the Bavarian armed forces, stiff and proper in his army uniform; Colonel Hans von Seisser, chief of the Bavarian state police; and State Commissioner

Gustav Ritter von Kahr, looking somewhat rumpled in his formal tie and tails.

"Yankee Leader, Yankee Base," Jaeger said. *"More cars are pulling up in front of the main door . . . a red Mercedes in the lead. This looks like it."*

"Confirmed, Chief," Gomez added. *"I can see them from the corner. Someone's opening the car door. There he is! It's Hitler!"*

The triumvirate of Bavaria's leaders had reached the stage. It looked as though the speech-making was about to begin. With Hitler just outside, the stage was set for the putsch.

"Hitler's talking with the police," Jaeger said. *"Wait! I just spotted Rudolf Hess. He's holding the front door open. Hitler's coming in now."*

"Yankee Base," Hunter said. "Can you get a shot at him?" The mission could be brought to a conclusion within the next few seconds. There was a long silence, heightened by the hiss of static in Hunter's ear.

"Negative. Negative. The crowd is too thick. There're people following him in. Their backs are to me. I can't get an ID on any of them but Hess and Hitler. . . ."

So . . . they would have to hit him as he left, according to plan. But with the hall this crowded, was he going to be able to see Hitler at all? In all the smoke and confusion, he could barely see the auditorium's main doors.

Someone was making introductory remarks at the front of the room, but Hunter couldn't hear him. He did see von Kahr step to the rostrum, a thick sheaf of papers in his hands. As the crowd fell silent, Bavaria's leader began to deliver his speech in a low, droning mumble.

It was a singularly uninspired speech, a pedantic ramble about the evils and inconsistencies of Marxism. Hunter found himself looking about the room, studying the crowd. Large crowds made him distinctly uncomfortable—a legacy of his Alaskan boyhood—and the temper of this one was worrisome. Not far away, an S.A. officer carefully poured white powder from a paper envelope onto the back of his wrist, inhaled it, then licked the remains. Hunter was forcefully reminded of the pathetic girl who had joined them in the cabaret the night before.

He turned away, disgusted. The use of cocaine and other drugs had been out of control just before America's collapse. He wondered if there was a parallel between this culture and his own.

He found himself looking into brown eyes that chilled him to the core, eyes that met his in cold, probing assessment. There was no mistaking the awry hair, the comical toothbrush mustache. Adolf Hitler stood a few feet behind him, next to one of the ornamental pillars at the back of the room.

Hunter found himself momentarily frozen, unable to move as his eyes locked with those of the man he had come to kill. *Der Führer* seemed nervous, still wearing a shabby trench coat and moving his hands restlessly. But those eyes . . . those eyes . . .

Hilter's companions gathered around. Hunter recognized Rudolf Hess, and Hitler's bodyguard, Ulrich Graf. The extremely tall man buying three beers for three billion marks at the auditorium's serving counter had to be Dr. Ernst Hanfstaengl, Hitler's foreign press advisor. A man he did not recognize from the briefings, with a neat mustache and thick, rimless glasses, stood at Hitler's side, speaking with him urgently.

Adolf Hitler is standing four feet away, Hunter thought. *I could draw my pistol and shoot him down right here.*

It was an unnerving thought. He had not seen Vladimir Lenin face to face, and the impact of this meeting was overwhelming.

He was close enough to hear the conversation. "We should bring General von Ludendorff in," the unknown man was saying in a low voice. "You will need him in this crowd."

Hitler accepted a beer from Hanfstaengl and looked around the room. "I can handle them, Scheubner. Five minutes and I will have them all in the palm of my hand. We don't need Ludendorff here."

"With respect, we do, *mein Führer.* He will sway the army people . . . and the police."

"You think so?"

"I *know* so, *mein Führer.*"

Hitler seemed to consider this. "Very well, Scheubner. Take care of it."

"Ja wohl, mein Führer."

The little man set his beer on a table, turned, and made his way through the crowd toward a side door. Hitler leaned against the pillar, nursing his beer and listening to von Kahr's speech.

Hunter was still wrestling with the knowledge that he could kill Hitler here, now. Would he be able to get away in the confusion after his shot? It was possible . . . if unlikely. Hunter glanced past the *Führer* and found Graf watching him without emotion. The eyes of Hitler's bodyguard seemed to be everywhere,

roving about the room, watching for threats. If
Hunter was to try to take Hitler down now, he would
have to do it when Graf was looking elsewhere. He
decided to pretend disinterest for now and watch for
an opportunity later.

When would Hitler make his move? Hunter
glanced at his watch, set that morning by the clock
on one of Munich's many church towers. It was
nearly 8:30. He glanced back and saw Hitler, a disgusted look on his face, remove his trench coat and
hand it to Graf. Underneath, he was wearing an ill-
fitting, formal cutaway, the Iron Cross he had won
in World War I pinned to his lapel. To Hunter's
practiced eye, the bulge under the coat at his hip
looked suspiciously like a holstered handgun.

Hunter casually turned his back on Hitler and
watched von Kahr. The politician was droning on,
reading from the papers before him. "The quintes-
sential evil of Marxism is that it raises man's expec-
tations by pandering to his innate indolence . . ."

"*Yankee Leader, this is Base,*" Jaeger announced.
"*Soldiers arriving outside.*"

"How many?"

"*I can't tell, Lieutenant. Several truckloads. Most
of the crowds have dispersed already . . . but there's
still some police in the street. It looked like there
was going to be a confrontation, but the S.A. just
bulled their way through. Ah! There's a truck unloading. The sign on the side reads* 'Stosstrupp-
Hitler, München.' *Hitler's personal guard! They're
coming in now.*"

"They have the place surrounded," Anderson
added. "*I was just told to get out of the way or be
gunned down. They're a mite belligerent tonight.*"

There was a stir at the back of the room. Hunter turned and saw steel-helmeted Storm Troopers squeezing in from the vestibule. With a shock of recognition, he glimpsed a Maxim gun being set up on the other side of the double doors.

A revolver appeared in Hitler's hand. With a sharp movement of his head, he gathered his companions and began moving toward the front of the hall. All of them brandished handguns.

"The first and foremost task confronting the German people today," von Kahr was reading, "is to regain their freedom. If they do not succeed in this, Germany will lose its place among the nations and disappear . . ."

Hitler was a perfect target . . . but no. The S.A. troopers near the entrance had their machine gun set up. A shot now would unleash a bloodbath in the crowded hall.

No. They would have to play this one as they'd planned it.

The crowd closed in front of Hitler, stopping him. A blue-coated police officer blocked his way momentarily, but the Nazi leader threatened him with the pistol, then pushed forward. Near the front of the hall, Hitler sprang onto a chair, then up on a table, towering above the heads of the crowd, his revolver waving toward the ceiling. The disturbance had interrupted the speaker, had caused the crowd's murmur to grow to a small roar.

"*Schweigen!*" he screamed above the tumult, his voice shrill, almost hysterical. "Quiet!"

The gunshot cut through the crowd noise like thunder, setting off a chorus of screams and yells. Plaster and dust sifted from the fresh bullet hole in the ceiling, as a half dozen people nearby overturned tables or tried to lose themselves on the floor.

"The national revolution has broken out!" Hitler continued, still waving the smoking revolver. Sweat poured down his face, plastering his hair and giving him a weirdly inhuman aspect. "The hall is surrounded! No one may leave!"

With a shout and a revolver shot, Adolf Hitler had just transformed von Kahr's putsch into his own.

Fourteen

A cabinet minister tried to crawl under a table. Dozens of men crowded toward the auditorium's exits but were forced back with cuffs and rifle butts swung by cursing Storm Troopers. Someone let loose with a shrill *"Heil!"* as Hitler climbed onto the speaker's platform. "What is this, South America?" someone else shouted, and there were numerous jeers and catcalls. Hitler looked drunk—or insane—a figure at once comic and deadly with his ill-fitted morning coat and waving revolver.

"Six hundred men have this hall covered and surrounded!" Hitler screamed at the room. "No one is to leave this room! If there is not immediate quiet, I shall order a machine gun posted on the balcony!"

The silence was nearly instantaneous. Hitler drew himself up straight, aware of the three thousand pairs of eyes turned on him and him alone. "I declare the Bavarian government deposed! The government is deposed! A provisional Reich government is being formed! The police and army have joined under our swastika banner, which is at this moment flying above the police stations and army barracks of the city!"

Hunter watched with keen interest. Hitler's statements were all, he knew, pure bluff. According to Todd's briefings, nothing had been done about the various police and army units in the city. Hitler was gambling on the prestige and authority of the war hero, von Ludendorff, to bring the army and the police over to the revolution once it had been declared.

Hitler spoke urgently with Kahr, Seisser, and Lossow, gesturing with his pistol. Bavaria's triumvirs looked shocked and pale, but stubborn. Hunter could not hear what was being said, but it was clear the three were being ordered to precede Hitler into a small room off the stage through one of the auditorium's side doors.

"Please, *Herr Major* . . . what is happening?" a voice pleaded at his side. Hunter looked down at a small, gray-haired man. It took Hunter a moment to realize the man was addressing him . . . until he remembered that he was wearing the uniform of one of the troopers occupying the hall.

Hunter wasn't sure what he could or should say, but the terror in the man's face was sharply evident. The panicky edge to his voice, the twitch at the corner of his eye, suggested that the man was about to break down completely.

"Everything will be fine, *mein Herr*," he said. The man seemed to respond to the calm authority in

Hunter's voice. "*Herr* Hitler is arranging everything with von Kahr and the others now."

"But all those soldiers . . ."

"I promise you, sir, no one will be hurt. This is all . . . all just a little show." He gestured to where the Nazis' press agent, Hanfstaengl, no longer waving a revolver, was standing on a chair, talking to a gaggle of journalists. "It'll all be over in a few hours."

The man seemed reassured. He thanked Hunter and made his way back through the crowd to his seat.

He opened his radio mike. "Yankee Base, Yankee Leader," he murmured. "What's happening?"

"*Storm Troopers everywhere Lieutenant,*" Jaeger replied. "*They have the street completely blocked and they're turning people away. They have a couple of machine guns set up on tripods right out front. The police just walked off and left them in charge. What's your situation?*"

"Hitler's just declared his putsch and marched the Bavarian government off into a side room. I'm trying to get through the crowd to that end of the hall. If I can get close to Hitler, maybe I can give him a message or something to get him to come out. Keep your comline open, and be ready if I give the word. Relay it to the others."

It took Hunter nearly fifteen minutes to circle the hall, despite the fact that most of the civilians gave way before the menace of his uniform. Many people blocked his progress with demands or pleadings that they be allowed to leave, that they be told what was happening, that they not be shot. A pair of burly troopers stood in front of the door through which

Hitler had vanished, stubby MP18 submachine guns cradled in their arms.

Hunter was torn. At this moment, Hitler would be bullying Kahr, Seisser, and Lossow into joining the putsch . . . a putsch which they had been on the verge of declaring themselves. History recorded that they would agree, after Hitler threatened to shoot them all and himself as well. History did *not* record an S.A. major entering the room during the scene and leading Hitler outside . . . there to be killed by a sniper's bullet. To enter that room was to change history.

That was, after all, why he was here, but the drama of the moment made him curiously reluctant to make any unalterable move.

"Stand aside," he said. "I've got to see the *Führer*."

"No," the guard said, looking down at Hunter with a distinct sneer. "Sir."

The man's uniform was different from those of the regular S.A. brownshirts, a *feldgrau* tunic worn with a black belt and a swastika brassard, with a death's head sewn to the front of his Norwegian-style ski cap. His SMG was pointed at Hunter's gut.

"That's insubordination, soldier. Stand aside, or . . ."

"No, sir." One finger casually tapped at the death's head on his hat. "Hitler Stosstrupp," the man said slowly. "His special forces. We take our orders from *Herr* Berchtold . . . or from *Herr* Hitler. No one else."

Hunter remembered hearing that the Hitler Stosstrupp was an elite band hand-picked for their toughness and skill at brawling. They were the direct precursors of another elite unit which would become well known a few years hence—the dreaded SS.

Through the closed, wooden door Hunter could make out Hitler's shrill voice. "If things go wrong, there are four bullets left in this pistol! One for each of you should you desert me . . . the last one for me! If I am not triumphant tomorrow, I shall be a dead man!"

So, the drama was being played out, and he was powerless to intervene. He turned back to the auditorium, where Hermann Göring, resplendent in a uniform aglitter with medals, was addressing the audience. "This is not an assault on *Herr* von Kahr," he bellowed. "Or on the army, who are already marching out of their barracks with flags waving! It is directed solely against the Jew government in Berlin! It is merely the first step of the national revolution desired by everyone in this auditorium!" Moments later, Göring was leading the audience in a booming chorus of *Deutschland, Deutschland über Alles.* Three thousand voices together made the walls ring . . . and must have added to the persuasive force of Hitler's threats in the side room.

The singing dwindled away, with claps and cheers and shouts of *"Heil Hitler!"*

"Besides, ladies and gentlemen," Göring added. "You've all got your beer!"

Loew looked up from the city maps spread across the folding table as the man entered the warehouse office. "Well, Comrade Major . . . how are things going at the beer hall?"

The mild-looking man polished his rimless glasses with his handkerchief, then set them carefully back on his nose. "Everything is on schedule and according to plan," he replied. "The beer hall was completely surrounded when I left. By now, Hitler must be lying his head off to Kahr and the others. I'm just on my way to get Ludendorff."

"Excellent. It sounds like it's time to get Röhm moving."

Rachel twisted uselessly once more against the ropes which bound her wrists behind her back. They had tied her to the upright wooden chair hours before. All evening, men wearing a variety of different uniforms had been gathering around the table, discussing the details of the plan they called Rising Star.

She was not sure why she had been brought to Loew's office after her attempted escape. After securely tying and gagging her, her captors had ignored her completely. She had been straining to hear their low-voiced discussions from across the room, but so far had heard little which made sense.

Loew glanced across the map table at Rachel. His icy blue eyes held no emotion she could identify. "Did you see any sign of the Americans?" he asked.

"No, Comrade Colonel. Perhaps we scared them off."

"I don't think these Americans will have given up that easily," Todd/Kulagin said. He had been hovering around the perimeter of the planning group all evening, though no one had been paying much attention to him. "You don't even know what they look like!"

Loew ignored the spy but gave Rachel another long, calculating look. "I don't believe the Americans will prove to be a large problem, Comrade Major. We will use the woman to control them.''

"Yes, sir."

Loew bent over the maps, his finger tracing a road. "Boychenko!"

A man in a gray uniform with a death's head on the front of his ski cap snapped a salute. "Yes, Comrade Colonel!"

"It seems we no longer need Röhm's entire detachment at the Burgerbrau. We will have him divert part of his force to take and hold the War Ministry. We will need it for Ludendorff's headquarters later."

"Yes, sir."

"Some of Röhm's troops can go to the Sanktannaplatz and collect the weapons hidden there."

One of the uniformed men at the table looked up at Loew. "What about the others, sir?"

"I want Röhm in position now. I don't trust that fool . . . and we have no agents close to him in his organization. Our people will join the other S.A. groups and give them their orders later . . . as originally planned." He pointed to a spot on a map. "You should be able to intercept Röhm here, somewhere along the Briennerstrasse. Use Göring's name on the order."

"Ja, Herr Oberst."

Loew looked at the major. "You'd better get on with it, Comrade."

"Agreed, Comrade." He looked tired. "That idiot Hitler . . ."

"Not much longer, and you can drop this Scheubner-Richter charade," Loew said. "Hitler will have served his purpose in just a few more days."

"Ja wohl, Kamerad Oberst."

"I believe it is a mistake to discount the Americans," Kulagin said as the two men left. "They may have already penetrated the beer hall."

"I do not discount them," Loew replied, contempt edging his voice. He walked around the table and approached Rachel.

"Comfortable, my dear?" he asked her, speaking English. He leaned over to check the ropes binding her ankles and arms to the chair. "Your people never really had a chance, you know. Not against the VBU."

Rachel twisted around, her eyes wide above the gag.

"*Vremya Bezopasnosti Upravlenie,*" he said. "I don't expect that you've heard of it. Our new branch of the KGB . . . the Time Security Directorate." He seemed to read her expression. "In case you were wondering, your people did not kill Lenin. He made it to Leningrad, as planned."

The words struck Rachel like hammer blows. Lenin . . . alive?

"Oh, yes," Loew continued. "We've had an operational time machine for some time, now. Our agents in 1917 made certain Lenin and his party boarded a different train. There were Bolsheviks on that railcar, certainly . . . but not the ones your team was looking for. *That* was our doing."

Satisfied that Rachel was still securely tied, he stepped back. "The VBU has planned all of this very carefully, you see. Operation Rising Star will be our death blow against the West."

Kulagin shifted uncomfortably on the other side of the room. "Sir . . . the American commandos . . ."

"Don't worry about the damned Americans!"

Loew whirled away from Rachel. "Sokolov! Your knife!"

One of the men in S.A. garb pulled a dagger from his belt scabbard and handed it to Loew. Kulagin paled.

Loew turned the knife in his hand, its edge glittering. He looked at the spy with cold calculation. "Perhaps there is a way for you to redeem yourself after all, Kulagin."

"Ah . . . Comrade Colonel . . ."

Loew smiled, then turned back to Rachel. She watched the knife with a terrified fascination. *He's going to kill me* . . . She struggled against the ropes.

"Gently, my dear, gently," Loew said in English. He reached down and plucked at the collar of her white blouse, then brought the knife up until it rested close by her throat.

"You're . . . you're not going to kill her, Comrade Colonel?" Kulagin's eyes were wide and staring. "I thought she would be useful . . . Her knowledge . . ."

With a swift, precise motion, Loew nicked the material of her blouse, then ripped it sharply down across her chest. Buttons snapped and clattered as they danced across the concrete floor. Loew pulled the scrap of fabric away, turned, and thrust it at Kulagin. "If Hitler made it inside the beer hall, it must mean the Americans are inside as well. Otherwise, they would have killed him out on the street." He handed the knife back to Sokolov. "We will make you useful, Kulagin. That piece of blouse if proof that we have the girl. Take Sokolov and Luzhin with you to the beer hall. Find the Americans. Perhaps you can persuade them not to interfere.''

Rachel sagged back against the back of the chair. She was alive! She opened her eyes and met Loew's pale stare. ''So long as she behaves herself, we will let her live,'' Loew said. ''She could yet be very useful to us.''

Over the course of an hour, the mood in the Burgerbrau had swung wildly from one extreme to the other. The crowd's enthusiasm after Göring's speech had faded as Hitler remained locked in the side room with Bavaria's government leaders. After a time, the *Führer* had reappeared on the speaker's platform.

Hunter could not remember ever having seen anything like it. Hitler, a wild-eyed Charlie Chaplin in baggy trousers and ill-fitting cutaway, was transformed as he began speaking. As far as Hunter could tell, the man didn't *say* much of anything beyond the fact that the deliberations with von Kahr and the others were taking longer than expected . . . but the thunder of his words, the power of his promises, his impassioned plea for the support of the Bavarian people, all drew the crowd to his side as if by magic. He strode from the room a conqueror, the three thousand prisoners in the hall on their feet, shrieking *''Heil Hitler''* and cheering wildly. The arrival of General Erich von Ludendorff seemed perfectly timed to mesh with the crowd's high spirits.

Those spirits plunged again as Hess read out a list of cabinet ministers and others who were now under arrest . . . and worsened as Storm Troopers moved among them, taking hostages. ''Some nationalist sal-

vation this is!'' someone in the mob shouted. "Hitler
and his people are swine!'' Sounds of struggle broke
out in the back of the hall as a number of people
tried to push their way past the guards and were
driven back into the auditorium by S.A. men swinging truncheons and rifle butts.

At last, Hitler marched back onto the stage, followed by Ludendorff, Kahr and the others. Kahr
announced in a subdued voice that an agreement
had been reached. The crowd remained restless until
Hitler stepped forward and began speaking once
again.

The magic returned, more chilling, more powerful
than ever. Hunter watched, amazed, as a hostile
crowd once again fell under the spell of Hitler's or-
atory. His voice, almost conversational as he announced appointments in the new government, rose
steadily to an impassioned crescendo, thundering
through the hall.

"In the coming weeks and months I will fulfill the
vow I made to myself five years ago as a gas-blinded
cripple in a hospital here!'' The crowd followed
every word, mesmerized. "I vowed never to rest until the criminals who betrayed us in 1918 are crushed,
until a Germany of power and greatness, of freedom
and glory, has risen out of the wretched rubble that
it is today! Amen!'' The crowd screamed approval.
"Long live the Bavarian government! *Hoch! Hoch!
Hoch!*'' The beer hall exploded in cheers and tumul-
tuous cries of *"Hoch!"* and *"Heil Hitler!"*

Hitler appeared as frenzied as the mob. "Long live
the German national government! *Hoch! Hoch!
Hoch!*''

The speeches that followed were anticlimactic by

comparison. Eventually, people began leaving, though the process was slowed by searches at the doors for Bolshevik spies and Jews. The Bavarian leaders were led back to the side room to discuss the details of the new government. Hunter saw the man Hitler had sent off after Ludendorff shepherding them through the door.

Hitler circulated through the still-crowded room, receiving congratulations and handshakes. The crowd had proclaimed him as the savior of Bavaria. Soon, he would lead them in a march on Berlin, bringing the National Socialist revolution to all of Germany.

Hunter was frustrated. The putsch was well underway, but not once had he had an opportunity to get close to the man. If he could only get close enough, his borrowed major's uniform might let him concoct a story that could draw Hitler outside and into Jaeger's sights.

"Let me through! I have an urgent message. Let me through!"

A minor commotion near the front door attracted Hunter's attention. An S.A. *leutnant* had been trapped in the press of people being forced to show identification at the main door.

An urgent message might be addressed to almost anyone in the hall, but Hunter felt a small twist of hope. Possibly . . .

"You there!" Hunter threw a major's authority behind his voice. "Let that man through!" Uniforms parted, and a disheveled lieutenant stepped into the auditorium, a folded paper in his hand. "What's your message, lieutenant?"

"Urgent, *Herr Major!* For the *Führer!*"

"I'll take it."

"Trouble at the Engineer Barracks," the lieutenant explained as Hunter unfolded the note and read through the scrawled handwriting swiftly. "The captain in charge won't give the Oberland Bund people their weapons. It's a standoff!"

He folded the note again, remembering the argument he'd overheard the night before. "I'll take care of it."

"Ja wohl, Herr Major!"

This might be the opportunity Hunter had been waiting for. "Yankee Leader to Yankee Base!"

"Go ahead, Yankee Leader."

"Stand by, Karl. I think I'm going to be able to steer the target your way."

"Ready and waiting. Keep us posted."

"Will do. Yankee Leader out."

Adolf Hitler stood near the auditorium stage, shaking hands and beaming at the people gathered around him, secure in the knowledge that his putsch was going off precisely according to plan. The timetable worked out with Scheubner-Richter called for select groups of S.A. and Stosstrupp all over the city to go into action now, gathering weapons from hidden arsenals, and marching on such key points as telegraph and radio offices, police barracks, and the old Bavarian War Ministry in the center of the city. With von Kahr now persuaded to support him, with all of Bavaria as a power base, the way was open now for a triumphant march on Berlin. He, Adolf Hitler, would be the ruler of a new National Socialist Germany. . . .

"Verzeihung, mein Führer!" An S.A. major was

pushing forward through the politicians and Storm Troopers in front of the stage. "I have an urgent message for you from the Oberland Bund!"

Hitler remembered seeing the young major earlier in the evening. The man's uniform did not fit him well . . . but there was a sharp look about the eyes, a look of competence, which Hitler admired. He reached through the crowd to accept the message.

"The situation is serious, *mein Führer*," the major said. "I was directed to tell you that only your presence at the Engineer Barracks can resolve the matter."

Göring looked up sharply. "*Der Führer* has far more important things to do than . . ."

"*Nein!*" Hitler said. "Everything has gone so well, we cannot let those fools interfere with the plan now!"

Hitler believed strongly in his own sense of destiny. The shouts and acclamations of the crowd were still ringing in his ears. "I will go at once! Quickly! Organize an expeditionary force! At least three trucks of S.A.! We will assist the Oberland Bund with artillery, if need be!"

Hunter watched the frenzied preparations from a distance. "Stand ready, Yankee Base," he murmured. "Hitler's in the vestibule, getting his coat. He'll be coming out the front door any moment now."

"*We're ready and in position. The streets are thick with soldiers, but I'll have a perfect shot when he steps out through the door.*"

"He's on his way. Get ready."

Still shouting orders, Hitler strode toward the front

door of the Burgerbrau. Hunter pushed past the people still milling about the auditorium's front door, following.

"Hunter!"

The use of his name froze Hunter where he stood. He turned toward the voice. He felt a thrill of shock as he recognized the speaker. "Todd!"

What had gone wrong? All he could imagine was that Todd had been sent through the portal to deliver some last-minute order or change in plans.

But why *now*, of all times?

Across the street, Karl Jaeger brought his rifle's scope to his face. People were spilling through the front door now; officers, mostly, waving, giving orders. S.A. soldiers were climbing aboard the three rickety trucks lining the Rosenheimerstrasse.

There! The face nearly filled his scope at 10× magnification. He recognized the straight, unkempt hair, the narrow, toothbrush mustache.

His finger drew up the slack on the trigger as he brought the sight's crosshairs into line with Adolf Hitler's forehead.

"Recognize this?" Todd was standing close to Hunter now, holding out a piece of white cloth.

Hunter frowned. The cloth gleamed in the light from chandeliers in the vestibule's ceiling. It appeared to be synthetic, a piece torn from a white blouse.

"We have her, Hunter. Call off your people, now!"

Hunter was paralyzed by shock. "Todd . . . what in hell . . ."

"Do I need to spell it out? Rachel is our prisoner! If you kill Hitler, she dies!"

Todd . . . the saboteur!

Hunter's hand dropped to the radio under the hem of his major's tunic. It might already be too late. . . .

"Yankee Base! Abort! Abort!"

Fifteen

The crosshairs centered squarely on Hitler's face.
Jaeger released a little of his pent-up breath. Just
relax . . . squeeze . . .

"Abort! Abort!"

Jaeger's finger came off the trigger. He fumbled
for the transmit switch on his radio. What the hell
was Hunter playing at?

"Aborted," Jaeger said. "Damn it, Lieutenant
. . . why?"

"Hold your position," Hunter said, the voice
tense in Jaeger's earpiece. Through his scope, he
could see Hitler talking with someone in a Stosstrupp uniform as he waited for a driver to bring
his red Mercedes around to the front of the beer
cellar.

"I've got a perfect shot, Lieutenant."

"Negative." Was that a tremor in Hunter's voice?
"Let him go."

The Mercedes drew ahead as the street filled with
soldiers piling into a trio of lorries.

The chance was gone.

"Excellent," Todd said. He was wearing a heavy
overcoat and kept one hand hidden in his pocket.
Hunter had no doubt that a gun was aimed at him.
"Now, you will do precisely what I say. Tell your
men to go to the alley west of the Burgerbrau . . . .
the one connecting Rosenheimerstrasse with the Kellerstrasse in the back. They will lay their weapons
on the ground and wait outside the kitchen door. You
will relay my instructions exactly, then give me your
microphone, earpiece, and radio pack. If there is any
resistance, Rachel Stein will die."

Hunter passed the instructions on to his men, then
unclipped the mike from his lapel and pulled the receiver from his ear. "So . . . the Russians have a
time machine, too," Hunter said as he handed the
communications gear to Todd.

"Shut up." Todd glanced back and forth across
the crowded vestibule, then jerked his head. "Back
into the auditorium."

Todd guided Hunter to a side door in the main hall
which opened into the Burgerbrau's kitchen. It took
them several minutes to make their way through the
milling press of people who still thronged the auditorium.

Hunter formed and discarded several plans for
turning the tables on Todd. In the noise and confusion it might be possible to take the man down. Was
Todd telling the truth? That piece of white, synthetic

fabric argued he was. If Hunter tried anything, he would have to move fast to find where Rachel was being held before her captors killed her.

Two large men in S.A. uniforms and carrying MP18 submachine guns joined them as they entered the kitchen, and Hunter changed his mind about trying to pin Todd in the swinging door as he went through.

The alley was a narrow canyon between bare brick cliffs. Trash cans stood sentinel amid heaped piles of refuse which had spilled out onto the mud street. Munich's main streets had, for the most part, been faultlessly clean. Perhaps the back alleys were reserved for the stench and filth of uncollected garbage.

Greg King and Eddie Gomez stood a few feet away, their submachine guns and automatic pistols lying at their feet, their hands open and carefully held clear of their sides.

Todd's gun slipped out into the open, a deadly little Beretta questing back and forth. "There were four of them," he snapped. "Sokolov! Check that way! Luzhin! Down there!"

"Easy, there, Todd!" King held his hands up, palms out. He spoke slowly and with great deliberation. "The other two are coming!"

"Where are they?"

"Hey . . . take it easy, okay? Jaeger was on the third floor of that flophouse across Rosenheimer. He's got to come down to street level, then get across Rosenheimerstrasse through a small army of your . . . friends."

"That's right," Gomez added. "And I saw Anderson. He got stopped by Storm Troopers while he was coming up the street.''

Todd hesitated, obviously suspicious. He gestured with his pistol at his two men, sending them up the alley to check around corners. A growl of noise drifted down the alley from the direction of Rosenheimerstrasse as trucks filled with soldiers gunned their engines and began moving up the street.

Get ready. King's hand signal was quick, almost invisible.

''All clear,'' Sokolov said, reappearing. Luzhin, too, returned from the other direction, shaking his head.

Todd's eyes continued to scan the surrounding buildings, as though expecting the missing men to materialize out of the bricks. It was dark in the alley, which caught only scattered light from streetlamps at either end.

''We will wait,'' he said. He gestured toward Hunter with his pistol. ''If they're not here in five minutes, Lieutenant, one of your men is going to die. If they try anything funny, I'll see to it that Rachel's last few hours are extremely unpleasant.''

''No need for that,'' King said. He pointed back down the street toward the Kellerstrasse. ''There they are!''

Todd and his subgunners swung about in unison, their weapons seeking targets down the alley. There was a shattering clatter a few feet behind them.

Roy Anderson burst up from one of the garbage cans parked beside the Burgerbrau's kitchen door, the silenced H&K at chest level, spitting fire as the garbage can lid rattled across the alley. Luzhin catapulted forward as bullets smashed along his spine from behind.

Hunter lunged for the ground as the first burst cut loose, his legs scissoring out and back, entangling Todd's ankles. Sokolov twisted to one side at the same instant, trying to bring his weapon to bear. A three-round burst caught him high in the shoulder and throat, spinning him around and slamming him backward into a wall already splattered with his blood. His MP18 stuttered flame and sent ricochets screaming up the bricks above their heads before Anderson corrected his aim and placed three more rounds squarely into the Russian's chest. The body shuddered with the impact, momentarily pinned to the wall, then slid to the ground along a smear of blood.

King and Gomez retrieved their weapons but the firefight was already over. Hunter scrambled around and grappled with Todd on the ground, levering the man's hand back at the wrist to pry the Beretta from his fingers.

Hunter flipped the pistol's safety on, then hauled Todd into a sitting position and shoved him back against the Burgerbrau's alley wall.

"You have some explaining to do, Mister," he said, the tone carrying fire and ice. "You can start by telling us where Rachel Stein is."

"It's happened!" Loew announced, setting the receiver of his telephone down. "That was Scheubner-Richter. Von Kahr and the others have joined Hitler's revolution!"

Still tied to the chair in the warehouse office, Rachel watched as Loew barked orders at the twenty-odd men in the room.

"We must work quickly now," he continued. "The Major says the Oberland Bund has already moved on the Engineer Barracks and run into trouble. Apparently, Hitler has already left to see to matters there."

"Does that change our schedule?" one of the men in S.A. dress asked.

Loew nodded. "Our timetable will be advanced by one hour. Each of you must be with the Nazi units assigned to you, ready to direct them, within two hours. We must be certain our people are controlling events tonight, and not that idiot Hitler. So . . . all of you, muster downstairs in the armory and draw your weapons."

The men, most of them in S.A. brownshirts and swastika armbands, a few in civilian clothes or the gray and black of the Hitler Stosstrupp, began filing out of the room. Loew stopped one man in S.A. uniform. "Mikhalin! You stay with the girl. Once we're gone and the streets are clear, take her to the *schloss*. After the Nazis win, we'll take her back to *Uralskiy Stantzeeya* and wring her dry."

"Yes, Comrade Colonel!"

The guard looked across at Rachel as Loew left the room, an open leer spreading across his face.

It was the same man who had escorted her to the bathroom only a few hours earlier.

"My name is Captain Pavel Alexeivitch Kulagin." He struggled to breathe as Hunter pressed him back against the wall. "I'm not telling you anything! You hurt me, and the girl dies!"

Hunter scowled and tightened his grip on the big man's collar. "Well, that's not going to help you much, is it?"

"You'll . . . you'll never find where she is."

Behind the scowl, Hunter felt a sharp pang of indecision. Kulagin was their only link to Rachel and the people who were holding her, and he knew it. If Kulagin didn't talk, and quickly, Anderson's fast thinking would go for nothing.

The ambush had been Roy Anderson's idea, worked out as the three of them hurried toward the back of the Burgerbrau, and implemented when they saw that the alley was deserted. It was still unclear to Hunter how Anderson had folded his lanky frame into the garbage can after the Texan emptied it on the ground, but the trick worked. King's announcement that the missing team members were approaching had been the signal for Roy to come out shooting.

Hunter appreciated initiative in a combat team, but he wondered if, just this once, his men had shown a bit too much. Their impromptu ambush might have wrecked their chances of finding Rachel . . . unless they could find a way to make Kulagin talk.

King came up behind Hunter. "Those two are dead," he said. "Eddie and Roy are covering the alley approaches. No sign they had any backup."

"This gentleman doesn't want to tell us where Rachel is," Hunter said as he retrieved his radio gear from Kulagin's pocket.

"Give him to me," King said. "He'll talk."

Kulagin gave a weak grin. "You . . . you Americans don't know the first thing about persuasion. You're too soft. Anyway . . . we have the girl."

A soft whistle sounded down the alley. Gomez

waved his MP5 as another figure appeared. "There's Jaeger," King said.

The German approached and handed Hunter the Uzi he'd left in the rented room. The distant street-lamps gleamed off the barrel of the Wa-2000 sniper's rifle cradled in his arms. "Just what the hell is going on?"

"It seems Mr. Todd here is a Russian," Hunter said. He had to fight to keep his voice from shaking. "Name of Kulagin. He claims his people are holding Rachel someplace nearby, but he won't tell us where."

Hunter noted the twist at the corner of Jaeger's mouth, the tightening of his knuckles against the Walther's pistol grip. That same hatred Hunter had seen on the ridge above the Werra kindled behind the German's eyes.

Hunter returned his full attention to the prisoner. "I'll bet you did lots of snooping, back when you worked at the Complex. Did you ever read Mr. Jaeger's personnel records?" He allowed himself to smile with humor he did not feel. "He doesn't like Russians, you know."

Kulagin's eyes widened slightly. At his side, Jaeger carefully slung his rifle, then reached under his jacket at the small of his back, drawing the knife concealed there. It was a Tanto, a short, heavy blade curved like a Japanese sword which shone silver in the dim light.

"Karl was a guerrilla fighter in Germany," Hunter continued. "He was quite good."

"Yeah," King added. "I've heard stories about those German partisans."

Kulagin had evidently heard the same stories. His

eyes were wide open now, staring at the blade in Jaeger's hand.

"What's your score now, Karl?" Hunter was surprised at how casually the words came out.

"Eighty-two." There was slow death in that voice.

"Well, here's eighty-three." He shoved Kulagin to the ground at Jaeger's feet. "Have fun. Us soft Americans will make sure you're not disturbed for a while."

"No! Wait!" The Russian struggled as Jaeger's arm snaked down, striking at Kulagin's throat. The knife hovered above his eyes. "Get him away from me!"

"You have something you'd like to tell us?"

The answer, it seemed, was yes.

Hunter was not entirely surprised to learn about the *Vremya Bezopasnosti Upravlenie*, or that the Soviets had their own time machine. He was dismayed to learn that Lenin had not, after all, died in the train wreck, and shocked to learn just how completely the VBU had penetrated Hitler's Nazis in 1923 Bavaria.

"You're telling us that the VBU is trying to help Hitler's putsch *succeed*?" Hunter shook his head. "Dammit, man, that makes absolutely no sense at all!"

Kulagin's eyes were fixed on Jaeger's blade. "Y-yes. If the putsch is successful, Hitler will march on Berlin . . . will call for a Nazi revolution throughout the country."

"What in the hell are Communists doing helping Adolf Hitler?" King demanded.

"We . . . the VBU . . . we have agents with . . . with contact among the local Communists. When the Nazis have Berlin terrified and the Weimar govern-

ment helpless, there will be a nationwide rising . . .
a counterrevolution.''

"So Germany goes Communist in the Twenties,''
Hunter said.

"That's right.'' Once started, Kulagin's words
tumbled out one upon the next. "Our historical fore-
casters expect civil war to break out within the next
month. In a year, Germany will be a Communist
republic . . . in ten, a member of the Greater Soviet
Union.''

Hunter heard Jaeger's sharp intake of breath at his
side. He wondered momentarily what Jaeger would
be like, born and raised in a world where Germany
had been under Russian rule for decades.

"World War II will pit France and England against
the overwhelming power of Communist Eurasia.
America will come in too late to help its allies. We
expect the United States will fall to a united Communist world no later than 1975.''

So the Communists had been trying to rewrite history in much the same way as the Chronos Project.
Apparently they had been at it longer, and with con-
siderably greater success.

He forced his mind back to the immediate problem
at hand. "Where's Rachel?''

Kulagin looked as though he were going to resist,
but he thought better of it as Jaeger's knife came
close again.

"Not far from here . . . on the Widenmayerstrasse . . .''

In bits and pieces, Kulagin described the VBU's
Munich headquarters, a warehouse located just across
the street from the Isar. They learned where in the
building she was being kept and that there could be

as many as thirty VBU troops on hand at any one time. Hunter pressed Kulagin for precise details. How many would be at the warehouse tonight? How many on guard? Even the threat of Jaeger's knife could elicit little additional information, however. Kulagin couldn't tell what he didn't know.

Hunter took King aside. "We've got to get her out," he said.

"What about the mission?"

"Killing Hitler?" Hunter shrugged. "Damn, how can we? God knows when he'll come back to the beer hall. Besides, it's starting to look like you were right, Greg. We missed Lenin. Maybe we're doomed to miss Hitler too."

"Hell, I don't know, Lieutenant." He reached out and struck the bricks beside him lightly with his fist. "We're here. It's real. I don't see what's stopping us. But you're right. We're got to rescue her." He grinned suddenly. "I knew that girl was going to be trouble!"

"You bastard!" Hunter was caught completely by surprise by the surge of anger, of raw emotion that boiled up at King's words. King's tone had been light, part of their usual good-natured bantering.

Was Rachel's capture affecting his judgment that much?

"Sorry, Greg . . ."

"No problem, Lieutenant." But there was no warmth in the words.

Sixteen

"They're gone, *devoshka*," the Russian said, his mouth close to her ear. His English was broken. "Is just me and you, *da*?"

Rachel flinched away from his touch. He snickered and roughly fondled one bare breast. She squeezed her eyes shut and fought to keep from trembling. Terror and loathing rose hot in the back of her throat. The rag held in her mouth by a length of packing tape choked her. She remembered four drunken Soviet soldiers smashing down her door in Boston, remembered them laughing as they knocked her down, as they dragged her to her bed. *Oh, God, don't let me be sick.* . . .

He tugged the remnants of her blouse down off her shoulders, then caressed her again. His fingers found the gold locket dangling between her breasts. "So

195

. . . what is this?'' His fingers closed on the chain, twisted sharply, snapping it away. ''Is gold, ha? You not need where you go, *devoshka*.'' The sight of the Russian holding the pendant up to the light, then dropping it into a shirt pocket, made her feel as violated as the touch of his hands.

He began caressing her again. ''They not care much at *Uralskiy Stantzeeya* if . . . if merchandise is used . . . *da*?'' He pinched her, hard. ''They use same way all time.''

The Russian laughed viciously, then let her go. Rachel heard him moving behind her. She opened her eyes and looked over her shoulder. In the corner he had found the mattress on which she'd regained consciousness the day before.

''Is good,'' he said, grinning at her. ''Now we be . . . how you say . . . get much comfortable.''

He began fumbling behind her. She felt the ropes lashing her arms to the chair back fall away, though her wrists were still tied. Then he squatted and began prying at the knots which bound her ankles to the chair legs.

Rachel gasped behind her gag, fighting back wave upon wave of panic. Her own terror threatened to hold her paralyzed, helpless. She wanted to strike out, to kick the Russian in the face, but one leg was still tied, her attacker at an impossible angle . . .

Then her legs were free. Her attacker stood, stepping in front of her to drag her to her feet by her hair. He leered, tugging at the waistband of her slacks. *No!*

The Russian's legs were spread slightly, bracing him when he pulled her to her feet. Rachel's knee came up, furiously driven by mingled rage and terror. The man gasped, his eyes bulging with the shock. He bent forward, doubled over. Her second thrust with her knee caught him squarely in the nose, smashing him up and back.

She dropped to the concrete floor, struggling to pull her bound wrists down past her hips. From the corner of her eye, she saw the Russian on hands and knees a few feet away, blood streaming from his shattered nose. Panic nearly claimed her again when she found herself doubled over as tightly as she could manage, unable to work her body through the circle of her arms. The Russian was getting up . . .

Rachel's scream was muffled by the gag as she forced her knees tight against her chest and dragged her feet past her wrists. Then she was up, her hands still tied, but in front of her now. Her attacker was nearly up as well when she grabbed the chair with an awkward, two-handed grip. She swung it as hard as she could, aiming for the side of his head.

The blow smashed the man to the concrete, splattering blood. Almost, he made it to his hands and knees once again when Rachel took another swing. This time, the back of the chair cracked. This time, he stayed down.

Rachel fought for breath, the gag choking her. She managed to peel the packing tape from her hair and face and pull the rag out of her mouth. It took her a moment more to work the knot at her wrists free with her teeth.

She couldn't tell if the man on the floor was dead or just spectacularly unconscious. But she was not going to let him keep her mother's locket. By hauling back on his limp arm, she was able to lever him over onto his back. The locket was in the right front pocket of the brown shirt. She stared blankly for a moment at the broken chain, then tucked the pendant into a pocket in her slacks.

Briefly, she considered taking the shirt as well. She had no idea how far it was from the warehouse to the Burgerbraukeller, but she knew she would have to venture out onto the city streets to try to find it.

She to get to Travis . . . had to warn him of what she had learned.

And that need decided her. She would waste precious minutes wrestling with the inanimate body on the floor, and if Loew or the others had heard any part of her fight with the Russian . . .

King jerked a thumb down the alley toward the Kellerstrasse. "We saw a truck parked back that way. Had a sign on it: *'Hitler Stosstrupp'*."

Hunter raised his eyebrows. "Keys?"

"Hey, Lieutenant! You're talking to the original tough kid from the Bronx . . . remember?" King's words seemed forced, as though he was trying to overcome the barrier raised by Hunter's earlier explosion.

The truck was a rattletrap of a lorry with a high, square cab and an open back, the sort of vehicle Hunter remembered as puttering about with comic speed in old, flickering, silent movies. It had the steering wheel on the right, with a license plate reading JM 4425 tacked onto the cab above the window. Anderson, Gomez, and Jaeger hauled Kulagin into the back of the lorry, while Hunter joined King in the front seat. King fished around under the steering column for a moment. "Uh oh."

"What's the matter?"

"No ignition. At least, nothing I'm familiar with."

Roy Anderson called down from the back. "Well shoot, Master Sergeant. This baby's got a crank."

"A what?"

"A crank! A starter crank!"

"Great," Hunter said. "We'd better walk."

"Hey . . . no problem," Anderson said. "My Granddaddy always told stories about the old truck on his ranch in Texas. Let me have a look."

It took a few moments to puzzle out the controls, despite Anderson's claim to understandings of things mechanical. "This here's gotta be the fuel lever," Anderson said, fiddling with a device on the steering column. "This over here oughta be the spark lever."

Hunter looked down. "Three pedals. Clutch, brake, gas?"

"Nope." Anderson indicated a button on the floor off to the side. "That there's the gas. Danged if I know what the extra pedal is for . . ."

"We'd better walk."

"Company coming, Chief!" Gomez's warning from the back of the truck caught Hunter by surprise. He looked up and saw an S.A. private approaching, his rifle slung carelessly over his shoulder.

Hunter climbed down out of the cab. The lone soldier might be their one hope of getting the antiquated machine running.

"You there, soldier!" he called in his best major's voice. "Give us a hand here!"

Their driving lesson took nearly ten minutes and left behind on the Kellerstrasse a private wondering at the intelligence of S.A. officers who didn't know how to drive. King favored an arm bruised by the starter crank's kick when Anderson opened the spark lever too far, while Hunter wondered again if it wouldn't be better to walk.

The Rosenheimerstrasse was nearly deserted by the time they made their way, in uncertain lurches and sputterings, down the hill toward the Ludwigs-brucke. There were S.A. soldiers guarding the bridge, and Hunter noticed a small field cannon parked near the bank of the river, but no one even threatened to stop the truck. Hunter was not entirely sure whether this was due to the Stosstrupp identifi-cation on the truck, or Anderson's uncertain driving.

Anderson turned right on the Munich side of the bridge and drove north along the river. Progress was slow. The streets were slick with freezing rain and patches of snow, and three times they were forced to pull over as small mobs of S.A. troopers surged into their path, brandishing torches, shouting, and sing-ing patriotic songs. The sounds of breaking glass rose above the noise of the mobs.

Hunter saw a young and desperate man scrambling for the imagined safety of an alley, a pack of S.A. thugs close at his heels. *"Jüdisch schwein! Halten Sie den Jude!"* A storefront window shattered under the impact of a brick.

"We've got to help him, Lieutenant!" Anderson's hands clenched the truck's steering wheel as though it were a weapon. The crowd caught the Jew, pulling him down, pummeling him with fists and clubs.

"How?" Hunter's reply was sharp and bitter. "Look." He pointed down the street to where a blue-coated Munich policeman was, with great delibera-tion, turning his back on the scene. Laughing and shouting insults, the crowd dragged their prisoner into the street, loading him into the back of a truck where other bloodied and battered citizens knelt under the guns of grinning soldiers.

"Keep driving," Hunter said. "We've got to find Rachel."

Beyond the suite of hallways and offices where Rachel had been held prisoner, the warehouse was a single vast, cavernous room. Stacks of crates gave it the aspect of a gigantic maze. Cartons, piled high, formed narrow, twisting canyons.

She drew back behind the cover provided by one of those canyon walls, shaking with pent-up frustration and fear. She had guided herself across the darkened floor by the remembered sound of a garage door. The warehouse had seemed deserted until she reached the main entrance.

A dozen men stood near the curiously antique trucks and cars parked behind the corrugated metal door. As she watched, two more men in S.A. uniforms joined them, cradling sleek automatic rifles. Rachel was no weapons expert, but she had seen enough Russian assault rifles in Boston to know a Soviet AKM when she saw one. Those lean, wicked-looking weapons with their curved banana magazines were the trademark of Communist forces throughout the world . . . at least, they were in her own time. The men had an unhurried air inconsistent with the weapons they carried. Several smoked, many were chatting in a casual fashion which suggested they would be staying put for some time. Rachel remembered Loew's timetable.

There was no escape that way and would be none for two more hours. She would have to find another way out.

Perhaps *this* way . . .

A metallic clatter just in front of her sent Rachel
ducking back into darkness. A man in civilian clothes
and a Nazi armband passed within a few feet of her,
snapping the magazine of his AKM into place. She
peered around the corner again after he had passed.
She saw the enclosed top of a stairwell ten yards
away. The door opened as two more S.A.-clad Russians emerged with their weapons.

That must be the door to the downstairs armory
Loew had mentioned.

Five minutes later she found the back door. For
once, it seemed that luck was with her. There were
no sentries, and when her hand turned the knob, it
opened easily, unlocked. There was no sign that her
escape had been noticed. Outside was cold, wind,
and darkness.

How far was the Burgerbraukeller? And where?
For a moment, she hesitated, uncertain.

She would worry about directions later. Gathering
the remnants of her torn blouse about her, she hurried out into the night.

"That must be it," Gomez said. "Look. Guards."

The warehouse Kulagin described was located just
across the broad Widenmayerstrasse from the Isar.
The Rangers had left their borrowed truck several
blocks further south, pulled off the street and out of
sight in an alley. Kulagin was tied and gagged under
a tarpaulin in the back.

" *'Fricht Importieren-Exportieren,'* " Jaeger read
the sign mounted on rust-colored bricks above the
big garage door. "That figures. Nothing like an im-

port-export warehouse as a cover for Communist spies.''

"Just makes you wonder what they're importin' from the future," Anderson said. "You figure we can spring Stein's daughter out of there, Lt.?"

Hunter ducked below the rim of the low, concrete abutment which separated the Widenmayerstrasse from the river bank. The Isar flowed black and icy a few feet behind him. "Two sentries," he said. "One on either side of the garage door. Looks like they're dressed as S.A.''

"Maybe they are S.A.," King suggested. "Damn it! How many time travelers can there *be* running around loose in 1923?"

"A good many," Anderson replied. "Thirty, if we can believe Todd . . . Kulagin . . . whatever the hell his name is. Anyway, would you trust S.A. thugs to guard *your* secret headquarters?"

Hunter glanced down at his S.A. major's uniform. "Right. Thanks a lot. Okay . . . Eddie? How much plastique did you bring? Do you have it here?"

Gomez patted the belt of his overcoat and grinned. "Right here, Chief. Enough to make a really nice bang.''

"How nice?"

"One kilo's worth, Lieutenant.''

"Enough to blast that garage door down.''

"No problem, Chief.''

A rattling sound rose from across the street. Hunter eased back up for another look over the abutment.

"Heads up, boys. Something's happening.''

They could hear shouts now, faint and confused, from inside the building. S.A. troops were opening the garage door, through which the IF Rangers could see several cars and trucks. A tall, distinguished-looking man in civilian clothes joined the two guards.

"Achtung!" They could hear him speaking plainly across the twenty yards which separated them. *"Die Fräulein ist gegangen!"*

"Rachel!" Hunter said. "She must have escaped!"

The man in civilian clothes questioned the guards, then began giving orders. Two men dressed as S.A. were dispatched up the Widenmayerstrasse toward the north. Three more headed south. The shadowy figures of other men could be seen moving inside the warehouse, evidently searching the place carefully.

"We've got to find her," Hunter said. "If she got out of there on her own, she must be out in the streets somewhere."

"How?" King asked.

"Back to the truck. We'll have to search the streets."

One girl . . . lost in the tangle of Munich's night streets. He remembered the scenes of terror he'd witnessed earlier, and shuddered.

Rachel hurried down the alley, gritting her teeth against the wet and icy wind that slashed at her each time she reached a cross street which opened up on the river. She was pretty sure she was heading in the right direction. From an alley between the warehouse and a looming brownstone apartment building, she had looked across a broad street and seen a concrete abutment which, she thought, must lie along the Isar. The blackness beyond suggested a park. If she was on the west bank of the river, close to Munich proper, that park might be the Maxmillananlagen, which, she knew, bordered the river just north of the Bur-gerbraukeller. She had to get to the Burgerbrau. Travis would be there . . .

Of course, if she was actually on the *east* bank, then she was totally lost. Her work on the coordinate system used by the portal for locking in on Munich, however, had given her a good understanding of Munich's topography. And if she was lost, she might still be able to find a policeman who could help her.

The alley opened onto a main street, narrow but well-lighted. A sign on the pole of a gas lamp at the corner read *Kochstrasse*.

The arm caught Rachel from behind as she stepped out of the alley. *"Was ist?"* a voice said in her ear. She heard someone laugh. Rachel gasped as the man behind her spun her around. Other figures emerged, men in S.A. uniforms, their swastika armbands bloody by the light of the gas lamp. She counted five of them, and it appeared they had been waiting there next to the alley.

Waiting for her.

Her hands shot up in a sharp, grip-breaking blow, and the man grunted with surprise as he released her. Another grabbed at her but missed as she twisted away. Desperate fear drove her. "You're not getting me again!" she yelled.

She was grabbed from behind once more as laugh-ter rang in her ears. Rachel screamed as loud as she could, striking back with her foot. She connected with her attacker's knee, eliciting a yelp of pain, but her captors maintained their hold.

"What's the matter, Fritz?" one grinning man said in German. "Is she too much for you?"

"Die Hure! She kicked me!" Someone struck her

from behind. Hands closed on her arms, plucked at the shreds of her blouse. They had her hemmed in, men in overcoats and ski caps. Two carried bolt-action rifles. The others wore holstered pistols or carried steel-tipped truncheons. She looked from face to face. They were young; teenagers, all of them. But their eyes were dangerous.

"It is a cold night, *nicht war*? And not safe on the streets for a pretty girl all alone. What do you say, *Kamaraden*? Shall we help the young lady?"

"*Ja*. It looks as though she needs warming."

"You know what I think, Willi?" another said, fondling her roughly. "I think we've caught ourselves another Jew."

More laughter. "*Ja* . . . what is our girl friend running from, dressed like that, I wonder?"

"Shall we take her?"

"Let's have some fun first. As you say, it is a cold night . . ."

Rachel struggled wildly, lashing out against her captors. She was beginning to realize that she had been wrong, that these Storm Troopers really were S.A., that she had escaped the Communists only to be picked up by a Nazi gang roving the streets of Munich.

She screamed again.

"Scream all you want, *Hure*," the one called Fritz said. He twisted her around to face him, forcing her to look up into eyes hard and cold with menace. "I like it. And, after all, *we're* the authority here."

"There's a place over there. An empty tenement. We could take her there."

"*Sehr gut*."

The hole appeared in Fritz's forehead squarely

above his left eye, as the back of his head disintegrated in blood and chips of bone. "Down, Rachel!"

That was Travis's voice! She dove for the pavement before Fritz had completed his fall. The sibilant rattle of a silenced submachine gun stuttered from down the street. Someone shrieked above her. She lifted her head off the brick paving, saw Karl Jaeger raising his odd-looking rifle. She didn't hear the shot, but another Nazi standing nearby lurched heavily against the wall, dropped the rifle he had been about to fire, and slumped to the ground with his fellows.

The entire firefight had taken three seconds.

Shakily, she rose to her feet. The bodies of her five attackers lay sprawled around her as though mowed down by an explosion.

Then Travis was there. "Rachel . . ."

She slid into his arms, clinging to him. She was sobbing and trying to stop and not able to stop and not really caring. He pulled off his major's overcoat and draped it around her shoulders, gathering her close.

"Lieutenant!" King whispered urgently. "That lot at the warehouse will have heard . . ."

A bullet *wheeed* off the wall a foot above their heads, showering them with chips of brick. Hunter dragged Rachel to the pavement as Gomez let loose a burst from his MP5. "Two of them, Chief! Down the alley!"

Another ricochet angled off the street from another direction. "And another one by the river," Anderson said. Full auto fire stuttered out of the night.

King slapped a fresh magazine into his gun. "They're going to rock and roll."

"They're Russians." Rachel said. "They had me

at their headquarters! They're carrying modern weapons . . .''

Bullets whipped overhead. ''Tell me about it,'' King said, rising far enough off the bricks to chop a three-round burst into the darkness. ''They're under cover, Lieutenant. We'll never take 'em like this.''

Hunter rolled one of the Storm Trooper bodies partway over, braced his MP5 across it, and loosed a burst down the alley. ''Any ideas?''

''Yeah. Cover me from the lone bozo down there.''

''Right. Go.'' Hunter shifted around, switched to full auto fire, and blasted away down Kochstrasse in the direction of the Isar. Anderson and Gomez joined in with long, ragged bursts down the alley. Full auto was a waste of precious ammunition, but it forced the Soviet gunmen to cover as King rolled across the alley mouth and slithered off, knees and elbows racing.

Their situation was not good, pinned down in a crossfire. If they stayed where they were, they were sheltered by the buildings from the two men in the alley, and from the other gunman by the S.A. bodies. But they didn't have enough ammo to carry out a fighting withdrawal, and if they stayed put, it could not be much longer before reinforcements arrived from the warehouse.

Hunter fired again, a long burst toward the river which ended unexpectedly as his magazine went dry. The lone Russian leaped into view, racing across Kochstrasse toward the cover of an automobile parked at the side of the street.

Jaeger, lying next to Hunter and Rachel, snapped his Wa-2000 to his cheek, the barrel of the weapon tracking the runner. The gun barked once, and the Russian stumbled, fell, a limp sprawl in the middle of the street.

"Dreiundachtzig," he muttered, half under his breath.

"They've stopped firing," Gomez said.

Hunter rolled over to the corner of the building and peered around, keeping his head down close to the pavement.

"Cease fire!" King called from up the alley. "All clear here!"

Minutes later, the six of them gathered at the truck. There was no sign of any further pursuit. For the moment, at least, the streets appeared deserted.

"We've got to get you out of here, Rachel," Hunter said. He climbed up in the back of the truck and lifted the tarpaulin. Kulagin glared at him over his gag. "We'll drive out to our DZ and dig up the beacon. We can get you and Todd here back to the Complex . . ."

"No," Rachel said. "No! There isn't time!"

"What do you mean?"

"The Soviets! I overheard them talking! They're trying to take over Hitler's putsch . . . controlling his S.A. forces all over Munich!" Quickly, she filled them in on what she had learned of the plan Loew had called Rising Star.

Hunter nodded. "Todd told us much the same," he said. "How long do we have?"

She shook her head. "Not long. Maybe an hour."

"And they're all at the warehouse now?"

"Except for a few who have already gone. There's a Russian calling himself Scheubner-Richter who's supposed to be with Hitler now. I think there must be others.''

''But this'll be our best chance to get most of them in one place.''

Her eyes widened. ''Travis! There are thirty of them and only five of you!''

Gomez grinned. ''Hey, no problem. It's only twenty-seven of them now!''

''Not funny, Eddie,'' King said. ''We'll have to leave her with the truck, Lieutenant. We can't get her to the beacon now.''

''Right.'' Hunter looked off in the direction of the warehouse. ''Okay. Here's what we'll do . . .

Seventeen

They're not leaving me back in the damned truck.
Rachel closed her fingers more tightly around the
grip of the MP5SD Gomez had given her. They had
wanted to leave her guarding Kulagin, but she had
insisted on coming along. "At least this way there'll
be six of us," she'd said. "I can help with the diversion."

She crouched behind the concrete wall opposite
the warehouse. Peering over the top, she could see
two guards armed with AK assault rifles, one on either side of the closed garage door. Shadowy figures
rose into view, arms sweeping about necks, knives
descending with choreographed precision.

The sentries were dead. Gomez crouched next to
the garage door, unraveling a length of plastic explosives and fusing which he had assembled from his

money belt as they'd made their plans moments before. Jaeger glanced up and down the Widenmayer-strasse, then picked up the AKMs dropped by the guards, and several magazines. The street was deserted. Unhurried, he strolled back toward Rachel.

There was blood on the sleeve of his suit jacket.

"He seems to know what he's doing," she said, nodding toward Gomez as Jaeger rolled across the wall and crouched down beside her. With his oddball sense of humor, Eddie Gomez had always struck her as a bit unstable. It was interesting to watch him now, working with sure, calm competence, attaching the explosives to the garage door between the two, still forms of the dead guards.

"He's good," the German agreed. "Ah, he's done. Get down."

Gomez sprinted across the street and vaulted the wall. Jaeger touched the transmit switch on his radio. "Yankee Leader, this is Yankee Three. The clock is running."

Gomez took one of the AKMs Jaeger had picked up and chambered a round with a ratcheting clack-clack. "Hold your ears!" he warned.

Hunter edged closer to the back entrance of the warehouse Rachel had described. Anderson and King took up positions on the far side of the door. They'd encountered one Russian in the alley behind the building, a man in civilian clothes carrying an AKM. King had silenced the man with a thrust from his Sykes-Fairbairn.

They checked the safeties on their SMGs, leaned back against the bricks of the building's back wall, and waited.

"Yankee Leader, this is Yankee Three," he heard through his earpiece. *"The clock is running."*

The explosion came moments later, a hollow, deep-throated boom which echoed through the building. "Now!" Hunter opened and pulled back. No burst of fire reached for them from the dimly lighted interior. King rolled around the corner and hurried silently into the warehouse, his weapon held ready. Hunter moved in after him, with Anderson bringing up the rear.

Inside was smoke and noise, the echoes of running men, and urgent shouts. They could hear the distinctive cracking of an AKM now, firing from outside the front of the building. Hunter gave hand signals. *Deploy! Go!*

They knew the layout, thanks to Rachel, knew where the stairs to the armory and the door to the office suite were. Moving separately through the maze-like canyons between the high-piled crates and boxes, coordinating their moves by radio, the three U.S. Rangers converged on the motor pool area. A dozen men in various uniforms were moving through roiling smoke toward a gaping hole that split the garage door. Several Russians were stretched out on the concrete floor near the breach. Others, seeking cover behind the parked vehicles, fired random bursts through the opening into the darkness outside.

Hunter felt a stab of worry. *Dammit! Rachel should have stayed with the truck!* After all she'd been through already, a stray bullet could cut short an already unpleasant visit to the past.

He was surprised at how much that thought hurt.

He dropped to one knee and brought his Uzi up. "Yankee Leader, in position!" he said, his voice scarcely more than a whisper. Anderson and King reported their readiness. "Ready . . . *go!*"

His subgun bucked in his hands, the chopping hiss of quick-triggered, three-round bursts scarcely audible above the clangor and din. A pair of VBU men pitched over as 9mm bullets drilled into their backs. King and Anderson opened up from other hiding places to either side, their short, accurate bursts cutting down man after man before the enemy even realized they were under fire.

"Pasmatreetyeh!" someone yelled above the racket, off to the right. *"Smatreetyeh!"*

Five S.A. troopers charged from the direction of the offices, shouting in Russian, carrying Soviet AKM assault rifles. Hunter flicked his selector switch to full auto, swung the heavy barrel of his SMG into line with the leader and squeezed the trigger. Spent brass clattered and danced against the crate beside him. Two of the disguised VBU men twisted and fell backward, then a third. Hunter's magazine went empty, but one of the other Rangers had already sighted on the charging Russians and chopped down the last two.

He clicked another thirty-two-round magazine into place, slipping the empty clip into a pocket. Only one more loaded mag after this. They hadn't come to 1923 expecting an all-out firefight; not counting the scrape behind the Burgerbrau, this was the second pitched battle this evening. He went back to short bursts, shredding the chest of a brown-shirted Russian and sending another diving for cover behind a massive black Daimler. Full auto fire ratcheted from behind a truck, punching ragged holes in the crate beside him and spraying splinters of wood past his face.

He'd been in one place too long. "Yankee Leader moving," he said. "Oblique right."

"You're covered," King's voice answered. *"Go!"*

Bursts from King's SMG drove the Russians' heads down. Hunter dove from cover, rolled across open concrete, and came up behind another stack of packing crates he'd already catalogued as a good spot.

"Yankee Leader!" Anderson's voice carried urgency. *"On your left!"*

A trio of VBU troopers rushed him. Hunter fired and missed as he rolled across the top of a crate to the shelter of the other side. A long burst from Hunter's left caught the three, sending them sprawling on bloody smears.

"Three down," Hunter reported. "Nice shooting, Roy!"

Working together, the Rangers closed on the motor pool, advancing from cover to cover, cutting down VBU agents as they flushed them. Hunter paused, reloading. The body of a VBU trooper in Stosstrupp grays lay sprawled across his path.

He stooped, picked up the AKM still clutched in the Russian's hands, then tugged a pair of banana magazines from the man's belt and transferred them to his own. There was no longer any need for silence, and using the Soviet weapon would save his Uzi's 9mm ammo for another occasion when silence might be necessary.

In true Storm Trooper fashion, the man had a bulky potato masher grenade tucked into the top of his jackboot. Hunter took that as well, then moved to a new vantage point, closer to the motor pool.

From here, Hunter could see the door which Rachel said led to the basement armory. That stairway presented the assault with a special problem. That was probably the only door; any VBU people trapped down there would fight all the harder if they knew there was no way out. A grenade like the one he'd just picked up would be an answer, but not a particularly good one since the Rangers had to assume that there were explosives in the basement. A sympathetic detonation could level the building, could take out a fair chuck of Munich, depending on how much demolitions gear was stored down there. Hunter wasn't prepared to take that risk.

Gunfire tore across the warehouse interior from atop a stack of crates on the far side of the motor pool, splintering wood and sending Hunter rolling out of the way. He came up shooting. His full auto burst shattered lights in the ceiling, then smashed into flesh and bone. Hunter saw the body roll off the crates, an AKM clattering on concrete a few feet away.

He considered switching his weapon to single shot. AKs on full-auto had a nasty tendency to overheat and were real bears to fire accurately. In these tight quarters, though, volume of fire was more important than accuracy.

"*Yankees, this is Two,*" Anderson announced. "*I got me a clear shot into the motor pool.*"

"Hit 'em, Roy!" Hunter ordered. "Greg! Swing right and behind them!"

More gunfire sounded from the left, followed by a keening shriek as a VBU agent clutched his belly and writhed in a spreading pool of blood. Anderson had climbed a stack of crates of his own and was firing down into a cluster of Soviets sheltering behind the vehicles. Bullets spanged and thunked into car bodies, shattering glass, and shredded the odd, spindly-looking rubber tires.

"*Eedetyeh s'youdah!*" someone shouted from the rear of the building. "*Skaryehyeh!*"

Shouted orders in Russian to come here and hurry brought him around, his weapon ready. A gang of men in various uniforms moved from the shadows, their weapons firing, as bullets whinned and howled, smashing crates, thudding into boxes. Hunter ducked for cover. This had all the signs of a massed charge, perhaps a last-ditch attempt to break out. The mob of Soviets was advancing toward the motor pool area, threatening to trap King and Hunter between two sizeable forces.

He pulled the captured grenade from his belt. It was an early potato-masher type quite different from any used by the American armed forces, but all Rangers were exposed to a wide variety of foreign and obsolete weapons. He unscrewed the cap on the base of the handle and fished out the porcelain ball on the end of its pull string.

"Yankees!" he yelled. "Heads down! Grenade!"

He yanked the pull igniter, let the grenade cook for a pair of seconds, then tossed it up and over the crates which sheltered him, aiming by ear at the greatest concentration of gunfire.

The blast was deafening in the enclosed space of the warehouse. Bits of wood and metal rattled across the concrete floor as the roar of the explosion gave way to the screams of wounded men. Most of the overhead lights were shattered by the blast, plunging the huge room into near darkness.

He swung his captured weapon up onto the crate, the stab of the heavy weapon's muzzle flash creating an eerie strobe effect against the boiling smoke. Stunned survivors of the blast jerked and whirled against the light as Hunter cut them down. The bodies of dead or wounded Russians lay strewn everywhere.

More AK gunfire erupted from behind the parked vehicles, but it was blind, wildly hurled into near blackness. Some of the charging Soviets had made it to the shelter of the vehicles. Hunter alerted his team, then moved again, sticking to the shadows. Any time now, some VBU agent might get the idea to use a grenade himself.

"Yankee Leader! Just around the corner, on your right."

"I've got him."

Hunter stepped around the corner firing, crumpling a surprised VBU agent. The Ranger ducked and rolled, coming up against smooth, rounded metal.

His new hiding place was a wall of ten-gallon steel drums, piled one upon another. Hunter felt a moment's cold fear. The drums were labeled *Turpentin.* He noticed the labels on some of the crates stacked nearby: *Anstrich*—paint. Hunter seemed to have found himself a particularly flammable part of the warehouse.

"Yankee Leader to Yankees," he said. "Look sharp! There's flammable stuff over here." That grenade he'd thrown could have caused a disaster. Several drums were holed already, oily liquid pooling on the floor. Hunter caught the pungent sharpness of turpentine in the air.

"Yankee Leader moving . . . fast!"

Something arced through the darkness, struck a steel drum, then clattered across the floor. Hunter dove behind a crate as the grenade blast roared behind him, hurling wood splinters like arrows. The light grew, wavering and uncertain at first, as flames danced amid shattered piles of fresh-cut kindling.

It wouldn't take long for the whole warehouse to blaze up, Hunter knew. Most of the crates were pine, and the interior of the building itself was supported by a framework of wooden pillars and exposed roof beams. And all of that paint and turpentine . . .

The smoke was growing thicker, moment by moment.

The roar of a motor drew his attention back to the motor pool. The soldier who had turned the car's crank spun away, wounded by a shot from Anderson, but the black Daimler was running now as fresh volleys of automatic fire chattered in all directions. The Americans blasted away at the vehicle as it started to move toward the ruin of the garage door.

The movement of the car exposed a huddle of Russians who had been crouched in its shadow. They rushed out now, firing their weapons and yelling. Hunter swung his weapon to cover this new threat but saw other Soviets bolting for the front door and the wide-open garage entrance, firing as they ran.

Rachel!

Rachel had the hang of firing the submachine gun now. Travis had cautioned her not to fire it on full auto, since the bucking, yammering kick of the weapon tended to drag its muzzle skyward. Three-round bursts, though, could be controlled. She squeezed the trigger and a Russian bolting from the front door toppled. Another VBU gunman dove through the torn garage door, then flipped over backward as rounds from Jaeger's AKM smashed into his skull and chest.

The garage door burst outward as a heavy black Daimler plowed through the gap left by Gomez's explosives. The car squealed on tires already hanging in ribbons from dented rims. Rachel had the momentary impression that nobody was driving.

No! She caught a glimpse of a face, the driver crouched down on the floor, sheltering behind the dash, steering wildly.

"That's him! That's him!" Rachel stood up behind the wall, swinging her MP5 up as the Daimler peeled right. She squeezed the trigger . . . and was startled by the absence of kick and buck.

"Get down!" Jaeger snapped.

"That's Loew! Get him, Karl!"

Jaeger was on his feet, his AKM chattering full-auto fire, but the car was already racing south far down the Widenmayerstrasse.

Rachel looked at her weapon in disbelief. "Damn! What happened to this thing?"

Gomez grinned at her out of the darkness. "They don't shoot forever, like in the movies, Miss Stein." He reared up above the wall and loosed several short bursts, then ducked down again. "Sorry. We have no more clips for it."

VBU troops were spilling from the building now, some firing, some simply running as hard as they could. A passing bullet thudded into the far side of the concrete wall. Rachel flinched at the sound.

"Down!" Jaeger snapped a fresh magazine into his AKM and added, "Please, Miss Stein! The Lieutenant wouldn't like it if anything happened to you now!''

"Looks like the good guys have the bad guys on the run," Gomez said. He held his hand to his earpiece, listening. "There's a fire in there. The Commies are running for it."

Fire! Travis was in there!

Her heart had stopped for a moment when they'd heard the dull boom of a grenade, but the radio reports had kept coming. Travis was alive, still fighting.

But if Travis was trapped inside . . . if he was killed . . .

It was surprising how much the thought hurt.

All resistance in the warehouse ceased as the fire spread, fueled by turpentine and wooden crates. The heat was intense, and acrid fumes were making breathing difficult.

"Yankee Leader, this is One," King said. "We'd better be moving, Lieutenant."

"*Roger,*" added Anderson, coughing. "*It's gettin' a mite uncomfortable in here.*"

"Right. Move forward, out the garage door. Watch your fire out that way. Ra . . . we've got people out there.

King hurried forward, joining Hunter near a pile of Russian bodies sprawled in the motor pool area. Hunter had very nearly said "Rachel," and that disturbed the Master Sergeant.

The Lieutenant was worried about the girl and rightly so. Civilians were always a liability on a combat mission. But Hunter's preoccupation with Rachel Stein could screw the mission, could screw *everything* if he guessed wrong. Greg King still wasn't sure what he thought about interfering with history, but he knew that the lieutenant needed a clear head to handle it and make sure they all came out alive.

"All Yankees," King said. "Hold your fire out there. We're coming out."

The clangor of fire bells was muted by distance, though the fire consuming the warehouse was visible by its ruddy reflection on the clouds overhead. Munich's fire department must be hard pressed tonight, Hunter thought. Roving gangs of S.A. would have started small fires all over the city. By the time fire trucks finally reached the scene, the Fricht warehouse was an inferno.

"We cleaned them out," Hunter said. He was exhausted, completely drained by the intensity of the firefight. The six of them stumbled up the Widenmayerstrasse toward the alley where they'd left the truck, each step requiring an effort of will. "Nazi bands all over Munich . . . the real Nazis . . . will be waiting for orders . . . and they'll never get them."

"So, what now?" Anderson asked. Of them all, he seemed the most energetic. The Texan always ran on adrenaline long after a firefight had ended.

Hunter forced himself to concentrate. "Back to the truck. We'll drive Rachel and Todd to our DZ, dig up the recall beacon and send them up home."

They rounded the corner into the alley where they'd left the truck. "Actually, it might be better if we all went back," Hunter continued. "If we didn't kill Lenin back in 1917 like we thought we did . . ."

He stopped in mid-sentence, his tiredness overcome by a numbing shock.

The truck, where they'd left Kulagin bound and gagged, was gone.

Eighteen

The Liebighaus was only four blocks away from the riverfront warehouse. It was small and less than clean, but it was close. That suited Hunter and Jaeger, who no longer had their overcoats. Best of all, it was cheap. The five Rangers pooled the last of their counterfeit 1923 banknotes and discovered they had just enough money left to rent one room for the night. Anderson, by this time the least disreputable-looking member of the team, took the accumulated hundreds of billions of marks in to the front desk, and later engaged the desk clerk in conversation while the rest of them slipped up to their room.

The room boasted cracked plaster and a single window looking out over the Liebigstrasse. King and Gomez dropped the bundled SMGs, which they'd hid under their overcoats, on the bed. Gomez removed

his coat, then offered his suit jacket to Rachel, who
was sweltering in the heavy S.A. greatcoat she had
borrowed from Hunter. She smiled her thanks.

Gomez went to the window and drew the curtain
aside. A trio of drunken Storm Troopers lurched arm
in arm out of a bar across the street, singing loudly
and off-key.

"Hell of a way to run a revolution," he said.
"Shouldn't they be taking over the radio station or
something?"

"As a matter of fact, yes," Rachel said, buttoning
up the suit coat. "And the telegraph office, and the
police barracks, and quite a few other key spots
around town. I overheard them talking about it at the
warehouse. Those fake Storm Troopers were supposed to organize all of that."

Anderson grinned. "So much for *that* Commie
plot."

"I don't know," Rachel said. "Their top leader—
Loew—got away. That major, Scheubner-Richter,
must still be with Hitler. They must have picked up
Todd when they took your truck. And others got
away during the fire. They could still try to change
history in their favor."

"What can they do?" Anderson asked. "We took
out most of them in the warehouse . . . and all their
imported weapons, too."

"They're still dangerous," Hunter reminded him.
He jerked his thumb toward the window. "Three men
might make a big difference in that pressure cooker."

"Can they?" King looked up. He had begun stripping the weapons on the bed, cleaning the parts with
a scrap torn from the bed sheet. "I wonder."

"What do you mean?"

"Isn't what we see out there pretty much the way . . . the way Todd told us it really happened? These VBU jokers wanted to make it so Hitler's putsch succeeded, to create the proper climate for a Communist rising in Germany, right?"

The others nodded agreement.

"But we stopped them. Just like they stopped us from killing Lenin. It's starting to look to me like I was right all along. History can't be changed."

Rachel looked stricken. "No! It *must* be possible . . ."

"We've got to find out," Hunter said. "We've got to *know*."

"By doing what?" Jaeger asked. "Are we still trying to kill Hitler?"

"Maybe the best thing would be to go dig up the beacon and call for a pick-up," Gomez said. "Let General Thompson figure out what to do next."

Rachel shook her head. "If changing the past is possible, if Loew and the others *do* manage to do something . . . the Complex, all of us . . . could be wiped out."

"No, we've got to act here . . . and now," Hunter decided. "It looks like our first responsibility is making sure the VBU doesn't change history in their favor."

"So we maintain the status quo," King said.

"Not quite. That wouldn't prove anything. If the opportunity presents itself, let's take out Hitler, too."

Anderson looked up sharply. "Whoa, there! What happens to history if we kill Hitler, but Lenin's still around to get the Bolshies organized in Russia? Seems to me Soviet Russia might be a bit stronger

later on if the Nazis don't invade them in World War
II!''

"Good point," Hunter said. He slumped. Fatigue
was dulling his thinking.

"That shouldn't be a problem," Rachel said. She
looked as tired as Hunter felt, with heavy circles under her eyes. "I've been thinking about how the temporal equations would vector out. Remember . . . it
takes time for a change back here to reach 2007. You
could kill Hitler in 1923, get back to Chronos, and
still have time to organize another mission back to
1917."

Anderson looked uncertain. "Wouldn't we undo
what we do to Hitler in 1923 by fooling around in
1917?"

"No," Rachel said. "Remember, the world is a
lot bigger here, in the early '20s, than it is in our
time. News doesn't cross borders as fast, or as completely. Events should proceed separately in the two
countries, without interfering with each other much."

Hunter nodded. "It's risky, but not as risky as
letting Loew and the others run around loose. And
if we *can* change history, we'd damn well better find
out now, before they change things and edit us out
of the history books."

"Okay, how?" King asked.

Rachel leaned back, her eyes closed. "Listen. If
you guys are going to talk all night, I'm going to
bed. I don't know about you, but I'm dead."

Hunter nodded. Rachel had been through hell . . .
and hadn't had much sleep along the way. "Go
ahead. We'll sack out on the floor later." The sounds
of chanting and raucous cheering filtered through the
window as a band of Nazis paraded up the street

outside. "Assuming we can get any sleep with that going on."

They cleared the weapons off the bed. Rachel was asleep before Hunter drew the blankets up over Eddie's rumpled suit coat.

"First thing we're going to need in the morning," Hunter said quietly, "is money."

They continued talking for another two hours, making their plans.

"You abysmally incompetent imbecile!" Loew's calm had deserted him with the realization that Rising Star was falling apart, shattered by the surprise commando attack at the warehouse. "You *led* them straight to our headquarters!"

"I had no choice, Comrade Colonel," Kulagin said stiffly. "Not after your people fell for their ambush in the alley behind the beer hall."

Loew's words broke like ice. "If I didn't need men, even idiots, I would shoot you myself!" He looked away from Kulagin, scowling. They were standing in a marble-floored hallway of the Bavarian War Ministry.

The surviving VBU agents had rendezvoused at the old ministry building on the corner of Schönfeldstrasse and the Ludwigstrasse, a few hundred yards north of the broad Odeonsplatz. Taken by Ernst Röhm and his men earlier in the evening, it had been the one putschist target to fall during the entire revolution. Four hundred men of Röhm's paramilitary Reichskriegflagge occupied the building now, which, it was planned, would become General von Ludendorff's headquarters once the putsch succeeded.

"Five men escaped from the warehouse . . . not

counting us," the VBU colonel continued. "Another four remain on guard at the *schloss*. Ten left out of thirty-six, plus one incompetent who can't follow orders without getting lost!"

Yelling echoed through the marble corridors of the War Ministry from a nearby room, shrill and insistent. Scheubner-Richter approached, looking worried. "He is upset," the major reported. "Things are not going as he planned."

Another burst of noise resounded down the hall, as Hitler redoubled his tirade against traitors, incompetents, and Communists. "As *he* planned? Our plans aren't going so well either. Not one putsch target taken tonight, save this building!"

"There's worse," Scheubner-Richter said. "Word has just arrived. Kahr, Seisser, and Lossow have renounced their part in the putsch. They claim they promised to support Hitler under duress . . . at gunpoint. By this time they will have gotten word through to Berlin. Orders will have come back to suppress the putsch."

"Damn! How did they get away from the Burgerbrau?"

The major shrugged. "Ludendorff allowed them to leave. They told him they were going to go make arrangements for the provisional government. He accepted their word as gentlemen, and they left." The little man pulled a pocket watch from his vest and glanced at it, the mild eyes cold behind his rimless spectacles. It was a few minutes before six in the morning, the end of a long, noisy night. "So far, comrades, events have unfolded precisely according to the history we know, with no significant changes.

If things continue as they have so far, Hitler's putsch will fail early this afternoon."

Kulagin looked distressed. "Perhaps, Comrades, it simply is not possible to change the past."

Loew's stare dripped contempt. "Indeed? History tells us that a march by Hitler's followers was stopped by the massed gunfire of the police at the Odeonsplatz on this day. We are going to change that." He paused, thinking. "You, Comrade Major, will return to the Burgerbrau. You must organize a march, a Nazi march to rally the people of the city."

"A march, Comrade Colonel? But that's . . ."

"Exactly what happened, I know. But the Bavarian State Police will be here in force this morning. They will surround the War Ministry . . . and if most of Hitler's troops are still squatting in the beer hall, they will surround them as well. But you have sensed the mood in the city. If the Nazis march, they will encourage the right-wing sympathizers, swell their ranks. What you must avoid, at all costs, is marching on the Odeonsplatz, for it is there that a confrontation between the marchers and the police will take place, according to the history we know."

Scheubner-Richter looked worried. "It may not be possible to exercise that much control."

"You have hostages?"

"Yes. There are city council members being held by Göring and his people in the dining room at the Burgerbrau. I'm told that the Nazis rounded up perhaps eighty people in Munich last night . . . mostly Jews and citizens with whom they wished to settle old scores. They have been taken to the Burgerbrau as well."

"Good. See to it that some are taken along with

the marchers. Explain to Göring. If there is resistance, use the hostages to get the marchers through. Most of the Bavarian police sympathize with the Nazis. The hostages will be our guarantee that the events of the original November ninth do not repeat themselves.''

"Yes, Comrade Colonel.''

"What of me, Comrade Colonel?''

"You will remain here with me.'' Loew's mouth twisted unpleasantly. "I wish to send people I can trust with the major.''

"Kulagin might be useful with me,'' Scheubner-Richter said. "He could identify the Americans should they attempt to interfere with the march.''

"*Nyet*. The Americans will be looking for me, now, thanks to this creature's incompetence. He will inform me should they approach us here.''

Scheubner-Richter frowned. "The police and army will have the War Ministry surrounded before noon. What can you accomplish here?''

"So far as Röhm is concerned, I am a wealthy local businessman, a contributor to the Party. I will volunteer to negotiate with the police when they arrive. As news of your march spreads, perhaps I can induce them to join the National Socialist Revolution.''

Scheubner-Richter shook his head. "It is desperate, Comrade Colonel.''

"These are desperate times. The Nazi putsch must succeed if we are to convince Berlin that they represent a serious threat. Only then can our people in Berlin move to open the door to the Communists. Rising Star can still succeed. It *must* succeed!''

A door slammed open nearby, echoing down bare

corridors. Hitler appeared, ridiculous in his formal, cutaway coat. Other Nazis spilled into the hallway with him. "I am prepared to die for my cause!" he shouted, shaking his fist theatrically. "We will go on as planned! I am returning to the Burgerbrau. Those who believe in me can join me there!"

Scheubner-Richter rolled his eyes toward the ceiling. "I must go, Comrade Colonel."

"*Da*. Stay with that idiot. And see to it that he organizes that march through Munich."

"It will be done. But I am worried. We struggle not only with the American commandos, but with the irresistible inertia of history itself."

"Bah! There is no 'irresistible inertia'! There are only people and events . . . and these we will shape to our will! We must ride history now . . . and change its course to one of our choosing."

"*Da*, Comrade Colonel."

Loew and Kulagin watched the major depart. Outside, a burst of singing erupted from a knot of half-drunken Reichskriegflagge men gathered on the War Ministry steps. Loew dragged his fingers across his face. "Fools," he muttered. "Fools and incompetents! What a way to run a revolution!"

"What shall we do, *Herr* Inspector?" The green-coated police lieutenant looked desperate. "Are they friends or enemies?"

Hunter frowned and looked off up the hill toward the Burgerbrau. Rowdy singing and political chants had sounded from that direction all morning as Hitler's supporters joined him there.

"They don't sound very friendly to me." Hunter tried to remain noncommittal. He had introduced himself to the lieutenant as a police inspector from Berlin. Hunter looked the part, wearing civilian clothes purchased that morning. His two days' growth of beard was gone as well. King and Anderson had set out early that morning in the midst of a snowstorm and returned with a fresh supply of Reichsmarks. They'd found their bank in an alley— three drunken S.A. troopers, pockets stuffed with the proceeds from a night's pillaging of Jewish shops. All of them, Rachel included, could walk the streets of Munich now without calling attention to themselves.

The lieutenant rubbed his hand across his mouth. He was young for such a command. "Many of these S.A. are *kamaraden* of my people," he said. "Hell, they were all drinking together a few nights ago. If we should be forced to fire on them . . ."

Hunter shrugged and tried to appear unconcerned. People kept asking him difficult questions, and he had no answers. But the police inspector role was essential to the plan they'd worked out.

There was no way to know for sure where the escaped VBU leaders might strike. Hunter and his team had learned that morning that Ernst Röhm's four hundred Reichskriegflagge troops had seized the War Ministry north of the Odeonsplatz. And Hitler was gathering an estimated three thousand supporters across the river at the Burgerbrau. Either spot was a potential target for VBU intervention.

Stopping the Russians was their main objective. King, Jaeger, and Rachel would watch the situation at the Odeonsplatz and at the nearby War Ministry. From there, they could guard against any VBU attempt to make use of Röhm's men.

Hunter, Anderson, and Gomez had joined the police line at the Ludwigsbrucke, a half mile away, where Hitler's small army from the beer hall would have to cross the Isar. If VBU agents were marching with Hitler, perhaps they could spot them here . . .

As for killing Hitler, that was a lesser objective, desirable if possible, but secondary to stopping the VBU. If history went according to schedule that afternoon, a battle would break out on the Odeonsplatz as police fired on the marchers. That would give them their chance. By then, Jaeger would be in position with his sniper's rifle to take another shot at Adolf Hitler. If history *could* be changed, Hitler would die in the Odeonsplatz.

If . . .

Göring cast a sour look toward Adolf Hitler, pacing restlessly near the Burgerbrau's entrance. "He has ordered that we not take hostages along, *Herr* Scheubner-Richter. He says he wants no martyrs . . ."

"Never mind," the major replied. "Take ten of the Jews and put them in a truck, back near the end of the column. You will need them to force your way through the police lines."

"But what about . . ."

"Leave *Herr* Hitler to me, Hermann."

A thunderous cheer rose from outside, a multitude greeting *der Führer* as he stepped out through the Burgerbrau's arched doorway. *"Sieg Heil! Sieg Heil! Sieg Heil!"*

"Our *Führer* has made his entrance," Göring observed. A nearby clock tower struck twelve above the roaring. He began buttoning the rubber coat he wore, arranging it so that the *Pour le Mérite* award for valor he was so proud of showed at his throat. "We should go."

"*Ja.*" Scheubner-Richter buckled his coat and placed his hat on his head. A band was playing *Badenweiler* rather badly.

It was beginning.

Hunter watched the column descend Rosenheimerstrasse toward the bridge, arrayed twelve abreast, swastika banners in the lead. The green police shifted, their rifles wavering uncertainly. Hunter could make out faces in the front line of marchers: Ludendorff, stiff and regal in a loden coat and a soft green hat; Göring, in a black rubber coat and steel helmet; Hitler in a battered-looking trench coat, his slouch hat in his hand; and there, at Hitler's side, the VBU agent, Scheubner-Richter.

Scheubner-Richter! The Soviets had indeed joined Hitler for the march.

"Form a line!" the lieutenant yelled. "*Schnell!* They will not pass!"

Thirty men faced three thousand, a fragile line stretched across the entrance to the bridge. The chill November wind snapped the swastika banners overhead.

"Halt!" The lieutenant stepped in front of his men. "Halt or be fired on!"

"Don't fire on your comrades!" Göring called.

Scheubner-Richter stepped forward, gesturing toward the rear of the column. "We have hostages," he told the police lieutenant. "Shoot and they die!"

Hunter followed the VBU agent's gesture, saw several trucks farther back amid the seething mass of

armed men filing the Rosenheimerstrasse. Most of
the trucks were piled high with men, and at least one
had a machine gun mounted over the roof of its cab.
But there was another . . .

Hitler looked surprised at Scheubner-Richter's
words, but events were rushing headlong now. There
were shouts. *"Nicht scheissen!"* The police line wavered, uncertain.

A bugle blared from the marching ranks, and a line
of gray-coated Stosstrupp raced forward, their bayonets leveled. The police line was swept aside.
Hunter saw rifle butts rise and fall, heard the crunch
of metal against bone.

Nineteen

"We've spotted the VBU!" Hunter's voice carried urgency as it came over King's earpiece. *"They've brought hostages with the column and are threatening to kill them if the police don't let them through!"*

"Understood," King replied. "I'll see what I can do here."

The Odeonsplatz was strangely quiet. The police had sealed off the plaza some time before. King, Jaeger, and Rachel had been allowed to remain only when King had insisted that the three of them were from the Reichswehr Ministry in Berlin.

The man in charge on the scene—one *Oberleutnant* Michael von Godin, acting commander of the 1st Battalion, 2nd Company of the State Police—had some one hundred thirty troopers gathered at the south end of the Odeonsplatz. There, the monumental Feldherrnhalle, memorial to two of Bavaria's hero-generals, dominated that end of the plaza. East, across the Residenzstrasse, was the vast and ornate bulk of the former palace of Bavarian kings, the Residenz. To the west lay the baroque facade of the Theatinerkirche, its dome and twin tower spires sharp against the gray November sky.

The squat steel shape of a wheeled armored car was parked in front of the Feldherrnhalle's broad steps, and a machine gun had been set up on a tripod nearby. It was expected that the Nazi marchers might try to march north, past the Odeonsplatz and on up the Ludwigstrasse to where army and police units held the War Ministry under siege.

"They are on their way, *Herr Oberleutnant*," King told von Godin. "I've just had a report from my people at the Ludwig bridge." He did not explain that he had received the report over a personal radio transceiver small enough to hold in the palm of his hand.

"Yes?"

"I'm told they have hostages with them."

The police commander's eyes widened. He was a young man, no older than his mid-twenties. Von Godin had an aristocratic assurance about him and appeared to King to be competent, but some of that assurance seemed to be slipping away now. "Hostages? We may have to let them pass."

"You can't do that! The Nazis must be stopped . . . here!"

The *Oberleutnant* shrugged and looked away. "How can we be responsible for the death of innocent hostages?" He turned suddenly, shouting orders at a detachment of police carrying MP18 submachine guns.

"Yankee Leader, this is King. We've got problems here."

"Go ahead." King could hear the thunder of cheering crowds behind Hunter's voice.

"The police here are wavering. Godin doesn't want to open fire if there are hostages with the marchers."

"Damn. Okay . . . stay with them. We'll see what we can work out at this end. By the way, Scheubner-Richter is here. That's confirmed. Any sign of Loew?"

King glanced across the plaza, to where Jaeger and Rachel were waiting in the shelter of a massive, equestrian statue of Maximilian I on the Wittelsbach-erplatz, at the place where the Briennerstrasse entered the Odeonsplatz. "No sign yet, Lieutenant. He might be at the War Ministry. We haven't been able to get close since the army surrounded the place."

"Okay. Keep me informed. Yankee Leader out."

Hunter returned his attention to the cheering crowds surrounding them. They were off the Ludwig bridge now, moving steadily toward the center of Munich along the Zweibrückenstrasse. They had joined the Nazi marchers after the police line had been brushed aside.

Anderson and Gomez marched beside him. "Start edging toward the side of the column," Hunter told them. "We'll drop back and see if we can rejoin it closer to the truck with the hostages.

The Texan looked back over his shoulder, to where

the trucks were crawling across the bridge. "Ain't gonna be easy, Lieutenant."

"Easy wasn't in the mission profile, Roy. Let's go."

It took time to work their way to a position adjacent to the trailing Nazi truck. The column had the precision of a military formation near its head, where Hitler and the others continued to march forward under their banners twelve abreast. At the trailing end, however, the parade was more mob than military, with civilian men, women, and children tagging along; stragglers from the front ranks carrying their rifles carelessly across their shoulders; and casual onlookers joining the march in the enthusiasm of the moment. A man in Stosstrupp uniform drove the last truck in the line, while two more with submachine guns rode in the back, watching the crowd with cold eyes. If the hostages were there, they would be in the back, lying on the floor.

By this time, the front of the column was streaming into the huge, open Marienplatz up ahead. Thousands of civilians lined the streets, waving swastika flags and cheering the parade. The plaza was thronged with people packed so thickly that three of Munich's blue-and-white trolleys were held immobile by the press, one behind another. Overhead, the red, black, and white swastika banner snapped from the flagstaff of the city hall's tower. The noise was deafening, with cars honking their horns, trolleys ringing their bells, and over all the thunder upon thunder of the crowd: *Heil! Heil! Heil! Ludendorff! Hitler! Heil!*

Ahead, the column, marching east, took a sudden turn to the right. In that direction, five hundred yards away, lay the Odeonsplatz and the waiting troopers under von Godin's command.

Damn that arrogant Prussian son of a bitch!

Scheubner-Richter scowled at General von Luden-dorff and wondered what had put the change of plan into the man's supposed mind. The column had been marching northwest, through the Marienplatz and in the general direction of targets missed by the putschists on the previous night—the police station at Ettstrasse, the telegraph office on Schillerstrasse, the train station. If the Americans had not attacked the warehouse, all of those targets would have fallen to the Nazis during the night. If they had kept going straight, perhaps the marchers, three thousand strong, might yet have se-cured those strategic points.

Why, in all of a good, atheistic Communist's non-existent hells had Ludendorff chosen to turn *north* at the Marienplatz?

The column was moving up Wienstrasse now, past the Neues Rathaus, the new town hall, which rose in spires and arches and nineteenth-century grandeur from the north side of the Marienplatz. Ahead lay the Theatinerstrasse . . . and the Odeonsplatz. How could he redirect the column now? He glanced side-ways at Ludendorff, taking in the stern, determined set to the war hero's face.

Before he had been assigned to the VBU, Scheubner-Richter had been a major in the KGB, op-erating in the chaos of central Europe. He was not used to this feeling of utter, complete helplessness.

Hitler was at Scheubner-Richter's side. *"Mein Führer!"* he said. "We can't go this way! The police station . . . the telegraph office!"

"Never mind, Scheubner," Hitler replied. *Der Führer* was smiling, basking in the adulation, the throbbing *heils* of the crowd. "The people, Scheubner! They are with us! Anything is possible now!"

"But, *mein Führer* . . ."

"Today we hold Munich in our hand!" Hitler exclaimed. "Soon, we will march on Berlin, and the country will be ours for the taking!"

There was no reasoning with such men. At least, Scheubner-Richter decided, they yet had a chance to avoid the curse of history. The hostages would allow them to pass the police lines at the Odeonsplatz.

"Okay, Rangers," Hunter said. He was speaking into his lapel mike because he, Gomez, and Anderson had split up to surround the truck, but he had to shout to be heard above the crowd. "On three!"

He pulled his Sykes-Fairbairn free of its sheath. "One . . . two . . . *three*!" Hunter took three running steps and vaulted onto the running board of the truck. His arm swept up around the nearest guard's body, yanking the man backward against the side of the truck. It was a clumsy angle for an attack. Hunter's knife hand punched up, sharp and short.

The guard shrieked as the steel blade pierced his coat and slipped between his ribs.

Using the guard's body for leverage, Hunter swung himself up over the side of the truck. On the floor, ten men in civilian clothes lay huddled shoulder to shoulder, looking up at him with sudden fear. Gomez straightened in the rear of the truck, the second guard at his feet, his Marine Ka-Bar slick with blood.

The people in the crowd nearest the truck reacted with a mixture of surprise, fear, and confusion. Most had seen nothing, though a few stood gaping as the truck lurched to a sudden stop, throwing Hunter off balance. In the cab, Anderson struggled with the driver. People were yelling all around, screaming against the waterfall roar of the crowd. Words were lost in the cacophony of noise.

The cab door flew open, and a Stosstrupp body flopped out onto the bricks. The truck began moving again, its horn blaring as pedestrians scattered in front of it.

"Roy!" Hunter yelled into his mike. "At the intersection! Turn right!"

As they turned right onto the Landschaftstrasse behind the ornate Rathaus, Hunter stood up straight, looking up the Wienstrasse to the left. Five hundred yards to the north, beyond the point where the Wienstrasse became the Theatinerstrasse, he could make out men blocking the way. That, he decided, must be the police line at the Odeonsplatz, waiting for Nazi marchers in the shadow of the twin towers of the Theatinerkirche. Several blocks north of the truck, the head of the column was swinging right on the Perusastrasse.

"Yankee Leader to King!" He called into his radio. "We've got the hostages! Tell the police the hostages are free!"

"Understood, Yankee Leader. Good going!"

"The hostages have been freed," King told von Godin. "I've just had word."

"How the hell would you know that?" Godin clutched a Kar 98 carbine in his hands. He looked harried and not about to believe the unsupported word of a man he didn't really know . . . even if he did claim to be from Berlin.

King jerked his thumb toward the equestrian statue across the plaza. Jaeger had climbed up on the statue's pedestal and was leaning against one of the bronze statues, aiming his peculiar-looking rifle with its telescopic sight down the Theatinerstrasse. Rachel crouched on the pedestal at his side.

"My man there has my agents in the Nazi column in sight," he explained, hoping he sounded believable. "He just got a signal from them. The hostages have been freed."

Godin looked uncertain and seemed about to reply, when a police lieutenant ran up from the direction of the Residenz. "Godin! Quick! Help! They're over here."

King followed as the *Oberleutnant* hurried across the Feldherrnhalle steps to the other side of the monument. Down the Residenzstrasse, the head of the marching column could be seen, a solid wall of color and movement filling the narrow street. The column had approached up one street, then shifted a block to the east, and was coming north on the parallel street.

The Nazis were flanking the main police line.

"Second Company!" von Godin yelled. "Double time! Double time!"

Police troops abandoned their positions across the Theatinerstrasse, rushing across the monument steps. The turret of the armored car clanked around to cover the threat from this new direction.

A thin line of green coats met the Nazi wall some distance down the Residenzstrasse and was shoved ahead of it, as if by an irresistible wave. The noise was deafening. The Residenzstrasse narrowed at its northern end, a tapering canyon between the clifflike stone walls of the Feldherrnhalle and the Residenz palace. The sound of thousands of tramping feet, of *Die Wacht am Rhein* sung or shouted at the tops of hundreds of voices, of wild cheering and screaming echoed and reechoed through the confined space, a roar of raw, savage sound. The march leaders came forward with linked arms. King saw Hitler striding forward between the towering figure of Ludendorff on his left, and a small, mild-looking man with rimless spectacles on his right.

"God *damn* it," Godin muttered. "That's His Excellency Ludendorff in the front rank of the marchers! We can't shoot a war hero!"

King took the police officer by the elbow, pointing. "Don't worry about Ludendorff! That little man next to him . . . with the toothbrush mustache! Concentrate on him!"

Godin nodded, then shouted orders at the troopers nearest him.

Stosstruppen were pressing past the leaders now, rifles lowered, bayonets fixed. The police fought with truncheons and carbine butts, and were swept aside, helpless to stop the oncoming tide.

"Reinforcements!" Godin yelled at King's side. "*Schnell!* They're breaking through!"

You will shoot what I tell you, when I tell you, and nothing more!

Jaeger brought his rifle's sight to his eye again, remembering Hunter's admonition. He was leaning against the rear end of Maximilian's bronze horse.

"They're coming," Rachel said. "I can hear them."

The 10× scope showed the mouth of the canyon-like Residenzstrasse clearly, beyond the steel helmeted heads of the gathering police troopers. He could not see the marchers yet, but he could hear them, a wall of noise thundering from the narrow street as the column squeezed its way between the buildings toward the Odeonsplatz. The forward line of police came into view past the corner of the Feldherrnhalle, in fragments now as it gave way before a charging line of gray Stosstruppen.

He lowered the rifle and opened his radio channel. "Yankee Leader, this is Jaeger."

"Go ahead, Karl."

"I have a clear shot at the head of the column, Lieutenant. They'll be in view in another second. Request permission to fire!"

Permission to fire . . .

The truck was well clear of the Nazi column now, though the streets were still crowded with civilians running toward the line of march off to the north. The hostages were sitting up now, somewhat bewildered at the sudden turn of events.

"Will the police hold now?" Hunter asked.

King, listening on the same channel, replied. *"They're trying, Lieutenant. They're shifting to meet the marchers!"*

"Here they come!" Jaeger added. *"There's Hitler! Do I take him?"*

Hunter considered. The VBU plan had been stopped cold. At least one of the Communist leaders was in the van of the column, but at this point, there was nothing he could do.

They could kill Hitler . . .

"Looks like we have the Commies stopped, Karl," he said. "Target Hitler! Take him down!"

The front of the column stepped into view past the corner of the Feldherrnhalle, side by side, arms linked. Jaeger brought the scope to his eye once more, drawing down on the leaders. His view wavered as he sought Hitler's face in the line.

The crosshairs centered instead on the man on Hitler's right . . . a mild-looking man with thick eyeglasses and a prim mustache.

No! God in heaven . . . no!

He remembered that face with a chill of twisting horror, with icy recollection of a torture cell in Hamburg.

Andrei Viktorovich Druzhinin, the Butcher of Hamburg.

The KGB murderer of his family strode arm in arm with Adolf Hitler. Two monsters side by side . . .

The rifle trembled in Jaeger's grip. Sweat blurred across the sight's optics. Hitler . . . Druzhinin . . . Hitler . . .

His finger clamped down on the trigger . . .

Twenty

Two Stosstrupp men stood squarely in the middle of the street. The one with the MP18 had his weapon at port arms. The other, a captain with a bulky C96 Mauser, held his hand up, palm out. "Halt!"

Damn! I thought we were clear! Hunter reached inside his coat for the Colt .45 holstered there. "Gun it, Roy! Heads down, everyone!"

The truck lurched forward. The soldiers in the street hesitated, their eyes widening. Then the man with the submachine gun brought the weapon to his shoulder and opened fire.

Glass sprayed from the front of the cab. Civilians on both sides of the street screamed and ran, streaming in all directions. The truck vented a shrieking clash of gears, skewed sideways, and shuddered to a dead stop.

Hunter dragged the .45's slide back, chambering a round, then leaned forward across the roof of the cab, gun braced in both hands. The Colt bucked once . . . twice . . . The subgunner pitched over backward, his weapon clattering across the brick pavement.

Gomez had his pistol out, drawing down on the second Storm Trooper, but the officer had already lunged for the cover of a nearby doorway. Behind them, fifty yards away, Hunter saw three more gray uniforms, forging ahead through the panicky crowd. "Roy!"

The truck door banged open, and Anderson rolled out, 9mm automatic in his hand. His face was slashed and bleeding and chips of glass glittered on his coat, but he signaled with a forefinger-to-thumb, "Okay."

A yammer sounded from the doorway across the street, and Mauser slugs hammered into the side of the truck. Gomez snapped off a shot which gouged splinters from the door's archway, driving the gunman back to cover.

"Everybody out!" Hunter yelled, propelling the nearest terrified ex-hostage toward the rear of the truck. *"Raus! Raus!"*

German civilians tumbled from the truck as Gomez placed three more shots into the doorway. The three Stosstrupp men down the street were closer now, obviously closing with the truck. Hunter vaulted out of the truck, landing beside Anderson. "You all right, Roy?"

The Texan wiped blood from his face. "No problem, Lt. Just cut a bit. I went down below the dashboard when that guy opened up." His mouth twisted under the smeared mask of blood. "Damn! Sorry, sir! When the shooting started, I stomped on the wrong pedal. Threw the transmission into reverse while we were going forward!''

He slapped Anderson's shoulder. "Don't worry about it. I wanted to walk anyway." Gomez rounded the rear of the truck, scattering confused-looking former hostages. Gunshots banged up the street, and a round slapped into the truck's cab.

"Eddie! You and Roy round up the hostages and lead them off south! Get them clear and turn them loose! Rendezvous at the Liebighaus. I'll draw them off and meet you there later."

Gomez and Anderson hustled the civilians around the next corner, heading south, as Hunter darted forward into the street. The hidden man with the C96 stepped onto the sidewalk, his heavy pistol raised.

Hunter dropped into a crouch, his Colt in both hands. The automatic barked, smashing the Stosstrupp captain back against the building.

"*Halt! Halt!*" The three new Stosstruppen brought their own weapons up. Hunter snapped a shot in their direction and ran, pounding across the bricks for the cover of the north side of the street. Roy and Eddie had led their charges south down the cross street. He would draw pursuit off to the north.

Bullets chipped flakes of brick from the wall close above his head.

His diversion was working.

The lone crack of a rifle across the plaza was followed by the volleyed roar of gunfire. King saw the mild-looking man next to Hitler jerk and drop, dragging the Führer to the street. He felt a shock of recognition; that was Scheubner-Richter, the VBU major

Rachel had described. Why had Karl disobeyed orders and shot him instead of Hitler?

Göring stood behind Scheubner-Richter's body, an expression of stunned disbelief on his chubby face. Ludendorff sprawled on the pavement at Hitler's side, his eyes wide while Ulrich Graf, Hitler's bodyguard, leaped in front of Hitler just in time to receive the full weight of the police line's volley. At the same moment, a bullet from the Nazi column passed between King and von Godin and smacked wetly into the forehead of a police corporal standing a few feet behind them.

King dropped to the pavement, chambering a round in his .45 Colt. All around him was smoke and noise and confusion. The entire front wall of marchers was dropping to the street now, piled four deep in places, scrambling for nonexistent cover, clawing at bricks now wet with blood. The machine gun in front of the Feldherrnhalle rattled away over the state police line, chopping into the gray stone wall of the Residenz, showering the mob with stone splinters and ricochets. Nazis crouched or sprawled in the mouth of the Residenzstrasse, some sheltering behind the living bodies of their friends, MP18s flickering fire at the police. There were shrieks and agonized screams above the thundering gunfire. All around the plaza, civilians ran for the cover of doorways and building corners, a surge of motion and panic.

From his position flat on the street, King could no longer see Hitler. "Jaeger!" he yelled into his microphone. "Can you see Hitler? Kill him! Kill him!"

• • •

Jaeger shut out King's voice yelling in his ear. He swept the confusion of the Nazis' front ranks with his telescopic sight, searching for his target.

Damn! Damn! Damn! The Butcher of Hamburg was dead . . . but he'd disobeyed orders to do it.

There! The crosshairs dropped onto Hitler's face, a white face stark with terror as the Nazi leader scrabbled on the bricks, half pinned by the bloody body of Druzhinin. He squeezed the trigger . . .

. . . just as Hitler's face was obscured by the legs and black rubber coat of another marcher.

It was hard to sort things out in the chaos at the mouth of the Residenzstrasse. Nazi marchers were surging back now, blindly fleeing the smoke and noise and carnage. Jaeger thought he saw someone rolling Druzhinin's body aside, pulling Hitler free . . . but a roiling cloud of white smoke from the gunfire blotted out the scene before he could find a target. The smoke cleared. He saw Hermann Göring twisting on the pavement, grimacing with pain as he clutched his thigh beneath his black coat.

The smoke closed in again.

Damn!

Hunter fired three quick rounds, snapping shots toward his pursuers and driving them to cover on the street. The slide of his .45 locked open on the last round . . . empty.

He turned and ran then, racing north up the Dienerstrasse as the Stosstruppen banged shots after him.

He thumbed the magazine release as he ran, letting it fall clear as he fished in his coat pocket for a loaded one. *My last clip,* he thought. He had only carried two seven-round magazines through the Chronos portal, since pistols were something less than ideal weapons for combat. *If I had my Uzi now . . .* But that was hidden back at the Liebighaus. It had not seemed wise to parade around 1923 Munich's streets by daylight, displaying a late twentieth-century submachine gun.

Another round spanged off the bricks near his feet as he slapped the fresh magazine home and chambered the first round. The building on his right, white stone with towers and windows, provided cover in the form of a low archway. He recognized the structure from his briefings on Munich—the Alter Hof, once a palace, now an administrative building.

He leaned around the corner, .45 raised. The trio of Stosstruppen had spread out cautiously along the street, and they ducked for cover as he loosed another round at them.

He fired again and saw one of his attackers drop just as he rose to his feet, but knew from the man's scramble for safety that he was not seriously hurt. The other two were moving apart, seeking to catch him in a crossfire. The chatter of an MP18 drove Hunter back to cover, slugs chipping into the corner of the archway and shrieking from the sidewalk.

Which way now? The archway led through the Alter Hof under the Affen tower, to an enclosed courtyard paved with cobblestones and lined with trees. There were doors, and other archways. He chose a likely opening in the wall facing him and bolted toward it.

His two pursuers entered the arch under the Affen tower, firing at the running man. Hunter changed course in mid-stride, ducking for cover behind the narrow shelter of a pilaster, an ornamental buttress extending a foot from the courtyard wall twenty-five yards from the arch. He fired and heard the whine of a ricochet. One of the gray-clad soldiers leaned around the corner and loosed a burst of MP18 fire. Glass shattered in a window to his left.

Both Stosstruppen broke from cover, rushing him, gambling that a man armed only with a pistol would be unable to hit a moving target at that range. Hunter dropped to one knee, aiming carefully with a two-handed grip at the submachine gunner.

The Colt roared as he panned with his target. Miss! He fired again and the running man's legs seemed to fly out from under him. His arms flailed wildly as he sprawled on the cobblestones in a limp heap.

The second man skidded to a stop, leveled his weapon, and fired.

Hunter heard the sharp chuff-chuff-chuff of silenced auto fire and jerked back against the building's wall in surprise. Silenced auto fire? When the gunfire stopped, he leaned around the corner and fired again, sending the enemy diving for cover behind a tree. Hunter had a glimpse of the man's gun as he moved and felt a shock of recognition.

The Vz 61 Skorpion was the smallest military-issue submachine gun in the world, a wicked-looking little weapon with a folding wire stock and a low-powered, easily-silenced round. It was also a Czech-designed weapon which did not see service until the 1960s.

His opponent was VBU.

With the enemy under cover, Hunter raced for another archway across the courtyard. The VBU agent came around the tree, the Skorpion hissing rapid-fire rounds in a burst which stitched scars up the wall in

front of the running American. Hunter ducked and
rolled, coming up facing the Russian, his Colt Commander raised. He fired and the VBU man's head
jerked back, exploding in blood and chips of bone.

Outside the courtyard, Hunter heard yells and
shouted orders, the approach of running, booted feet.
He rose from the cobblestones and headed the other
way.

Post-combat fatigue dragged at him as he made his
way north from the Alter Hof, moving toward the
looming mass of the Residenz. Perhaps he could
reach King and the others. He had tried to contact
him and found that one of his rolls across the pavement had broken his radio.

No matter. The battle appeared to be over.

All of the streets were filled with people now; running, screaming people streaming back from the direction of the Odeonsplatz. There were soldiers in
the crowds, S.A. and Stosstruppen, most without
guns, many stripping off their uniforms as they ran.
Some were bloody, while a few limped up the street,
supported by comrades. A squad of mounted lancers
clopped past on nervous horses, herding panic-
stricken civilians in front of them.

Across the Maximilianstrasse, tucked up against
the south wall of the Residenz, was the broad plaza
called the Max-Josef Platz. Remnants of the putsch
march poured out of the narrow opening of the Residenzstrasse and across the plaza, fleeing for safety.

Exhausted, he sagged against the base of a marble
pillar, one of the ornamental columns lining the portico of Munich's National Theater, and part of the
Residenz complex. A few feet away, a car, an old
gray Selve with a red cross banner fluttering from its

hood, was parked at the curb, its motor running. Two men with Nazi armbands waited inside.

Hunter watched, empty of emotion, as a cluster of men approached the car, hurrying across the plaza from the Residenzstrasse.

One of them was Adolf Hitler, white-faced, wild-eyed, his left arm cradled in his right.

For a moment, Hunter thought Hitler must have been shot in the arm, but there was no blood. Perhaps he had been injured in the press of the crowd.

Adolf Hitler turned his back to Hunter, five feet away.

Somehow, something had gone wrong at the Odeonsplatz, and Hitler was still very much alive. But here was one chance more . . .

The .45 was still gripped in his hand, hanging loose at his side. He brought the weapon up, aiming for the back of Hitler's head.

Only then did he see that the slide was locked open, the pistol empty. Hitler was helped into the Selve, which then pulled out from the curb and moved off through the crowds, carrying *der Führer* to safety.

Hours later, the six of them huddled in the chill damp of the woods some miles outside of Munich. Just as it was growing dark, they had reached the spot where they'd buried the recall beacon, and they waited now for the device's signal to travel the years to 2007 and alert the Chronos Complex that they were ready to return.

Hunter closed his eyes, lying back on the cold, black soil. Depression, an utter and complete emptiness of spirit, hung black above them all. As nearly as they could determine, the events of November eighth and ninth had followed exactly the pattern of history they knew.

The Nazi marchers had exchanged fire with the police in the Odeonsplatz for all of sixty seconds before breaking in utter rout. Only von Ludendorff, proud and regal, had risen from the street after that first volley and pressed forward, walking, incredibly, unmolested into the plaza where a police lieutenant had arrested him. Not a single Nazi had followed him.

Hitler's bodyguard had been found, still alive, with eleven bullets in him. Hitler himself, his shoulder dislocated by his fall to the pavement, had been among the first to flee, helped by accomplices who had spirited him away. Within days he would be arrested, convicted, and sentenced to a five-year term in Landsberg Prison, though he ultimately would serve only eight months.

Ernst Röhm had surrendered the forces at the War Ministry shortly after the battle on the Odeonsplatz. Most of those with him had been allowed to turn in their weapons and disperse.

They had stopped the VBU, certainly. Hunter had seen Scheubner-Richter's body on the Residenzstrasse.

He frowned. Had the VBU been beaten by the Rangers or by history? Perhaps the Russians had been able to affect events no more than the Americans.

"So changing the past was impossible all along," Hunter said. "We had three chances at Hitler and screwed every one."

Jaeger shook his head slowly. "I am sorry, Lieutenant." His voice was thin and far away. "I tried. I . . . tried, but . . ."

"That's okay, Karl. My responsibility. And . . . I had a chance too."

Rachel's face was a mask of anguish. She was clutching something small and golden in her hand . . . her mother's locket. "I was so sure . . ."

"Predestination," King said. "You can't change history because it already happened. Que será, será . . ."

A blue glow shimmered in the air nearby. Wearily, the six gathered their weapons and staggered across to where it waited, beckoning.

"It'll be good to get home," Anderson said. The bandages on his face were white in the near-darkness.

Hunter stepped through. Around him was the tang of ozone, the low hum of power fed through massive busbars and power cables. The bare rock walls of the chamber closed about him.

Bare rock?

The chamber was different . . . shockingly so. It was smaller, more cramped, more primitive.

Hunter's second shock limped toward him, leaning heavily on a cane. General Thompson looked older, haggard, and wore a black eye patch. His uniform was different too, camouflage fatigues, rumpled and mud-stained.

"Welcome back, gentlemen," Thompson said. His eye fell on Rachel. "Who is this?" Jaeger came through next. "Who are these people?"

"Oh, God," King said, his voice an awed whisper. "History can be changed!"

Twenty-One

It took several hours for them to overcome the dull shock of discovery. The universe they had known, the *history* they had known, had all been swept away, replaced by something else.

General Alexander Thompson was the same Thompson they had known . . . except that he had lost an eye during the Battle of Denver and had suffered a shattered kneecap from shrapnel taken when the Soviets stormed Jackson. The Chronos Complex had been built under Mt. Bannon as before, but it was smaller, with fewer people and fewer resources. The Soviets were hammering much more loudly at the gates of America in this version of the universe. Instead of U.N. Occupation Forces in the cities, there had been an all-out invasion in 1990. Instead of a more-or-less autonomous region in the Rockies, Free

America's holdings had been reduced to a scattering of bases and guerrilla camps . . . and the fortress under Mt. Bannon was under siege, daily shelled and bombed by the encircling might of the Soviet Red Army.

"And I thought it couldn't get any worse," Hunter said. "Everything is changed! What went wrong?"

"You were sent back to kill Lenin," Thompson told them. He had joined the six time travelers in one of the Complex's briefing rooms . . . a concrete-walled bunker through which the dull *crump* of Soviet artillery shells could be felt as the bombardment continued far overhead. A light mist of cement dust sifted from the ceiling with each muffled detonation. "Are you saying the mission failed?"

"*Something* failed," Rachel said. "You say there has never been a Dr. Stein working with your project?"

"Certainly not. Dr. Phillips is the science team leader here."

"Dr. Phillips! He's alive?"

Thompson looked at her warily. "Yes. Look . . . I would say you people owe us some kind of explanation. Did you kill Lenin or not? When will the . . . the change take effect?"

Hunter tried to smile, and failed. "Well, General, it's like this . . ."

The universe they had known had changed into something else during the early '30s. According to the history Hunter and his companions remembered, Adolf Hitler had emerged from prison after his failed putsch, reorganized the discredited and ailing Nazi party, and gone on to become Chancellor of Ger-

many just ten years after the Munich putsch. It was
a moody Karl Jaeger who remembered that the fire
in Berlin's Reichstag in 1933 had been blamed on
the Communists and used as a pretext to bring Hitler's Nazis to power.

Thompson had ordered history books brought to
the bunker. He thumbed through a thick volume—
William L. Shirer's *The Rise of the Third Reich*.
There had been no Reichstag fire in *this* history. The
Nazis had come to power in a landslide victory in
the elections of 1930.

There was another detail . . . a fascinating one. In
this transformed universe, Germany's Chancellor was
not Adolf Hitler. That minor Bavarian politician, it
seemed, had died shortly after his release from
Landsberg Prison, victim of the political violence
which swept the country as two rival branches of the
National Socialists—left and right—fought it out.

Hitler's version of Nazism, it seemed, had been
wiped out, while that of leftist Gregor Strasser had
won. After Strasser was injured in an auto accident
in 1926, leadership of the Nazi party fell to a tall,
distinguished man, a millionaire, a powerful orator
who had been heavily funding the Nazis since 1923.

His name was Walther Loew.

"Walther Loew!" Rachel exclaimed. "But he was
a Communist agent!"

"Indeed?" Thompson nodded understanding.
"That has been theorized but never proven. It would
explain a great deal, actually. Before Loew became
Chancellor, or course, the Communists and Nazis
were at each other's throats. It was Loew who ne-
gotiated the Non-Aggression Pact with Stalin in

1932. That led to the full-scale federation of Nazi Germany with the Soviet Union in 1938.''

Hunter listened, stunned. In the history he remembered, a pact between the two had been signed in 1939 . . . and broken two years later when Hitler invaded Russia. "You mean . . . Germany *joined* the Soviet Union? It went Communist?''

"Basically . . . yes. The Nazis under Loew were already strongly left wing . . . and they held many of the same ideals as the Soviets. The Federation started as an alliance, but by the time World War II ended, it was a lot firmer than that.''

"When . . . was World War II?''

Thompson gave Hunter a hard look. He was obviously having as much trouble coping with the situation as they were. "Are you seriously telling me none of this happened in your . . . the way you remember it?''

"We had a Second World War,'' Hunter said slowly. "But it sounds like things happened a bit differently in *ours*.''

"Hmm. Ours started in September of '39, when Germany and Russia invaded Poland.''

"And then France and England fought a united Germany and Russia . . .'' Hunter added.

"Then it was the same!''

"No. *No*! We remember America, England, France, and Russia as allies. Fighting Germany, Japan, and Italy.''

"God. Japan stayed neutral. Italy was on *our* side . . . for a while. America joined the fighting in 1943, but not before England and France had both fallen. The armistice came in '47, right after they dropped the Bomb on New York. Reparations nearly crippled the United States for five more years." Thompson shrugged. "The Federation was unbeatable after that. We've barely been holding on for sixty years. Most of the world is either part of the Soviet Empire or openly allied with them. There's talk of a World State. When America was invaded in '90, most resistance to the Communists simply collapsed . . . except here."

"Except here." Heavy artillery echoed far above the room. How much longer would this final pocket of resistance last?

And Loew had been Germany's ruler, the man who had led Germany to its transformed destiny.

"We had hoped that your team would change history, Captain," Thompson said heavily. Hunter looked up sharply. Evidently, promotions came faster in *this* version of the world. "We thought that by assassinating Lenin, we could block the rise of communism in Russia. We had planned to go after Loew after you got back. With both dictators gone, Dr. Phillips contends the twentieth century might turn out to have been quite peaceful. Apparently, we were mistaken."

"So were we," King said. "We'd about decided that history couldn't be changed."

"It hasn't," Thompson said. Then he gave a wry smile. "At least, it hasn't from *my* point of view. You, and the Project, were our last hope. What the hell are we going to do now?"

Hunter and Rachel sat together on a sofa in the common area of the barracks assigned to the team. They were alone. Anderson was at the dispensary having the cuts on his face treated, while the rest slept off the exhaustion which had been hammering at them for hours upon hours.

"You should sleep, too," Rachel told Hunter. She could see the circles under his eyes, the deadness in his face.

"I couldn't," he said. "I keep thinking it's . . . it's all my fault."

"Why?"

"We should've ignored Hitler, tried for a clean sweep of the VBU in Munich . . . gone after Loew . . ."

"Munich is a big city," she said. "There was no way to know where he was. Maybe he wasn't even in Munich during the march. I heard him talking about a *schloss* . . . a castle he was using as headquarters. He might have been there."

"Maybe. I doubt it. He would have wanted to keep an eye on things, especially after we showed up. Oh, *dammit*, Rachel! I screwed it up for all of us! For the whole country! I let Loew go . . . and knocked us clean into some damned parallel universe!"

"Not parallel," she said gently. "As near as Father could figure it, time doesn't branch, like in science fiction stories. It just . . . changes." She motioned in the air. "You change an event *here* . . . it changes the events which touch it *here*, and on and on."

He shook his head. "Isn't that the same thing?"

"No. When you change an event, it reconfigures everything down the time stream from that point. Remember me talking about the Transformation Wave? A kind of ripple moving down the time stream, caused by the change? That is the reconfiguring of history."

"Yeah . . . but that took time. Six days, you said, for the changes caused by us killing Lenin to reach 2007. We missed Loew in 1923 and stepped into a brand new universe a few hours later."

She sighed. The question had been gnawing at her. "I know. There are some points we must not understand as well as we thought we did." She sagged. "My best guess is that Loew was making changes in time—little ones, maybe—a good week before the Beer Hall Putsch. The Transformation Wave was already moving, building, by the time we beat them in Munich."

"And we stepped right into it." He shook his head. "Doesn't change anything. I screwed up . . . and the United States is in a hell of a lot worse shape now than it was when I left 2007. My fault . . ."

Rachel reached out and touched Hunter's face. She could read the pain there, the indecision.

"You did the best you could."

"Which wasn't good enough." His hands clenched. "Some second chance I turned out to be."

"So? There's always a third chance." She gestured vaguely at the walls. "Even with this junk, I should be able to do the calculations. It'd be a breeze if they had the equipment I had back . . . back in *our* Chronos Complex. The computers they have here are Dark Ages stuff, twenty years out of date. But even so, we should be able to go back and try again."

He drew back from her. "Again? No way! I've done enough damage back there already! Hell! What do we find next time we come back through the portal? The KGB, demanding our papers?"

Rachel bit back anger. She couldn't understand his

passive attitude. Where was the decision, the strength he'd shown in Munich?

She had leafed through Thompson's copy of *The Rise of the Third Reich* earlier. Shirer's description of the virtual extermination of the Jews in the '40s and '50s, of Soviet death camps and anti-Semitic pogroms which the Russians had used to strengthen their stranglehold on Europe, explained why Thompson hadn't know her.

Rachel Stein was Jewish. She remembered stories her father had told her once, stories about *his* father's survival in the hell of Auschwitz.

In *this* history, there had been no survivors.

The pause lengthened. Artillery thundered far overhead.

"We can change history," she said, her voice cold and steady. "We've proven that. We have the ability. Don't we still have the responsibility?"

"What . . . we just keep going back again and again?" He laughed, a flat, bitter sound. "Until we get it right?"

"Damn you, Travis! Okay! You screwed up! Are you just going to sit there feeling sorry for yourself?"

He looked at her blankly. "I could wipe us all out . . ."

Rachel reached inside the blouse they'd bought for her in Munich, pulling out the locket. Gomez had used a pair of needlenose pliers to knit the chain where it had been broken, back at the Munich warehouse, and now it was around her neck again.

"Travis . . . I used to think the most important thing about all this . . . The Chronos Project . . . was the chance that I might get my mother back.

Now I've lost my father too. But there's one hell of a lot more at stake here than our personal feelings! There are millions . . . *billions* of lives involved! If what has happened *was* our fault, don't you think it's up to us to make it right?''

She watched Hunter's face as his gaze shifted from the locket to her eyes. The artillery's dull thunder sounded closer now. "I wonder if we still have time?''

"It'll take a week to rewrite their programs here,'' she said. "If they can hold out that long up above . . .''

Hunter was nodding. There was a new light in his eyes, a new strength. "We'll have to find the exact point to strike . . . the exact *time* . . . We'll have to find Loew before he came to power.'' He paused then, his voice sobering once more. "We'll *have* to get him, Rachel. If we miss this time, we won't have a Chronos Complex to come back to. This really will be our last chance . . .''

Then they were in each other's arms, seeking, holding. He crushed her against his chest, and she felt herself lost in his embrace. Their kiss lingered . . . deepened. . . . She realized how much she needed him.

Only much later did a small shudder take her as she lay there in his arms.

My God, I could lose him too.

Twenty miles southwest of Munich lay the Fünfseeland—the Land of Five Lakes—a rugged area of scenic vistas, forests, and deep Alpine lakes. The Ammersee stretched for ten miles beneath the brooding silence of the Benedictine priory of Andechs on

the heights of the Heiligerberg. Above the rock cliffs
along the western shore opposite Andechs rose the
walls and towers of a small castle, summer retreat
for Maximilian in the days of Bavaria's glory.

Shirer identified the site as Adlerschloss, the Eagle's Castle, the Alpine retreat of *der Adler*, the name
this universe had bestowed on Germany's dictator.
The records indicated that Walther Loew had purchased the place early in 1923 and had used it for
many years thereafter. Rachel had heard Loew and
the others mention a *schloss* several times while she
was a prisoner. Adlerschloss must have been what
they'd meant.

On February 14, 1926, an important meeting of
the leaders of the Nazi party had been held in Bamberg, not far from Nuremberg. In the reality the six
of them were coming to call Universe B, Walther
Loew made his dramatic appearance there, at the
head of a company of Storm Troopers, frustrating
Adolf Hitler's bid to regain control of the Nazi party.

Shirer's account recorded a meeting of Loew and
his top supporters at Adlerschloss two weeks before
Bamberg. That meeting, Hunter and Thompson
agreed, was the point which gave the Intervention
Force its best chance to get Loew and all of his people together in one place.

Hunter remembered the military doctrine of mini-
mum applied force. Take out Adlerschloss before
Bamberg, and history might develop along the lines
he knew.

Hunter strode across the bare rock floor of Time
Square. Rachel stood before one of the massive, upright cabinets housing a computer tape drive, going

over the translation of a section of program code from one computer language to another.

"Hello, Raye . . ."

Rachel turned her head, a swirl of black hair across her shoulders. She was still wearing the blouse and long skirt the team had bought her in Munich and was carrying Roy Anderson's H&K MP5. "Hi, Travis."

She looked tired. Rachel had been working with Dr. Phillips and the Project's technicians for eight days, rewriting the Control Programs used by this version of the time portal. The equipment was different here, cruder and less sophisticated, but the equations which governed its operation were the same. The portal in Universe B lacked the fine control made possible by her father's equations. When she was done, she could promise that the IF Team would be able to land within a few miles of their target . . . and within a few hours of their chosen time.

"I heard it's about ready to go," he said, looking past her at the cabinets that lined the room.

"Well . . ." She followed his gaze. "The program seems to be running okay, but it's so *slow*! Did you know they still use magnetic tape for data storage?"

The technician shrugged apology. "We didn't have that moon landing project you told us about to help us along," he said.

"As long as you can get us back there," Hunter said.

They heard the echoing of many booted feet on the rock floor behind them. Sergeant Jenkins was leading columns of men into the portal chamber, soldiers in ragged and battle-stained camouflage fatigues, carrying a hodgepodge mixture of weapons. Hunter saw numerous American weapons but the majority were captured Russian pieces: AKMs, Soviet German H&K assault rifles, and even a few RPG rocket launchers. In this universe, even more than in their own, the remnants of the U.S. Army were heavily reliant on equipment liberated from the enemy.

One hundred volunteers fell into formation. Thompson had been reluctant to draw so many defenders from the fortress on the surface, but it was obvious that the IF team would need more than six people to take on a castle.

Six people. Rachel was going, too. Hunter watched the one hundred men falling into orderly ranks and chewed his lip. He was not at all happy about taking Rachel back into the past, especially a past which promised to become a combat zone.

But the alternative might be worse. No one, not even Rachel, was certain what would happen to her if she stayed in Universe B and the Rangers succeeded in getting things back on track. Would Rachel vanish with Universe B when Universe A became reality once more?

"Looks like we're about ready to move out, Raye," he said. "God, I wish you didn't have to go."

"You think you could keep me away?" She patted the SMG slung over her shoulder. "I can take care of myself."

He made himself smile and nod. He looked away, seeking the other Rangers where they waited with the volunteers. Jaeger wiped his Wa-2000 with a rag, a look of utterly bleak and grim determination on his face. The German had said very little since Munich, and it was obvious that he was brooding. Could he be trusted now? *I'll have to watch him,* Hunter thought. *He blames himself . . . and that's not good.*

King and Gomez cradled their SMGs. Both were festooned with grenades and pouches carrying fresh magazines for their weapons, and Eddie carried a satchel stuffed with plastique. Anderson hefted an M-60 machine gun. Like Hunter, they wore their combat blacks and harnesses, carried unused through Munich in their satchels. All looked subdued, and there was none of the banter which usually marked the beginnings of other missions.

"Power is building, Captain."

"Huh?" Hunter still hadn't gotten the hang of being called "Captain." Still, one hundred men was a captain's command. Perhaps it all worked out. "Uh, right, Doctor."

What bothered him more was the knowledge that their success would condemn Phillips to death. General Thompson, presumably, would become himself, his *original* self, when history reconfigured.

But Rachel had seen Phillips die.

"Are you sure you don't want to come with us too, Doctor?"

Phillips gave him a thin smile. "Absolutely, Travis. I am needed here, to man the controls. Besides, there's no guarantee that I would survive, even if I accompanied you."

"I still don't understand that."

"If we're successful, Universe B will never have happened," Rachel said. Her voice sounded wistful . . . even sad. "We're still not sure what would happen to people who . . . who remembered growing up with this version of history, but our best guess is that they will . . . simply vanish. Jenkins, over there, is the same Jenkins we knew back in Universe A. He just has different memories, because he grew up in a history different from the one we remember. When the universe is reconfigured, so will he.''

Hunter glanced across to the one hundred volunteers. ''Maybe so. But as far as they're concerned, they're about to wipe themselves out of existence. Do they know . . . ?''

''They know,'' Phillips said. ''It's their choice, really. To die fighting the Russians on the surface . . . or give their lives, their *pasts*, for a chance at a better world . . .''

And Phillips, Hunter realized, would be reconfigured as a corpse.

The scientist seemed to understand what Hunter was thinking. ''Don't worry about it, my friend. It's a small enough price to pay. It is you who will have the hardest part.''

''What do you mean?''

Phillips smiled. ''Whatever happens as a result of your intervention, you will have to live with the results.''

Twenty-Two

"If any of you have second thoughts, now's the time to say so." Thompson stood erect, his hands clasped behind his back, surveying the ranks of silent men. No one stirred. "I want to make it clear; this operation is strictly for volunteers. If you want to back out now, it won't be held against you."

Hunter stood with the others in the front rank. The room was silent save for the growing, pulsing hum of power from the portal behind them. Their weapons were checked, their equipment secured in pouches and backpacks. They were ready.

Are we? A hundred men against a fortress. Against time itself . . .

"America has been fighting a holding action against the Russians for years," Thompson continued. He paced along the line, limping heavily.

"Some of you have been fighting since they launched their invasion seventeen years ago. In all that time, never has there been the slightest hope that, ultimately, we would win, that we could drive the invaders from our shores once and for all.

"But now you men have been offered a priceless opportunity, something few soldiers can ever hope for. You have been given the chance to strike that one, critical blow which could make the difference between freedom and slavery, between life and death."

He paused in his walk and turned his gaze on Rachel, where she stood at Hunter's side. "If you succeed, we're told that we will . . . be transformed. We will forget what we are here . . . will become different people, with different pasts, different memories. But we will live in a better world, a world where there is hope." Thompson's voice rose above the power hum, echoing from the rock walls. "I, for one, am willing to accept what looks, to us on this side of the change, like oblivion, like death."

Hunter's eyes met those of Dr. Phillips. In this portal chamber, there was no raised control booth, only a rough-and-ready collection of computers and instrumentation half smothered in a spaghetti tangle of wiring and cables at the back of the room. Phillips smiled and gave him a thumbs up.

Hunter nodded and returned the gesture. For some it would be, not oblivion, but death.

"I think all of us are willing to die," Thompson said. "To die, or accept oblivion . . . if it means that America will have a new chance, a new freedom. You men are Freedom's Rangers, returning to the past to strike at the heart of the tyranny that threatens to engulf us all.''

And if we fail, this is the new universe. The universe we created. Can we fight against the tide of history?

''I am proud to have been a part of this . . . prouder still to have commanded men such as you.

''Good luck. God bless you.''

The room resounded with the crash of cheering men. Hunter turned his head, saw the flush of excitement on young faces, saw Anderson and Gomez and King joining in.

With men such as these, history didn't stand a chance.

Then it was time. Hunter barked the order, and the columns turned and began filing up the ramp.

The way to the past was open.

The truck chugged up a winding road through stands of evergreen trees. It was dark and cold, a layer of snow on the ground. Ahead, lights blazing from ranked windows, stood their target, Adlerschloss.

They'd ambushed the truck on a road far down the mountain earlier that afternoon, taking the uniforms and papers of the men they'd found aboard. Their history briefings had established that truckloads of Nazis had been arriving at Adlerschloss throughout the day.

Hunter, seated next to Anderson, checked his appearance. The borrowed uniform coat covered his combat blacks and the pair of grenades on his harness. It was crowded in the cab; the Texan's big M-60 rested between them, wrapped in its tarpaulin cover. Hunter kept his eyes on the sentries at the castle's gatehouse. Those guards wore black uniforms and steel helmets which marked them as Loew's S.K.

According to the histories they'd read—the Universe B histories—Walther Loew had spent the twenty-seven months since the Beer Hall Putsch organizing his own, left-oriented branch of the Nazi party. The S.K., the *Sturmkommandos*, had begun as *der Adler's* elite bodyguards, trained by him personally here at his castle. Eventually, they would evolve into something very like the SS of Hunter's world.

Unless the Rangers could stop them here . . . tonight.

The conference at the castle tonight—February 10, 1926—would be their one opportunity to get all of the S.K., the Nazi leaders supporting Loew, and *der Adler* himself. Tomorrow, they would leave for Bamberg. After that, Loew's people would scatter across Germany, and events would move unalterably toward the pattern that led to Universe B.

"We're coming up on the gate," Hunter said quietly. His radio, newly repaired, relayed the warning to Gomez and Jaeger in the back of the truck with six of Universe B's commandos. King, Rachel, and the rest of the strike force were already deployed in the woods around them, waiting for Hunter's signal to attack.

Anderson slowed the truck. The Texan drew his silenced pistol and placed it on his lap. Hunter drew his own weapon and chambered a round.

The America of Universe B had never developed the 9mm hush puppy variant of the Smith & Wesson automatic, but their Mark XV silenced .22s had been designed for the same type of work. With the "Ivan-offer," you had to get in close and shoot often, but it was good for taking out Russian sentries quietly.

"Halt!" One of the black-uniformed sentries stood before the lowered, iron bar gate, his hand raised. Hunter noted the weapon slung on his shoulder—a Soviet AKM.

The sentry shone a flashlight on Anderson's and Hunter's faces. "Papers, *meinen Herren . . ."*

Hunter handed him the sheaf of papers taken from the body of the man who had occupied the seat Hunter was now sitting in. The sentry inspected them, returned them. "All is in order, *mein Herr*. Proceed."

The iron gate raised, and Anderson edged the truck into the arched tunnel beyond. At the far end was another gatehouse, and more sentries, though it was unlikely that there would be another check.

"Two sentries at the front gate," Hunter murmured into his radio. "Armed with modern AKMs. We're approaching the inner gate now. Stand ready. Yankee Team, this is Yankee Leader. Do you read me?"

"We hear you, Yankee Leader," King's voice was tense. *"We're in position, ready to go."*

"Any time now."

The inner gate was raised. Another guard stood aside, waving them through, pointing across the courtyard to where other vehicles were parked. From the number of cars and trucks lined up under the floodlights, the conference must be well under way.

An S.K. officer stepped out of the guardhouse

doorway. "Where have you people been?" he demanded. "You're two hours la . . ."

The officer froze the moment his flashlight beam fell on Hunter's face.

It was Kulagin.

"Achtung! Achtung! Halten Sie jene Mannen!"

Hunter brought his .22 up as Kulagin lunged for cover behind the guard house. The weapon hissed, rounds cracking off stone.

"It's gone up!" Hunter yelled into his lapel mike. "Go! Go!"

He banged the cab door open and rolled to the ground. "Catch!" Anderson yelled as he tossed Hunter's Uzi to him. Hunter dropped the .22 and snicked off the SMG's safety. A guard stood three yards away, mouth open in astonishment, hands fumbling for his slung AKM.

Hunter squeezed off a burst that smashed the S.K. trooper to the ground. Somewhere, an AKM hammered. Glass exploded from the front of the truck, but Anderson was already on the ground, his massive 60-gun in his hands. The weapon thundered, spitting flame into the night. Running S.K. guards screamed and spun and fell as 7.62 rounds chopped through them.

Men piled out of the rear of the truck and raced toward the outer gates. The plan had called for them to sneak up and take the outside sentries quietly at the same time that Hunter and Anderson took the inner gate, but surprise was gone now. An alarm shrilled. AKM fire spat, knocking down one of the American commandos. Gomez dropped into a crouch, his H&K whispering death.

"*Outer gate secure!*" Gomez said over the radio net.

"Right," Hunter replied. "Okay, Yankees, come on in!"

The bulk of the commando force had been drawn up in a semicircle reaching from cliff to cliff on either side of Adlerschloss's perch above the Ammersee. At Hunter's command, King, Rachel, and seventy commandos raced for the castle gates. The rest waited silently in the darkness to catch any of Loew's men who escaped from the trap.

No one escapes this time, Hunter told himself. He and Anderson stripped off the S.K. jackets that had gotten them this far.

It was bad—very bad—that the alarm had been sounded so soon, but the plan had been designed with the possibility of an early discovery in mind. Adlerschloss was not large as Bavarian castles went, scarcely larger than the Alter Hof in Munich. The main *residenz* loomed above the edge of the cliff, flanked by towers, while north and south wings extended to smaller towers, the west palisade, and the gate.

The plan had called for Hunter's group to seize the gate area and hold it for King's force. Once inside, the attackers were to split up, cross the courtyard, and move through both wings toward the *residenz*. Loew and his supporters, most of them almost certainly VBU, would be gathered in the great hall at the back of the building, overlooking the lake. The idea had been to infiltrate the castle before an alarm could be given, burst in on the conference, and kill Loew and his people in one swift, sudden strike.

Now it would have to be done the hard way.

A pounding of feet heralded the arrival of the main force. "What happened, Lieutenant?" King demanded. Rachel was just behind him, her eyes wild, her H&K tightly held.

"Kulagin," Hunter replied. "He must've been checking the guard."

AKM fire banged across the courtyard. "Damn bad luck."

"Organize your people here, Master Sergeant," Hunter said. "Start the flanking teams working through the castle wings. Roy and I'll see what we can do to regain surprise."

"Sir!"

Anderson's M-60 hammered, and glass smashed in the distance. Hunter's eyes locked with Rachel's, as commandos streamed in from the dark. "You stay here with the gate force, Raye," he said gently. *She should be safe enough here.*

Twenty of the commandos had been detailed to hold the castle gate, the cork in a bottle. As long as Rachel stayed inside the gatehouse . . .

Her eyes showed agony. "I'd rather be with you."

"We've been over this before. I want you safe." A bullet cracked into the stones of the gatehouse somewhere overhead. Hunter took Rachel's elbow and steered her to the shelter of a buttress at the corner of the tunnel. "As safe as possible anyhow. I'll be back."

Hunter pulled himself away. "Roy! Mount up! Gomez! Jaeger! Grab six men and get in the truck!"

The truck was still running. Anderson climbed back in the cab, his machine gun smoking where it rested on the seat. The truck's windows were gone now, and broken glass covered everything.

Anderson gunned the engine and launched the truck forward. AKM fire probed from the walls surrounding the inner courtyard. Rounds spanged off the roof of the cab, stitched pockmarks along the side. Ahead, surprised guards dove to either side of the front door of the *residenz*, seeking cover behind the ornate pillars which supported the courtyard portico.

The truck smashed into one of the pillars, canting to one side as it came to rest in front of the door. *''Arriba!''* Gomez yelled, and the commandos came boiling out of the rear.

Hunter and Anderson rolled clear of the cab. Glass smashed from a window to the right of the doors as the Americans vaulted up the *residenz* steps. Anderson's M-60 spat flame, driving through the window frame and the body of the gunman behind it. Gomez sprinted to the wall beside the window and tossed a grenade through. The blast was followed by shrieks from inside.

Hunter crashed through the *residenz* doors, his Uzi blazing, the rest of his team close behind. There were scattered S.K. bodies sprawled on the marble floor inside. Potted plants had been hurled across the room by the blast, spreading dirt everywhere. Two broad, carpeted staircases mirrored one another as they swept up either side of the foyer to a second-floor landing. A trio of S.K. men leaned over the railing, AKMs spitting flame.

One of the commandos screamed and lurched backward into a wall. Hunter's Uzi fired, catching one of the attackers in the face and torso, while Karl Jaeger cut loose with his Walther. A hole opened in a second S.K. man's forehead. The railing splintered as he pitched forward in a less-than-graceful swan dive to the foyer floor. One of the commandos mounted the right-hand staircase, his M-16 blasting into the third ambusher.

A door banged open off the second-floor landing. Hunter caught a glimpse of black S.K. uniforms, of spurting flame, of a hand grenade arcing out and down, bouncing with a sharp report along the marble floor of the foyer.

"Look out!" One of the commandos shouldered Hunter aside and dove onto the rolling grenade, gathering it under his body. The blast lifted the man off the floor, tearing him in bloody horror, but the concussion and shrapnel were muffled. The rest of Hunter's men remained standing, weapons hammering at the second-floor landing.

More S.K. erupted from doors along the upstairs hallway. Through the roar of gunfire, Hunter became aware of a new sound, a long, drawn-out keening which he took at first for one of his men in agony. Then he saw Anderson, now halfway up the left-hand stairs, his 60-gun swinging in an arc at waist level, his head thrown back and his mouth open in a wild rebel yell.

There was no more movement on the upstairs landing.

"Anderson! Take two men! Secure the upstairs! The rest of you with me!" He paused, looking at the torn body of the man who had thrown himself on the grenade. *I never even knew his name. . . .*

Double doors, painted white, were set against the far wall under the railed landing. Their research had placed the *schloss's* great hall there.

• • •

The battle for the courtyard was over, though stray sounds of gunfire still crackled from the north wing of the *schloss*. King made his way along the south wing, his H&K probing shadows.

A few work lights gleamed harshly from an open area on the ground level which had the look of an old stable converted to a motor pool machine shop. Three bodies in S.K. black lay sprawled nearby where they'd been gunned down as they emerged from a storeroom. Vehicles were lined up along the covered portico, together with random stacks of crates and machinery. King was reminded of the warehouse in Munich.

Sergeant Jenkins approached, slapping a fresh magazine into his M-16. "The motor pool is secure, Master Sergeant," he said. "There's something over here you'd better see, though."

The something was scattered over much of the machine shop; cables and instrument casings and plastic packing crates empty except for foam linings. The massive stones of the southeast tower made up one wall of the old stable area, and there were signs that recent excavations had been made into the stable floor and the tower foundations. Armored cable, as thick as a man's thigh, extruded itself from floor to tower wall.

King picked up one of the plastic boxes and examined the oddly-shaped cutout in the foam. Surely, nothing like this had been used in 1926.

The VBU had been working at something in the tower, that much was certain. King's mind turned over several possibilities, discarding each in turn.

Except one.

He opened his radio channel. "Corporal Randolph! This is King."

"Randolph," the voice of the man in charge of the gate force replied in his earphone. *"Go ahead."*

"Get Rachel Stein. Have her meet me at the southeast corner of the courtyard." He looked at the plastic case in his hand, with growing horror. "I need her to take a look at something here."

They followed a grenade through the double doors, bursting into the great hall through smoke and screams and the shatter of breaking glass. Hunter had a blurred impression of the long room, of windows stretching from floor to ceiling, of a huge stone fireplace, a flag displaying a swastika and eagle device hanging above the mantle. A massive, hardwood conference table had been smashed apart by the blast. Bodies lay sprawled on the floor. An S.K. officer staggered through the smoke, blood streaming from nose and ears.

The conference table had caught and deflected much of the blast, unfortunately. More S.K. officers remained standing, weapons ready, than lay on the floor. AKM fire barked through the smoke. The commando who had tossed the grenade shrieked, kicked, and fell, torn from crotch to throat by a long burst of fire.

Hunter fired back, killing two. Movement to his right caught his eye. He had not seen Loew in Munich, but he had studied the face enough times in the history books of Universe B . . . the proud, aristocratic features, the hawk-like visage of *der Adler.* He was wearing a black S.K. officer's uniform. "Loew!"

He triggered a three-round burst, saw splinters snap

out from the door frame as the Nazi leader plunged through.

An S.K. *oberleutnant* rose up behind the ruin of the table, AK in hand, aiming at Hunter. Jaeger drilled the man with his Walther, catching him full in the chest, sending him back through an unbroken window pane.

More gunfire roared from the left. Hunter took cover behind the table, his H&K hissing response. A last S.K. officer and a man in civilian clothes collided with one another and a closed door, trying to escape as Hunter cut them down.

Then the hall was silent. Gunfire continued to echo through from the courtyard, and a cold wind rattled at the broken windows. Someone moaned on the floor. Gomez and a commando appeared on either side of him, their weapons smoking.

He opened a radio channel. "Yankee Leader to Yankee Team. Greg, how's it look out there?"

"*Courtyard secure,*" King's voice replied. "*But we've got something strange here.*"

"What?"

There was a confusion of voices in Hunter's earpiece, someone talking in the background. "*I'm in the southeast corner of the courtyard,*" King continued. "*Rachel's here with me. She thinks we've found the main power conduit for a Russki time portal.*"

A time portal . . . here?

He remembered his glimpse of Loew, vanishing through a door leading . . .

. . . toward the southeast corner of the *schloss*!

Twenty-Three

"You and Rachel see if there's any way to unplug the damn thing."

"Doesn't look like it, Lieutenant," King replied. "Rachel says the main generator must be buried. All we can see is the main power cable . . . and that's armor plated."

There was a pause, the muffled sounds of orders given in the background. *"Right. I've sent Gomez with his bag of tricks. Keep me posted."*

Glass exploded from a window across the courtyard, yanking King's attention to the north wing. The flickering muzzle flash of a machine gun winked from a third-floor window. Gouts of splintered stone and dirt tracked across the courtyard, tangling the feet of running commandos, tripping them, spinning them down.

King lunged, knocking Rachel down into the shadow of a stack of wooden crates. Bullets stitched through the wood above his head, showering him with splinters. He twisted, thumbing his transmit switch. "Lieutenant! We're taking fire out here! Heavy MG on the north wall!" From the sound of the gun, it was a PKM.

"Pull back into the south wing," Hunter said. *"I'll try to reach the tower from here! Yankee Leader out!"*

The machine gun continued to sweep the court-yard. King saw a commando crouch behind a parked car, unlimbering a Soviet RPG, saw shards of glass spray from the vehicle's windows like a white mist under the court floodlights, saw the man clutch his face and sprawl backward in blood and torn flesh. The RPG lay on the pavement, ten yards from King's position.

King rolled off Rachel. "Jenkins!" He yelled. "Pull the men back inside the stable, there! Rachel! Go with them!"

Rachel hesitated. "What about . . ."

"Dammit, lady, get the hell out of here!" He reared up over the boxes and rattled off a full clip of 9mm rounds toward the enemy gun.

The PKM was silenced long enough for Rachel to bolt for the sheltering darkness of the stable behind them. Then the MG opened up again, stitching lead across the stacks of boxes, shattering lights, rico-cheting from the building wall in a barrage of fire that went on and on and on. King flattened himself on the ground, painfully aware of the inadequacy of his shelter. The packing crates were being smashed to splinters, as substantial against that drumming fire as cardboard.

With several of the work lights gone, it was darker in the southeast corner now. King reloaded, then broke from cover, darting out into the courtyard toward the riddled car and the body of the soldier behind it. Taking cover behind the car, he slung his H&K, picked up the RPG where it had fallen, and set it on his shoulder.

The range was less than one hundred yards.

More muzzle flashes stabbed from the darkness underneath the MG site, and King heard shouts, the sounds of running men. A whole pack of VBU and native S.K. troops were gathering under the cover of the PKM, preparing to rush the front gate.

One problem at a time . . .

He took aim and squeezed the trigger. The rocket-propelled grenade kicked away from the launcher, then swooped up in its peculiar, dipping flight path as the engine fired. A line of sparks arrowed upward toward the third-floor window.

The explosion blew the window out in a cascade of rubble and glass and smoke. The elegant perfection of the north wall's courtyard facade was abruptly marred by a gaping hole where the window had been.

Charging men surged into the courtyard, weapons blazing. King could make out numerous civilians, as well as black-clad S.K. soldiers, under the glare of the floodlights. The north wing, it appeared, had been a barracks area, and the surviving troops had massed for a last-ditch attempt against the castle gate.

Gunfire met them from the gatehouse, where Corporal Randolph's men crouched behind windows and barricades along the west wall. The fire was augmented by a stuttering roar from the *residenz*. King recognized the staccato thunder of Anderson's M-60, firing now from a second-floor window above the *residenz* door.

The courtyard was transformed into a slaughterhouse.

King raised his H&K to add his fire to the rest. Then the pounding of a new outburst of autofire sounded from inside the south wing, somewhere behind him. With a curse, he whirled and plunged inside.

"Where's Karl?" Hunter looked about the great hall, at the ruin and the twisted bodies. "Where did Jaeger go?"

The one soldier remaining with him pointed toward the splintered door . . . the door through which Loew had run moments before. "I saw him go through there, sir."

"Oh, shit," Hunter said. Jaeger had been silent to the point of sullenness since Munich, and Hunter had not been able to talk with him, to find out what was going on in the German's mind.

Other thoughts crowded in. Rachel was under fire in the courtyard . . . but Jaeger was chasing Loew without knowing that the VBU leader must by trying to reach the Russian time portal . . .

"Shit!"

He slapped a fresh magazine into his Uzi and started after Jaeger.

Rachel screamed. Autofire burned through the corridor gouging chunks from plaster walls and tearing men into bloody rags. She tried to bury herself behind the scanty shelter of a corbel projecting into the hallway as plaster dust and chunks of wood sprayed past her face. Jenkins spun and twisted, chest and face pulped as a Soviet light machine gun stuttered from behind the improvised cover of an upturned table at the far end of the hall.

Three other men in the squad were down, four more crouched in niches or behind pillars along the corridor. The hail of fire from the end of the passageway had all of them pinned. One man plucked a grenade off his combat harness, only to be cut down by a long burst which sent him sprawling onto the carpet before he could pull the pin.

Silenced rounds hissed past her head from behind. She turned, saw King kneeling, his MP5 spitting fire. Then the line of chattering death connected with the master sergeant, bowling him over, blood splattered across his legs.

"Greg!"

One of the commandos leaped into the open, blazing away with his M-16, covering the wounded man. Rounds slammed across his torso, nearly cutting him in half.

King was still moving, dragging himself to the cover of a doorway. Another soldier grabbed his combat harness, trying to tug him to safety. Rapid-fire slugs cut him down, sending him sprawling across King's back. Rachel squeezed her eyes shut and tried to back her way into the wall as gunfire thundered in her ears.

Jaeger pulled back behind a corner where the hallway jogged right, pressing a fresh 6-round magazine into the bullpup receiver of his Wa-2000. Another

short burst tore past his head from up the hall, where
his quarry had turned and fired a Skorpion.

He wasn't going to let Walther Loew escape.

Karl Jaeger was no longer motivated by revenge.
Since Munich, since his failure at the Odeonsplatz,
the burning hatred for the Communist bastards who
had murdered his family had somehow evaporated,
leaving only a dull deadness, a blackness that threatened to engulf him. Druzhinin was dead . . . killed
by Jaeger's own hands . . . but the KGB monster's
death had done nothing but leave Jaeger feeling
empty and utterly, completely alone.

The only purpose he had to drive him now was the
mission. He had pursued *der Adler* from the main
hall, exchanging fire at every corner, twisting back
toward the south end of the *residenz*. Loew must not
escape.

He chambered a round from the new magazine,
steeled himself, then rolled off the corner and into
the clear. Nothing in sight. He ran, swinging left
around another bend in the hall . . .

. . . and nearly collided with four S.K. men huddled behind a pile of furniture, blazing away down
another passageway with an RPK machine gun. Beyond, a door hung open, revealing stone stairs and
the curved walls of a castle tower.

Walther Loew was there, reloading his Skorpion.
"Achtung!" the VBU leader yelled, pointing. "Stop
him! Stop that man!"

Jaeger's rifle kicked in his hands as he snapped off
two shots from the hip. The S.K. machinegunner
smashed back against an upturned table, as his loader
shrieked agony and clutched his belly.

Another man fired, the bullet clutching at Jaeger's

sleeve. The German guerrilla fired a third time, and the S.K. trooper's head split open in a spray of blood and gore.

The fourth S.K. soldier's shot caught Jaeger in the side.

He spun back against the wall, holding himself, firing one-handed. The last target pitched up and back in a clatter of furniture and weapons and lay still.

Left hand clenched to his wound, Jaeger pushed away from the wall, the Walther's hot muzzle seeking the door and the stairs. The ripping-cloth rattle of Loew's Skorpion caught him in the chest, lifted him up, spun him into the frame of the tower doorway. His head lay on the stone steps.

He heard the sound of boots hastening up the stairs. The darkness closed in . . .

The battle in the hallway was over. Rachel crossed to where King lay under the bodies of a pair of dead commandos. She'd feared the worst, seeing all of the blood, but King's legs were moving, and he levered himself up to help her roll the bodies clear. "Hit in the calf," he said. His face was a mask of blood . . . but it was not his.

She fought back the twisting in her stomach. She'd taken a first aid course through a community program during the war scare of the late nineties; there had never been any mention of there being so much blood.

Rachel removed King's combat knife from it sheath on his harness and cut away at the seam of his bloody trousers. She tore the cloth to expose his lower leg. The long skirt purchased in Munich would provide material for compresses. She began cutting strips from the hem and applying them to the wound. The blood was welling and dark . . . no arteries hit . . .

"I don't think anything's broken," she told King. She unbuckled his combat harness and gunbelt, helping him get comfortable.

The master sergeant grimaced, shifting the leg. "Feels like it just went through the muscle. Thanks . . ."

Rachel heard movement behind her and turned. "Travis!"

Hunter paused by the tower door, bending over Jaeger's body. He looked up at her cry.

"Rachel! Are you okay!"

"Fine! Greg's shot in the leg . . . but he'll be all right. Loew went through that door . . ."

Hunter nodded grimly, hefted his Uzi, then stepped past the open door, across Jaeger's body and into the tower.

Step by silent step, Hunter moved up the stairs as they circled the inside wall of the castle's southeast tower. A babble of conflicting emotions rose . . . Jaeger dead . . . King wounded . . . Rachel alive! He pushed them to the back of his mind as he took the stone steps one at a time, concentrating only on what awaited him above.

Loew must not escape.

He felt the presence of the Soviet portal before he heard it, a familiar prickling across the hairs of his skin. The assault force's plan had been designed to prevent VBU agents from escaping the castle into the surrounding woods.

No one had considered the possibility that they had a portal of their own, here in the *schloss* in 1926 . . .

The stairway emerged through the floor into a circular room which filled the tower. Through the railing beside the stairwell, he could see a low platform at the center of the chamber. Cables snaked across the floor, and the room was filled with tables, metal cabinets, and unidentifiable pieces of electronic apparatus. Four metal uprights rose from the platform, where the flickerings of a shifting blue haze came and went. He heard the low hum of power, smelled the sting of ozone . . .

Movement to the left caught his eye. He swung sharply, his weapon tracking the black uniform as it lunged behind a table. Hunter fired, 9mm rounds splintering glass and striking sparks from the stone wall beyond with the shrilling of ricochets.

A pair of beefy arms closed about his shoulders from behind.

Hunter struggled, twisting in his attacker's grip, wrestling for control of the submachine gun. He felt the man's breath hot against his neck. Hunter pulled forward, ducking his head as though attempting to pull away, then snapped his head up and back as hard as he could.

His head rang with the concussion, but he heard his attacker yell with surprise and pain, and the grip was loosed. Hunter spun around, bringing his Uzi up to the ready.

Kulagin!

There was a roar of gunfire from across the chamber, and Hunter felt a piledriver blow smash him high in his left arm. The impact staggered him, driving him sideways to the floor in a haze of violent pain, as his Uzi skittered out of his grasp and across the room.

He had a confused impression of Loew standing behind a table at the far end of the room, a Skorpion machine pistol in his hand. Then the massive form of Kulagin descended on him, a fist cracking down into his face.

King picked up his H&K, snapped in his last 9mm magazine, and chambered a round. His right leg burned and throbbed where the RPK round had gone through, but he could stand well enough. He took an experimental step, then another. So far, so good.

"Okay," he said. Rachel stood beside him, her eyes wide with fear. They'd heard the burst of machine gun fire upstairs, heard sounds of a scuffle now. "You stay here! If Gomez comes through, send him up!" he turned and began limping heavily toward the tower door.

"I'm coming with you!" There was rebellion in her voice.

"No, dammit!" The Lieutenant was facing Loew upstairs . . . alone. "Stay put! I can't watch you and him both!"

Kulagin's fist slammed into his wounded shoulder, and Hunter screamed with the pain. The Russian agent squatted heavily on his chest, holding him down, smashing him with blows. Beyond, Loew worked at an instrument console, as the blue glow between the platform uprights intensified.

"*Oobyat yevoh!*" Loew shouted at Kulagin in Russian. "Kill him!"

Grinning, Kulagin reached across Hunter, groping

for his holstered .45, pulling it clear. Hunter grabbed Kulagin's gun hand with both hands and nearly passed out with the pain in his left arm. Kulagin grasped the weapon's slide, snicked it back . . .

Hunter let go of Kulagin's wrist, the surprise move catching the VBU agent off guard. Hunter's arm shot up, striking with all his power with the heel of his hand into his attacker's face. Kulagin's head snapped back, suddenly bloody. Hunter twisted, rolled, and kicked free as he grappled again for the Colt in Kulagin's hand. They faced each other on their knees for a long second, straining, the pistol between them. His arm throbbing, Hunter forced the gun and Kulagin's hand up . . . up . . . then smashed it down, slapping the wrist across the edge of a table. The gun fired, the roar deafening, as the bullet whined from the far wall. Hunter brought the hand up again, smashed it down again . . . Kulagin screamed.

With the third blow, the Colt flew from Kulagin's fingers, clattering across the floor. Hunter's knee caught Kulagin in the stomach, eliciting a heavy oof of surprise. Then Hunter's elbow whipped around, taking the Russian in the side of the head.

Kulagin smashed backward, overturning a table with a crash of instrumentation.

Across the room, Loew looked up from a low, jury-rigged console, then slapped at the holster on his hip, drawing his Skorpion. A noise on the stairs diverted him, making him turn away from Hunter, the weapon coming up.

King was there, his back to Loew.

"No!" Hunter screamed, leaping.

The distance was too great. The Skorpion spat fire, spent casings flashing in the light. Splinters chewed along the wooden railing as King jerked aside, turning . . .

Hunter collided with Loew as King went down, the remainder of the Skorpion's magazine punching a line of holes across the ceiling. The two men crashed back into the tower wall, arms locked. As they seesawed back and forth, he caught a glimpse of King, sprawled on his side at the top of the stairs, fresh blood flowing down his face from a ragged gash in his head.

King stirred in a sea of thundering, blinding pain. His head pounded, the pain searing, twisting, sickening . . .

Through the warm wetness of trickling blood, shapes moved. He saw Loew and Hunter locked together against the wall, saw Kulagin staggering upright, stooping, rising with Hunter's .45. The muzzle wavered toward Hunter's back. "Get clear!" Kulagin yelled in Russian. "Knock him away!"

Feebly, King felt about for the H&K he had dropped. No . . . there it was . . . three feet away.

It might as well have been a mile.

Movement . . .

Then Rachel was there, King's Colt clutched in both hands, enormous.

"*Todd!*" She shouted. "Todd, you bastard!"

The Russian turned. The pistol wavered . . . came up . . . came around . . .

The bark of the automatic was shattering, close above King's head. A white star appeared against the stone above Kulagin's shoulder. Her second shot roared . . . and her third. Kulagin was slammed back into the wall, teeth bared in an agonized grimace.

Rachel kept firing, the Colt steady in two hands. King's ears rang with the concussion as the girl squeezed off round after round.

Kulagin's body slid down the wall, leaving a red trail on the stone. Much of his face was gone.

"My God, lady," King managed to say at last. He felt his consciousness slipping away. "I'm glad you're on our side. . . ."

They struggled face to face as gunfire thundered from the stairs. Then Loew pulled his hand free and lashed the empty Skorpion down hard on the American's wounded arm. The machine pistol swung again, striking Hunter in the side of the head, knocking him backward across a low table.

The VBU leader tossed the Skorpion aside and vaulted for the platform. The power hum was steady. The portal was open. Beyond was Uralskiy Station. There would be reinforcements. . . .

Hunter heaved himself up on hands and knees, the scene frozen for him in time. He saw Todd slumped against a wall, his face blown away, saw Rachel kneeling above King's body, her hands clutching a smoking .45, slide locked open, the gun empty.

He saw Loew jump onto the platform, silhouetted against the blue glow.

King's H&K lay six feet away. Hunter dove for it, landing and rolling on his injured shoulder as he scooped up the weapon. He came up hard against the wall next to Rachel, the submachine gun wobbling in an unsteady, one-handed grip. He squeezed the trigger.

Autofire raked across the room, probing after

Loew. *Der Adler* had already stepped into the blue glow. There was an instant's glimpse of Loew staggering . . . twisting . . .

Loew vanished.

Hunter pulled himself to his feet, his back against cold stones. He dropped the H&K to the floor, then reached with his good hand for one of the grenades clipped to his harness.

VBU reinforcements might appear at any moment. He yanked the pin, staggered across the room, and tossed the grenade into the blue haze.

Seconds passed. Then, in absolute silence, the glow winked out.

Elsewhere throughout Adlerschloss, the battle came to an end. Gomez arrived in the tower chamber minutes later, followed by Anderson and a handful of the surviving commandos. Roy Anderson crouched at the top of the stairs, tending King's head wound.

Rachel, her face still pale, examined the electronic equipment wired to the central platform. "This isn't the main Russian portal," she said after a moment.

"Didn't think it was," Hunter said. He slumped against a table, utterly drained. "Not nearly as much gadgetry here as at Time Square. What is it?"

"This must be their alternative to a recall beacon." She passed a hand over her eyes, smearing the blood and smoke stains on her face. "They were working on something like this at the Complex, a couple of years ago. The idea is . . . you ship people back into time with enough equipment and supplies for them to build a downtime link . . . a kind of receiving station at the other end of the portal opening. The main portal system is locked in here. It's clumsy . . . We settled on the recall beacon concept instead.''

Hunter looked up at the platform, where the glow had been. "Then . . . did my grenade get the Russian portal? Up in 2007, I mean?''

She shook her head. "I don't know. You must have damaged it, at least.'' She smiled. "You pulled the plug.''

He nodded. "And we're going to keep it pulled. Gomez!''

It took thirty minutes for the strike force to pull out of the castle and into the woods to the west. Eddie had planted his charges on the deactivated Soviet equipment. Now he waited at Hunter's side, waiting to trigger the radio detonator which would set them off.

Hunter felt a touch at his side. Rachel was there, looking up at him. "We'll be going home soon,'' he said. "We'll have to stay a few days, make sure we got them all . . .''

"We'll have to allow time for the Transformation Wave to reach 2007, too,'' Rachel said. "*Our* 2007.''

"All set, Chief,'' Gomez said. "Let's blow it!''
Hunter nodded.

The detonation split the southeast tower with a flash which briefly lit Adlerschloss, painting black spires against white fire. The low, rumbling boom reached them a moment later, followed by the slithering hiss of debris cascading down the cliff into the lake.

The first blast was followed by another. Flames leaped against the night, illuminating the tree tops and flashing from the surface of the lake. They could see the stately facade of the old *residenz* slumping, crumbling in dust and smoke and fury. The walls fell, roaring. Spray rose beyond the cliff, mingling with the column of smoke crawling into the night sky.

King, his head heavily bandaged, pushed himself up on his elbows on an improvised stretcher nearby, trying to see. Roy Anderson knelt beside him. "You just lay yourself back down there, Greg." He grinned in the flickering light. "Damned hardheaded master sergeants!"

The low-velocity Skorpion round had creased the side of King's head. They would have to get him back to 2007 to determine whether or not his skull was fractured, but he seemed to be out of danger. The jokes were already circulating about the master sergeant with the skull thick enough to stop a bullet.

King ignored Anderson. "Nice fireworks," he said. "Ought to make Eddie happy."

"It made a nice bang," Gomez agreed. Thunder roared from the Ammersee.

Hunter looked at Rachel. Her face was smeared with blood and smoke. Firelight gleamed in her eyes. She was beautiful.

"Well . . . did we do it?" he asked her. He shifted his arm uncomfortably in its sling. "Do you think we've set things straight?"

She smiled. "You've stopped Loew. I think history will be able to take care of itself, now."

Hunter nodded. He knew from experience that it took considerable effort to redirect the forces which shaped the flow of history. Now that the VBU had been defeated in the early '20s, perhaps things would get back on track.

Rachel's hand went to the locket at her throat. "Now we know we *can* change the past," she said softly. "Given time . . ."

Epilogue

Hunter stepped from the blue glow, followed by the others. He blinked into sudden light.

"Good God, man! Where the hell have you been?" Thompson strode forward, cane, limp, and eyepatch gone. Around him was the gleaming efficiency of the portal chamber Hunter remembered. Sergeant Jenkins, alive again, stood nearby. "Did you get Hitler?"

The universe, *their* universe, was back.

As Rachel had predicted, the survivors of the Universe B commando team were gone, vanished in the step from 1926 to 2007. The historical events which had led up to Universe B had never happened.

Or had they? Hunter had long since given up trying to unravel the bizarre cause-and-effect chaos of time travel. History was so complex, with so many

309

places where a missed step while trying to change things could lead to disaster . . .

"It'd *still* be great to get rid of all the dictators," Anderson said. The six of them stood outside, on a ledge overlooking the late spring beauty of Jackson Hole. The Texan made a chopping gesture with his hand. "Wipe out the Commies and the Nazis, all at once!"

"Someday we will," Hunter agreed. It disturbed him that Hitler had survived after all, that their history still recorded Lenin and Hitler, communism and the Third Reich. *Someday* . . .

The decision had been made only after a week of debriefings and discussion. Their understanding of the dynamics of history was too imperfect, too incomplete, to allow them to make wholesale changes . . . yet. They would have to study the past carefully to determine the one place, the one time where their intervention could eliminate communism and the VBU . . . without replacing them with something even worse. When they found that point in the past they would strike, overwhelming the VBU with a wave of changing history before they could strike back.

Of course, the VBU would be using the very same tactics against them. While they studied and learned, they would have to mount guard, protecting history from the VBU's attempts to manipulate time to their own advantage.

It promised to be a long and bitter war.

Hunter took Rachel in his arms. A cool breeze off the mountains stirred her hair.

Back in the night above the Ammersee, Rachel

had said that history would take care of itself now, given time.

He smiled. Given time . . . and Freedom's Rangers.

And they had all the time in the world.

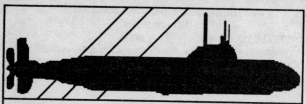